The Lessons of Magik

The Descendants Series Book 1

SLMcGinnis

Castle Drum Publishing

Castle Drum Publishing

Printed in the United States of America.

First Printing, 2023

ISBN 979-8-9872153-4-0

Castle Drum Publishing

www.castledrumpublishing.org

This novel's story and characters are fictitious. Certain long-standing institutions, agencies, and public offices are mentioned, but the characters involved are wholly imaginary.

Contents

1. See Me After Class — 1

2. Can I Borrow That? — 9

3. Found Magik — 15

4. Intimidation Is Not An Option — 19

5. Parties. Magik. Feelings. — 27

6. Hello, Are You There? — 32

7. Operation Tutor is a Go — 36

8. Unknown Number — 44

9. Teach a Man to Fish — 50

10. Failing! — 54

11. Executions and Brothers — 64

12. To Be Or Not? — 72

13. Anxiety Times Ten — 77

14. Another Dead End — 82

15. Dinner With Devil(s) — 88

16. With All Due Respect — 96

17. Put Your Hands Up! — 107

18. A Helping Hand — 114

19. The Truth Comes Out — 123

20. Old Acquaintances — 134

21. The Smuggler — 138

22. A Favor — 153

23. An Unwelcome Stranger — 159

24. His Decision — 164

25. Curious Questions — 167

26. How to Catch Fire — 181

27. Late Night Escapades — 184

28. He's Coming — 196

29. Failure to Protect — 198

30. Declarations of War — 205

31. A Temporary Setback — 211

32. Haven — 213

33. New Enemies — 221

34. Chaos — 229

35. A Whole New World — 236

36. An Extended Hand — 244

37. The Mark of a Descendant — 248

About the Author — 256

See Me After Class

KARA

K ARA STOPPED AT HER teacher's desk, and he tapped some papers before pushing them over. She stared down, clasped her hands in front of her, and forced a smile. She messed up. Students weren't told to stay after class to get a pat on the back.

"You know why I wanted to talk?" the bearded man asked.

Kara shook her head as the classroom door shut behind the last students. "Because I did such a good job on my homework," she said. Her voice faltered. Half of the work still needed to be completed.

"Quite the opposite. Normally, I don't pull students aside, but your parents are... influential." The man sighed and rubbed his eyes. "You're failing."

Kara's heart sank. She fought to control her trembling fingers and made herself nod. If she pretended not to panic, maybe she wouldn't.

"You know what that means." Mr. Barclay's voice softened.

She nodded again. Her tongue was too heavy to speak.

The sun shone through the barred classroom window, casting shadows across her pale skin as if she were in jail.

"I want to help. I can recommend a tutor. If you pass the final, it'll bring your grade up," he said, holding out a slip of paper.

Kara tried to take it, but her body wouldn't move. She was failing out of her program. If Angel found out, she would send her to reform school.

"Take it. Call him." Mr. Barclay waved the slip in the air. "I know he'll help."

Kara gulped and reached for it. Her hand shook, and panic clogged her throat. She swallowed past it and scanned the four-digit number. "Wait a minute, this is-"

"Yes, and if anyone asks, I didn't give it to you." He shouldn't risk his life for her.

Kara tried to give it back. "I can't."

"Your parents saved me once. Call."

She looked at the stack of papers as she slipped the number into her pocket. Her fingers fumbled through half-finished equations, blank scraps of homework, and wrong answers.

"The only chapters on the test will be the first thirteen. Focus there."

Kara gathered her assignments and managed a brisk nod. "Thanks." She hurried out of the room as tears slipped down her face.

The last bell rang, and everyone filtered out of their classes and down the hall. She barely registered when someone bumped her elbow or pushed her out of the way to reach their friends. She couldn't fail, but she couldn't call either. There's no way Ryan would help. He was at the top of the class. Her eyes widened, and she stopped walking. *Oh no, did he tell Ryan I was failing? Then he knows I'm an idiot. I can't get a tutor who thinks I'm incompetent.*

One of the older kids knocked her down, and her papers flew across the hall. She let out a panicked yelp and crawled around on the cold white tile floor, trying to gather everything before anyone could see her failure.

"Hey, you alright?" His voice made her freeze.

She looked up into bright emerald eyes as Ryan handed her a few pages of their last assignment. They were in the first and fourth hours together. He would know what those papers were.

Kara snatched them and pressed them to her chest, using her free hand to wipe the tears from her face.

"Fine, totally fine," she said. "Thanks, I don't need help. You can go. I mean, it's a waste of time, but I appreciate it."

Ryan smirked and held a hand down when he stood. "Up you go."

She wanted to fall into a fiery hole. That would be less painful. Unable to find a reason to reject his help, Kara set her hand in his. His skin was burning like he maybe had a fever, but he didn't look sick.

Ryan was a different sort of person. His skin was sun-bronzed, and his hair a sandy blonde. He wore too bright clothes and always overdid the bracelets and earrings. A lot of rumors surrounded the enigma that was the boy. Some said he wasn't from the city, and others said he worked for Angel.

Kara mostly ignored rumors because kids liked to talk, but there was one thing people never mentioned. She stared into his green eyes peppered with brown. *He's kinda cute.*

"Come on, I don't wanna be here any longer than I have to." Killian stopped next to them and scrunched his nose when he saw her. "Oh," he said.

Her panic prevented her from taking offense.

Dealing with Ryan was one thing, but dealing with his identical twin brother was different. The only thing they shared was basic appearance. Their personalities were like the sun and moon. Ryan might've been the fighter, but Killian was much more intimidating with his straight back, stoic gaze, and tight lips.

"Be nice," Ryan said, walking off with a wave. The twins vanished into the crowd.

Kara's heart pounded as she waited for one of them to turn around and laugh. She squeezed her eyes closed, taking a few deep breaths. There was one rule to survive high school: avoid those two. She shook her thoughts off and hurried outside. Her phone vibrated, and she pulled it out of her pocket with a frown.

A small text from her mom popped up on the screen:

Be home late. Make dinner and bed on time. Love you.

Kara whimpered and put the phone away. A kid from homeroom stopped in front of her to hock a wad of spit on the black concrete. Her stomach churned as she gagged and stepped past the long-haired nuisance. *Why are boys disgusting?*

Students filed out of the shabby, two-story school building, trading its thin, prison-like windows for black fences and gravel paths. Kara hurried down the steps and onto the road that would take her home. Her eyes caught Mr. Barclay across the bumpy, black road, and she disappeared behind a trio of girls trying to lie low. Dread picked apart her stomach as she chewed her lip and reached into the pocket of her jeans, fingering the slip of paper.

Moments later, a bell chimed in the distance, and a hologram appeared in the sky. Angel. Yorklyn City's leader. Her fiery red hair flowed down her shoulders as she stared into the camera. Her face popped up above the people as a floating video. When the sun vanished with her appearance, shadows flew across the ground and bathed them in a dim darkness.

"Hello, my subjects. Today has been a wonderful day. The forecast calls for sun. Regarding any illegal activities downtown, my men are working around the clock to keep you safe. If you see suspicious activity, report it to your neighborhood watch.

"I wish you well. Remember, the 10 p.m. curfew is still in effect until we catch our perpetrator. Until next time." Her image faded, and the world brightened after it pushed back the encroaching shadows.

Kara tucked a strand of raven hair behind her ear and frowned as idle chatter continued. Nothing new - just another day.

Before she could get to the residential district, chanting caught her attention. She looked around and saw a bunch of boys circling around a fight. She inched closer and frowned when she saw Ryan's neon green shirt through the gaps.

"Fight! Fight! Fight!"

He didn't give that long, did he?

Ryan caught her eye through the crowd and smirked. A cocky little thing, like she should be impressed. He wasn't that great. Even with his adorable freckles.

I think I'm making a grave mistake asking him for anything. Send me a sign that this is wrong.

One patrolman saw the fight and rushed to it. The kids immediately parted ways. With a rough grip, his hand closed around the back of Ryan's neck and pulled him off his victim. "No fighting," the robotic voice said.

The patrolman's face remained covered by a green helmet that clicked into place behind his ears and hid his identity. He could speak without removing the dark piece of plastic from his mouth. The soldier wore basic army attire and a black rod at his hip. There was also a large circular device on his back.

Ryan murmured something, and everyone scattered like little boys. The patrolman let him go. "Behave yourself."

Kara froze when Ryan looked at her again. Her lips pressed into a thin line when he waved and walked over to her, shoving his hands in his pockets.

"What're you doin' out this way?" he asked.

"I live out here," she said.

"You live in the shopping district?" he asked.

Kara opened her mouth to argue and stopped. She wasn't going home; she had to get groceries for dinner. "*You* live in the shopping district," she blurted and hurried off.

"That doesn't make any sense," he called, amusement coloring his voice.

Kara didn't have time for boys. If she was going to pass, she had to study. She stopped at one of the small grocery shops and bought supplies with her mom's corporate card.

Angel entrusted them to the higher-ups. She gathered her bags and flicked her hair out of her face.

The sun was setting, casting long shadows across the ground by the time she made it home. She heaved a sigh and hurried home but stopped in her driveway.

Their house was like every other on the street. A two-story building painted all white. There were few windows on the front and no garage as most people didn't have cars. It caused too much pollution. There was gravel around the structure and a small stoop leading to the front door. No color, no individuality, just a place to sleep for the night.

Dawson, her little brother, stood on the stoop with a sheepish smile. "Forgot my card."

Kara leveled him with a stare. "You've gotta stop doing that. I should be glad you're home, I suppose." She swiped a keycard across a panel next to the door with her free hand, granting them access.

Kara went straight to the kitchen, bypassing the quiet living room that dropped from the dining room and its expansive window. Her bag bumped into a brightly colored vase in the front hall, but Dawson caught it before it could topple and shatter. Her mom spent money on the most ridiculous things. Kara huffed in annoyance, adjusted her load, and hurried into the kitchen before she could break anything.

She opened some cupboards and began shoving cans of beans and jars of tomato paste inside. "Now, what do you want to eat? Make it simple. I don't feel like cooking."

Dawson hopped into the seat at the bar in the kitchen and rested his chin on his palms. He blinked at her with his dark blue eyes and shook his head occasionally to keep his hair out of his eyes.

"You need a haircut," she muttered, closing the thick wooden door of the cupboard and swiping some crumbs off the marbled countertop.

"If I let you cut it, will you put the blue back in?" he asked.

"Will you stop spray painting walls in the alleys?"

He cleared his throat. "I would never do such an illegal thing."

"I found the mask and ruined shirt in the laundry," she said.

Dawson sighed and tapped his fingers on the bar top. "Fine, I'll stop for two weeks if you do the color."

Kara wished he would cut the crap, but seeing as that wasn't part of her brother's nature, she would take what she could get.

With a nod, he clapped his hands and pointed to the fridge. "There's leftover meat pie from the other night. Warm it up and grab the scissors," he said.

She hesitated for a minute before shrugging. Leftovers weren't ideal, but they were easy. Dawson slid off the chair and got some plates and cups while she reheated the goopy mess of meat, gravy, and frozen vegetables.

They talked a little as they ate, and Kara cut her brother's hair after. She colored his bangs dark blue, though the black dulled the color. When she finished, it was half the length. It barely brushed the tops of his ears.

"Thanks, gonna read me a story before bed?" he asked.

"Aren't you too old?" she countered.

He shrugged and began gathering the dishes. "I like it when you read. The story sounds better in your voice," he said.

Kara smiled despite the worry and exhaustion running through her body. "I'm tired. It was a long day. I'm gonna clean and sleep," she said.

"Fine, but tomorrow you're reading," he said.

She smiled. "Deal."

They spent a few more minutes together before she gathered her school bag and retired to her bedroom upstairs.

Family pictures hung on the walls in the hall, and she stopped to stare at one photo of her brother and their best friend. A chestnut brown-haired kid with a tooth-gapped smile and olive skin. Her fingers skimmed the glass, and she cracked the smallest of smiles. "Night, Tory. Miss you every day."

Dawson's bedroom door closed, and she slipped into hers. She dropped her stuff by her desk and sighed. Kara brushed the white lace curtains aside and peeked out the window at the city's dark streets.

A few soldiers walked up and down the district, ensuring nothing was happening. Kara let the curtain fall back into place and unpacked her bag. She set everything on her desk and sifted through her math book and half-finished assignments. A book of old fairy tales rested on her bedside table with her bright pink lamp with no shade. She stared at it longingly. There were so many other things she would rather be doing.

Kara changed into a soft pair of blue pajama bottoms and a silky tank. She brushed her hair out with her fingers and sat in the uncomfortable wood chair to get some work done. After a few hours of studying, she would go straight to bed.

Can I Borrow That?

"HEY, CAN I BORROW your-" Killian stopped in the doorway of their shared bedroom. "What're you doing?"

Ryan had the pieces of their alarm clock spread out on his bed. He peered at each gear, wire, and switch before setting it down and moving on to the next piece. "I'm fixing it," he said.

Killian nodded. He walked in and looked down when something skittered across the hardwood floor. He took a step back to avoid broken glass and nails.

A shattered mirror rested face down, and one shelf was no longer a shelf. Instead, it was in pieces against Killian's bed.

"What'd you do?" Killian asked.

Ryan didn't look up, pressed a finger to his lips, and picked up another piece of the ruined clock.

Killian rubbed his eyes and walked across the bedroom floor, trying to avoid anything dangerous. "Okay, what's happening? I'm supposed to be the unpredictable one," he said. He sat on the end of Ryan's bed and snapped his fingers until his brother looked at him.

Ryan's dark emerald gaze was unfocused and glazed over.

"Were you drinking?" Killian asked.

Ryan shook his head. "Haven't slept in about twenty-eight hours."

"Right, insomnia. You know you can always ask for help. I have spells that keep you from doing - well, this." Killian said.

"It's not."

"What do you call it, then?" Killian asked.

"A stroke of inspiration. I can get outside the walls," Ryan said. He gestured to the parts. "I just need to fix the clock. We reverse time, boom. Done."

"Just say you were drinking." Someone knocked on the front door, and Killian sighed. "Please, stop destroying things. I'll be back," Killian said. He got off the bed and hurried down the hall.

Ryan mumbled something behind him in their native tongue, but Killian was out of earshot before he had a proper comeback.

The walls in their one-bedroom flat were bare. As were the wooden floors, he padded down. He insisted on getting a few rugs to avoid slipping, but Ryan enjoyed running up and down the halls of the tiny home and sliding in his socks.

Killian opened the front door and stared down at a black-haired child. Dawson brushed his moppish hair out of his face and beamed.

"How did you get here? Tell me you didn't walk."

The boy shrugged. "K, I didn't."

Killian grabbed his bicep and dragged him inside. "What are you doing here?" he asked.

"Ryan texted me about needing supplies for some invention." Dawson held up his backpack. "I just brought what he asked for."

Killian snatched the bag and tossed it onto the couch. "Dawson, you know you're supposed to run this stuff by me," Killian said.

"You act more like his mom than his brother. What's the problem with having some fun?" Dawson said.

It has nothing to do with fun. Killian couldn't say that out loud. It would lead to more questions, and Ryan's activities could be treasonous. "If you keep giving Ryan stupid shit, I'm gonna tell Kara." He didn't want to use the sister card.

Dawson sent him a scathing glance. It wasn't like Killian wanted to be the responsible one. One of them *had* to be.

"Stop giving me that petulant stare. You're like a kid," Killian growled.

"I *am* a kid. And, by the way, so are you," Dawson said.

"Uh-huh." Killian wasn't going to play the game.

"You're like my sister. You two would be such good friends," the kid muttered as he rolled his eyes.

Killian glared and opened his mouth to argue, but Dawson covered his nose with his shirt sleeve and grimaced. "Is that smoke?"

A chill swept through Killian's veins, and he bolted to the bedroom.

Ryan held dancing flames mixed with burning clock pieces in his palm.

"Ryan," Killian shouted, lunging forward. He forgot about the broken mirror and sliced his foot. Pain surged through his leg, and he cursed. Killian slammed the side of his fist into the wall beside him, making Ryan jump.

Dawson peeked into the bedroom and raised his eyebrows. "What's goin' on?" he asked.

The flames vanished when Dawson spoke, and Ryan blinked. His eyes cleared, and he looked at Killian. "I didn't know we had company," he said. Ryan's gaze flicked to the blood-soaked sock, and he cocked his head to the side. "You're bleeding."

"No shit, I'm bleeding. Why'd you break the mirror?"

"It looked at me wrong," Ryan said.

Dawson chuckled and pointed to the living room. "I'll get the broom."

"How did it look at you wrong? It's your reflection." Killian shouted. He was over it. Killian limped to his bed and tore his sock off to see the damage. Blood dripped onto the floor, and he prodded the laceration.

"How'd you cut your foot?" Ryan asked.

Killian narrowed his eyes and kept his gaze on his injury. He was afraid he would punch his brother if he looked at him. "On the glass you left on the floor. Thanks, by the way," Killian said.

Ryan smirked, climbed off his mattress, and flicked his wrist. A small flame appeared on the tip of his index finger. "Want me to fix it?"

"Touch me, and you'll never wake up again." Killian leveled Ryan with a glare that could kill.

His brother chuckled, and the flame disappeared when Dawson returned with the broom and dustpan. He began sweeping up the mess without a word. That should have been the first thing Killian did, and he silently chastised himself for it.

"I can do it, Dawson. Don't worry about it," Ryan said.

"Why don't you get some bandages? I don't feel comfortable going through your things," Dawson said.

"Sure thing. Whatcha doin' out here anyway?" Ryan asked as he moved past Dawson into the washroom across the hall.

"You asked me for parts."

Ryan was quiet, and Killian heard a cupboard snap shut. When his brother returned, his smile was gone, his lips pursed.

"You don't remember, do you?" Killian asked.

"Guess not. Don't really remember trashin' the bedroom, either. Why'd you let me do that?"

Killian didn't think about punching him this time. He just moved. His fist connected with Ryan's jaw, and pain shot through his hand. He shook it out, and the frustration faded a little.

"I deserved that," Ryan said, rubbing his cheek. "Come on, kid. I'll walk you home."

Killian muttered to himself as Ryan tossed him bandages.

Dawson finished sweeping and set the broom aside. "You sure that's a good idea?" he asked.

"Better than staying here," Ryan said.

They left, and Killian fell back onto his bed with a sigh. Ryan was back to normal. He closed his eyes, and his foot throbbed. For a moment, he wished he hit him harder.

Killian jumped when something landed on his chest. He blinked in the dim light and groaned when he sat up. A paper bag fell into his hands. His foot and head hurt. "I feel horrid."

"You always do when you nap. Haven't seen you do that in a while," Ryan said, gesturing to the brown sack. "I got dinner."

Killian yawned.

Ryan sat on his own bed and fell flat on his back.

Killian dug into the bag and pulled out one of the pre-made sandwiches from the deli across the street. Food was food. He bit into the ham and cheese dinner and nodded a thanks. He looked around the room, wondering where to start cleaning, but found everything back to normal.

The ruined shelf was put back together and set between their thin mattresses, the glass had been swept off the floor, and the dirty clothes were thrown into the hamper by the door. Ryan's clock project had vanished and was replaced with a blanket.

"Sorry about the mess. Haven't been sleepin' too well," Ryan said. He looked away when he noticed Killian scrutinizing the room.

That was one less thing he had to do. Killian said, "You mentioned something along those lines."

"Yeah, well. What're you gonna do?" Ryan grumbled.

"I dunno. Maybe tell your brother who has magik abilities that make you sleep? Seems like the logical thing. Then again, you fail at logic." Killian rolled his eyes.

Ryan chuckled under his breath. "I get it."

"No, you don't."

Ryan didn't argue. Instead, he shifted his weight onto his side and propped himself on his elbow. "What stupid thing did I do? Aside from breaking everything?" he asked.

"We need a new alarm clock. You were trying to make a time machine," Killian said through a mouthful of food.

Ryan opened his mouth to say something but stopped himself. He just snorted in amusement and shook his head. His voice was weary, and dark bags clung to the skin under his eyes. "Guess that didn't work as well as I'd hoped," he said.

Killian finished the sandwich and wiped his fingers on his pants. "No big deal can't be any worse than when you're trying to stop me from killing. I gotta get some sleep. Big test tomorrow."

"Can you cast some of that lovely magic on me?" Ryan asked.

Killian snapped his fingers. "Dusk to dusk. Wipe the memories until morning's light." A zing of energy twinged from his fingertips, and Ryan's eyes closed. Killian flicked the lights off and rolled over in his bed. At least one of them wouldn't dream.

Found Magik

J ustin's hand lingered over the pot, and he waited for steam. He counted the seconds in his head until tiny drops of hot water popped into his palm. He patted along the countertop until his fingertips brushed a wood cutting board.

Footsteps padded around upstairs, and the man smirked and shook his head. Cody would be asking for dinner soon. The front door creaked open, and Justin's back went rigid. Something metal clinked as the intruder walked down the hall. Their footsteps barely brushed the wood floors.

Justin held his hand over the pot again. He forced a strand of energy from his palm and throughout the house. There were a few silver and gray energy glimmers, mostly Cody's. Justin furrowed his brow in annoyance, and the feet shuffled closer. He couldn't get a reading on the stranger. No one should be able to cross his spells without him knowing.

The person knocked into one of the tables in the hall, and Justin's free hand traveled along the countertop. He grabbed the handle of his cutting knife and pulled it down by his side. The scent of homebrewed ale assaulted his nostrils, and his stomach churned. *Alcoholic, great.*

As soon as he heard the slap of bare feet on the kitchen tile, Justin turned and threw the knife. There was a loud curse, and the ground rolled underfoot. Justin flew to the floor and slammed his elbow into a drawer someone had left open. He exhaled sharply and moved out of the way when he heard the chink of metal being withdrawn from a sheath.

Justin snapped his fingers, and his bow appeared in his palm, but a familiar voice caught him off guard. "I didn't come for a fight."

He paused momentarily, and the bow vanished before he was tempted to use it. "What're you doing here?" he asked.

Nicholas' footsteps got closer, and a hand touched his shoulder.

Justin knocked his hand away with a snarl. If his floor was trashed, he would be pissed. He turned to inspect the damage without acknowledging his brother.

"I need to talk to you," Nicholas said, pain coloring his tone.

"I told you I didn't want you coming around here," Justin said, a scowl deepening his features. He didn't find anything wrong with the wooden floors, so there was a plus to this meeting.

Nicholas sighed. "It's important. Things are starting to go south again."

Justin crossed his arms against his chest as he stood once more. He was afraid he was going to throw the first punch.

Nicholas's energy backed up as his brother took a step away. "You're not even gonna hear me out," he said.

"No, I'm not. You smell like booze. Get out."

"This isn't about me. It's about you and your screw-up ten years ago," Nicholas seethed.

"*My* screw-up? You better be joking. The only mistake I ever made was trusting a bunch of humans. That failure had nothing to do with me."

"You're the one who let the plan fall! Even now, you're being arrogant if you would just listen–"

"Get out of my house!" Justin roared.

Nicholas stopped and took a deep breath.

Justin didn't hear footsteps leaving, so he assumed his brother was still there. His energy was hidden, so he couldn't rely on the only sight he had to analyze the situation. He opened his mouth to demand Nick's exit again, but Cody's excited voice washed over him. He cursed to himself and flicked his wrist, throwing an invisible wall between Nicholas and Cody.

"Cody, stay where you are," Justin said.

"Uncle Nicky! I talked about you at school today. How are you?" Cody asked with excitement.

"Go back upstairs," Justin said, trying to keep his voice level. He might've not been the best dad, but he wouldn't fight in front of his child.

Nicholas scoffed. "You can't be serious. Jay, I want to talk. This goes beyond us. People are in trouble."

"I don't give a damn about people. The only person I care about is in this house. Now leave."

Cody's voice shook. "Don't make him go, please. Let him stay for the night. You guys can talk. I won't interrupt."

There was nothing to discuss until Nicholas decided to clean up his act. Justin was sick of bailing him out. The man wasn't a teenager anymore. It was time for him to take responsibility. "This doesn't concern you," Justin said. "Now, go to your room."

"Fine, I'll leave!" Something hard was slammed on the counter, and Nicholas tapped the invisible wall. The vibration ran up Justin's arm. "Let this down."

Justin complied, and the wall vanished.

Nicholas walked out of the kitchen, mumbling to himself. Cody scuttled to his uncle's side, and Justin felt along the top of the counter as their footsteps got further down the hall.

Justin fought the urge to drag Cody away from his uncle, but they hadn't seen each other in two years. He would let them say goodbye. His hand brushed a piece of stone on the counter with something engraved in it. A message of some sort. When Justin first lost his sight, Nicholas used to communicate with him like that. He scoffed and shoved the rock away before turning to the stove to check his water. Droplets hit his palm, signaling its completion. A soft, meaty aroma wafted through the kitchen.

The front door shut, and soft footsteps padded back to the kitchen. Cody sniffled.

"I'm not trying to be cruel," Justin said.

"You wouldn't even listen to him. Why won't you give him a chance?" Cody asked.

The pain in his voice cut through Justin, but a kid wouldn't understand. He ran a hand down his face. "I need you to finish this. Let it sit a moment more and pull it off the heat."

Cody rummaged on the counter and put the stone in Justin's hands. "Only if you promise to read it."

The message was short. He exited the kitchen and walked down the hall to his bedroom.

When the door was shut firmly behind him, he walked to his bed and sat down on the edge with a deep sigh. He ran his fingers across the tablet and closed his eyes. He tried to make out the letters and piece together what was being said. After a few minutes, Justin frowned and set the tablet aside. It was simple and to the point:

I've found more Descendants.

Intimidation Is Not An Option

KARA

HER ALARM BLARED TOO early. Kara cracked her eyes and peered at the sheet of paper next to her head. *Fell asleep. Great.* She pushed herself up and walked to the bedside, where a small, circular device blared noisily. A high-pitched tone emitted from it as it bounced around on the wood, telling her it was time to get up.

She picked it up, and it stopped squealing and moving. When she set it back down, it chimed. "Alarm set for same time in twenty-four hours, thank you."

"Didn't ask for a wake-up call," Kara grumbled as she rubbed her eyes.

She stared at her untouched bed with the pink comforter and itched to crawl into it. She was already failing, wasn't she? Kara slapped her cheeks and hurried out of the room before she could be tempted further. It wasn't hard falling into her morning routine. Shower, brush hair, pick out clothes, get dressed.

She walked past the stairs and banged on Dawson's bedroom door twenty minutes after her alarm rang. "Time to get up, don't make me come up again."

Kara returned to her room; the plush white carpet tickled her bare feet. She threw on socks and black sneakers before packing her bag and hurrying downstairs.

She had ten minutes to figure out what to make for breakfast. Kara opened cupboards and rifled through them. "Too late for cereal, not enough bread for toast, what the hell... that's expired." She tossed an old, crushed can on the counter.

Kara turned to the stove and pressed a big red button. A holographic menu appeared. "Welcome to the first-class menu of Angel's city. What can we prepare for you?" the robot asked.

"Quick and easy," Kara said.

"Do you want protein with that?"

"Sure, whatever."

The menu disappeared, and the glass paneling slid away on the stove. Two brown bars popped up, and she grabbed them before rushing back upstairs.

"Dawson, come on." She banged on his door again. "We're going to be late."

He grunted within, and something heavy hit the floor. She hoped he fell out of bed. Kara grabbed his bag from beside the door and went back downstairs. She set it on the counter and put one of the bars beside it.

She bit into hers and made a face. The bitter bar was packed with gritty powder and tasted like broccoli. Her mom needed to recalibrate the machine.

Kara grabbed some milk out of the fridge and downed a glass. When she rinsed the cup, she filled it with ice and water and returned up the stairs. This time, Kara didn't knock. She opened the door and walked to the bedside; Dawson was curled up on the floor next Jit. She sipped the water and poured the rest over his head.

He scrambled off the ground, shaking the wet out of his black hair. "What the heck."

"We're going to be late," she snapped again.

She stepped over dirty clothes and empty cans of paint. One of these days, she needed to get in there and clean out his Helwe hole.

Before she closed the door, Dawson ran from closet to dresser to find appropriate clothes.

Kara returned to the kitchen, washed the cup, and placed it back in the cupboard. She wolfed down the rest of the disgusting breakfast and looked up when Dawson bolted down the stairs.

He sniffed the protein bar and frowned. "What's this?"

"Machines on the fritz. Let's go," she said.

Dawson sighed, took a hesitant bite, and a look of pure disgust crossed his face. "What the..."

She grabbed his wrist, and they hurried down the front hall and out the door.

"I'm on time today," Dawson said with a smile as the door locked behind them.

"Uh-huh, by, like, two minutes," she said.

They strolled down the street by all the cookie-cutter houses with no yards. Some cars, mainly big boxy vehicles that polluted the air faster than the factories, were parked in driveways. Most people in the city walked. It was a small area, and walking was an excellent exercise.

Gravel and boulders made up a patchwork of lawns, split by black streets and gray, concrete sidewalks. She had always found the lack of color dull but, unlike her brother, had never been tempted to disturb the cityscape.

The sky was powered by electricity. Not even the sun was natural. It was a bright light, and the heat was from the factory's spires. Most people took pills to ensure they got all the nutrients they didn't otherwise get.

"What are we gonna do this summer? School lets out soon, and I wanna make plans," Dawson said.

Kara shrugged. She had little planned. She figured she would hang out at home if she wasn't doing homework. She asked, "What plans do you have?"

"We are gonna hit the watering hole and library," he said.

She chuckled darkly and shook her head. "The library burned down five years ago." It was a bitter memory she didn't want to deal with.

Dawson mumbled under his breath and crossed his arms against his chest.

They arrived at school, and Kara stared glumly. All the anxiety from the day before rolled back to the front of her brain. Another day to survive. She still needed to ask for help in math.

"Hey, there's Ryan!" Before she could stop him, Dawson ran over to the blonde, a skip in his step.

Kara forced a smile as she followed her brother. Maybe she could casually slip in asking for a favor. Even if it was odd that Dawson had senior friends, she should try to be nice.

Ryan wore a horrendously orange shirt and a pair of baggy black shorts. Killian was in a button-up, long-sleeved shirt and a pair of slacks.

She couldn't believe they were related.

"I can see your eyes. Got a haircut?" Ryan asked. "Mornin' Princess, I see you're as sunny as always." He cracked a smile when he saw her.

She pursed her lips and narrowed her eyes. "Don't call me that."

"That's right. You don't like nicknames," Ryan said. He smirked, not at all put off by the venom in her voice.

She expected nothing less. They stared at each other. The stupid smirk never left his face, and she knew it was a challenge. He was daring her to get mad or lose her cool.

Well, she wasn't going to give him the satisfaction. Kara tossed her frizzy raven curls over her shoulder and turned her chin up. She had better things to do. "See you after school, Dawson."

Dawson waved her off and grabbed Ryan's arm. They disappeared into the growing throng of students, and Kara forced herself to look away.

She didn't trust Ryan. For some reason, he enjoyed her brother's company as much as Dawson enjoyed him.

She hurried across the scuffed tile floors to her locker and tapped the combination into the remote on the door. It beeped before clicking open, and she unloaded her bag. She would spend her first three hours in math, so she only needed some of the five books.

"Kara, we gotta talk."

She jumped when she shut the door and saw one of the twins standing there. Her heart lurched, and she clutched the book to her chest. Kara searched his face and noticed he didn't have earrings. Nor was he wearing a neon-colored shirt. Killian.

Ryan was tolerable. She really would rather not be left alone with the other. "You want to talk to me?" she asked. "About what?"

"Your brother."

Kara sighed and turned her back. She didn't have time. If Killian had a problem, he could figure it out.

The blonde matched her stride and shoved his hands in his pockets. "Just two seconds. It's important," he said, keeping his voice low.

Kara frowned and chewed the inside of her cheek. Dawson might have been in some sort of trouble. "What?" she asked.

"Private. Come to the third-floor stairwell. It goes to the roof," Killian said.

She stopped and stared. It wouldn't be that far-fetched of an idea for him to push her off the roof. Then again, it was probably the anxiety talking.

His face remained emotionless, making it hard to ascertain his intentions.

Kara nodded, and they walked out of the thinning crowd of students. Her cheeks burned at the whispers of her classmates as she passed. People were going to get the wrong idea about her.

They stopped at a thick black door, and he shoved it open with little trouble. He stepped aside and held it like a gentleman. At least he wasn't calling her princess.

Kara stepped across the threshold and stared at the wide, flat roof. Her eyes widened, and she hurried to look at the city. A small smile painted her lips as she gawked at huge steel skyscrapers and brick shops. Kara rested her hand on the railing that separated her from a fifteen-foot drop and leaned forward to take in the sight.

"You don't come here," Killian said. He walked over to her, and the door shut when he let it go.

Kara glanced at him and studied his profile in the bright sunlight. It was amazing how similar he was to his brother. Something clinked when he gripped the rail and pressed his back to it. Kara looked down and studied a set of rings on his left hand.

A silver one on his middle finger and a black and purple one on his thumb. They were shiny and sparkled. Something weird pulled at her stomach, and she wanted to touch one.

She reached out until he crossed his hands against his chest. Kara startled and looked up, breaking free of whatever trance she had been in. "What did you want to talk about?" she asked.

"Dawson and Ryan don't need to hang out. They cause too many problems," Killian said. He still didn't look at her.

She shrugged. Kara agreed, but he found another way whenever she hid a can of paint or removed the apps from his phone. "And what would you like me to do?" she asked.

"Make him stay away before I do," Killian said, brushing his hair back.

Kara's brow furrowed, and she clutched her books until her knuckles went white. Anger flickered to life under her skin. "Is that a threat?" she asked.

He raised a slim, blonde eyebrow and turned his head. His face was passive, but something swirled in his bright eyes.

She tried to read the emotion that lingered, but before she could, it was gone. A spike of pain tore through her temple, and she winced, pressing a palm to her head.

"You can make it whatever you want. Tell Dawson to mind his own business. He's a bad influence," Killian said.

The slow-burning anger roared to life, and she dropped her hand as the pain vanished. "*My* brother is a bad influence? Do you even know what they say about yours?" she snapped.

A bitter smile tugged at the corner of Killian's lips, and she shivered.

She knew there was a reason she avoided him.

"Who's worse? Me for trying to control my brother, or you for letting yours hang out with a criminal?" Killian asked. His tone stayed the same during their conversation.

"I can control my brother about as well as you can yours. Now, if you don't mind. I have a class to get to." She turned to leave. "Oh, and if you lay a hand on my brother, I'll hurt you."

Killian snorted in amusement as she threw open the door and slammed it behind her. She couldn't believe the audacity of some people.

Parties. Magik. Feelings.

RYAN

RYAN FLICKED THE BEDROOM light on and kicked aside a dirty shirt. Killian grumbled from his bed, and Ryan smirked. *Asleep already? Your day wasn't that bad, lazy bum.*

"I'm going to a party. Do you wanna come?"

Killian talked into his pillow. "Do I have to?"

"No, I'd much rather you didn't, but it's rude not to ask."

Killian cracked an eye and stared. No emotion passed across his face, so Ryan crossed his arms and leaned on the doorjamb. That was a familiar look. He was burnt out.

"Is Kara going?"

Ryan's eyes widened for a fraction of a second before he got control of his emotions. He smirked and swiped his thumb across his nose. It was a party regardless of who was there. "She might be. I dunno," he said.

Killian closed his eyes again and mumbled something Ryan missed. *Whatever his loss.* He waved and walked out when Killian raised his voice. "I've got a bad feeling. You shouldn't go."

Ryan cocked his head to the side and stopped in the hall. He wasn't one to believe in fate or destiny, but sometimes Killian had some weird premonitions. "Is this one of those bad feelings like the burned-down library? Or you not wanting to leave the house?" he asked.

Killian mumbled something, and Ryan sighed. He walked back to the door and looked at the lump. "Answer the question."

"Bad dream. Lots of people died."

Ryan ran a hand down his face and shook his head. "Guess I'm not going."

Killian pushed himself up and rubbed his eyes. "We can find something else to do."

Ryan chewed on his lip. He wanted to get hopelessly drunk and forget all life's problems. It wasn't a habit he should get into, but he had done worse. "Don't worry. Guess I'll get some studying done."

Killian yawned again. "Wanna practice magik?"

"Yes!"

Killian chuckled under his breath and got off the bed. There were few places where it was safe to use magik. Considering their existence was illegal, Ryan and Killian tried to play it safe. Well, Killian wanted to play it safe.

"The usual place?" he asked.

Ryan nodded and stepped back.

Killian waved his hand over the floor. "Darkness unite: teleportation," he said. A charged violet circle appeared on the wooden floor, and Ryan grinned. Black and purple melded into one until a dark door rose and opened into a black abyss. Killian held out his hand, and Ryan took it as they crossed the threshold into nothingness.

It passed in the blink of an eye, and before he knew it, they stood on a rocky shore beside a pool of clear water. The only place in Yorklyn connected to the outside was the watering hole.

Ryan wasn't sure anyone knew about their special spot, but they often practiced magik there to avoid being seen.

"Kara doesn't hate you," Killian said.

"That came out of nowhere. Why?" Ryan couldn't curb his curiosity.

"She wants you to help her in math. Heard some others talking about it in class," Killian said as he dropped his hand. He snapped his fingers and whispered a spell. Daggers appeared in each of his palms.

Ryan nodded, took a few steps back, and prepared himself. "She would die before she asked," Ryan said.

Killian threw one, and it whizzed towards Ryan.

He flicked his wrist, and a wave of fire threw the weapon off course, and it landed in the water before dissolving in a purple light.

"She might." Killian shrugged. He threw the second dagger, and Ryan caught it between his fingers.

He stared at the intricate blade and let it drop to his feet. "I don't need friends," Ryan said. He clapped his hands, and fire sparked to life as energy blasted from his palms. The ribbon of flames snaked through the air and snapped at Killian.

His brother jumped away from the crackling fire and winced when an ember brushed his cheek. "Divine protection of shadows: barrier," Killian said. A black wall appeared before him, and the flame exploded upon touching it. "What will you do when someone wants to be your friend?" Killian asked. "Do what you did to Avery?"

Ryan stopped smiling and bit his tongue. "You afraid someone's gonna steal me?" Ryan asked. His voice darkened, and he narrowed his eyes at the rocky ground.

"Don't be stupid. It'd be great if someone would take you," Killian said.

Ryan flicked his wrist, and a ball of fire tore through the black wall.

Killian gasped in pain and dropped to the ground before the ball hit him. He clutched his chest, and Ryan walked over to him with a nod.

"Never use a shield unless you can manage it. You risk damaging your heart," Ryan said. He held his hand down to help Killian up.

His brother scowled and slapped it away. Killian pushed himself up and ran a hand through his hair. "That was overkill."

Ryan shrugged. "You're the one who wanted to practice."

Usually, a situation like this would end with them punching each other. Luckily for Ryan, Killian didn't jump to attack.

He just brushed his shirt off and waved his hand. "Back up. Let's do it again."

Ryan raised a brow. "Do what again?"

"I'm gonna get this shield thing down," Killian said.

"Did you hear what I said?" Ryan growled.

Killian repeated his spell, and another wall appeared. "You had no problem doing it two seconds ago."

Ryan scratched his cheek. He acted without thinking. "If I apologize, will you drop it?" he asked.

Killian beckoned to the wall.

Ryan sighed and shook his head. They practiced late into the night. Killian only decided he was done when Ryan drew blood.

"How's your foot?" Ryan asked as they stared at the glitching stars in the sky.

Killian shrugged. "Fine. Nothing but a scab now."

"I meant to ask earlier," Ryan admitted.

They went silent again. Ryan watched the sky and let his thoughts drift.

When they were ten, they came to the city from The Wilds seeking their mother. It didn't take long for them to realize they were safer outside. Any wrong move in Yorklyn could get them killed. Ryan should have taken his chances with the animals.

"Is mom still alive, you think?" Killian asked.

Ryan didn't have an answer. Even if he did, he wouldn't say what he thought out loud. "We should go. We've broken curfew," Ryan said. Killian turned to stare, but Ryan forced himself to his feet.

"If Kara asks for help, what will you do?" Killian asked when they got back home.

Ryan fell onto his mattress and closed his eyes. "I suppose I'd help." Or maybe he wouldn't. As he fell asleep, rattling gunfire sounded in the distance.

Hello, Are You There?

ANGEL

THE RIVERBED GURGLED, AND she stared down at her reflection. A dark creature looked back at her with red eyes and sharp teeth. When the water rippled, the thing below didn't.

Angel brushed a strand of fiery hair behind her ear and held her hand over the shadow. Hands reached up and stopped at the waterline as if it were stuck behind a glass sheet.

"I'm tired of waiting. No more waiting. Find me pure ure blood," a voice hissed. It had no mouth, but Angel heard it clear as day.

She blinked at the image that refused to fade. The woman clenched her fist, and the water churned, swirling back and forth. "It won't be long, Lord Malsumis. Please, be patient," Angel whispered.

"Your energy is not enough to sustain me. You must find the one with the pure bloodline." The shadow rippled in the water. Its eyes glowed.

Angel peered into the darkness and wondered if she was seeing the proper form of her master. A wisp-like shadow that plagued the chilly waters. "I can't," she said.

The shadow hissed and faded.

Angel huffed at her reflection and straightened. When she first began her quest to fix the world, she didn't expect this. The old texts spoke of gods and goddesses beyond their world, but they didn't say how to summon those deities. For a decade, Angel tried to unite with her master by searching for pure-blooded magik Descendants in Yorklyn.

She tapped her bloody fingers against her thigh in rhythm with her pulsing heart. It would take time. The last interrogation of a Descendant didn't go well. When she got prisoners, she could bleed them dry without getting a spark of wisdom from them.

She would have to leave the city to find someone who was not afraid of her. It would be hard to leave. "I need someone reliable," she muttered. "An ally."

A bitter laugh made her jump. Angel whirled around and eyed the man. He tucked his hands behind his back and looked at her as if she were meat. She bared her teeth and tossed her fiery red curls behind her shoulder. "What the Helwe do you want?" she asked.

"I saw the chance to cut a deal," the man said. He wore a gray suit and a black mask rested against high cheekbones. His skin stretched too tight across his bones.

Angel curled her lips into a snarl and held her hand out. A frozen spear was transported to her palm, and she held it in front of her defensively. The cold metal burned, but she wouldn't leave herself defenseless. "What deal?" she asked.

The man took a step forward, and she pointed the sharp end of her weapon at his chest. He stopped and cocked his head to the side.

Her eye twitched, and she gripped the spear tighter. His hands didn't move, but she didn't trust it. There was something up.

"We have a common interest, Angel. I've been watching you, and your abilities benefit me. With some fine-tuning, no one will stop you. Not even the Descendant of Wind you're so tired of," he said.

Angel's throat tightened, and it burned when she swallowed. "Havoc, I'm in no mood. You know I won't cut a deal with a snake," she said.

"Not even if I, too, wish to bring Malsumis to our world."

Angel lowered her weapon but narrowed her eyes. There were a lot of worshippers of the primitive religion outside the city. Not all of them shared Lord Malsumis' vision. He might have been playing with her.

"How do you know?" she asked.

He smiled, his lips curled up like a crooked cat and revealed stained yellowed teeth. She shivered at how his black eyes crinkled and gleamed like hot coals. "My work goes well beyond yours. I've been studying the deities for many years. There's even a story about two people that tells of the end. Do you wish to hear it?" he asked.

Angel chewed the inside of her cheek and nodded.

"A man saw ten years ago. Before his wife gave birth, he told her she would have twins. The combination of their magik and pure bloodline would bring balance to the world," Havoc said, his eyes darkening. "Ask me what their magik is."

Angel scowled but played along. "What's their magik?"

"Light and dark," he said.

Angel furrowed her brow, and she let the spear vanish. It is a story of siblings bringing balance to an entire world. That wasn't in any of the old texts she found or read.

"The boys will be powerful; one will command the entire faction of light while the other will command the darkness. In the end, one of them is going to die." The man stopped, and she clicked her tongue.

She didn't have use for kids who end up killing each other. "How is one person supposed to handle the entire faction of light or dark? Descendants only control one element," Angel said, picking some dried blood from under her nails.

"The story will come true. I don't know how, but I know it will," Havoc said, his voice deepening.

"How?" she asked.

"Because I'm going to make sure it does."

Angel pursed her lips and thought for a moment. "How does this play into what I want?" she asked.

"You need a sacrifice. Someone with a magikal bloodline that spans generations. These boys have a long line of magik. Imagine how that would sustain your God," Havoc said.

Angel stayed quiet as she thought. She was foolish if she made a deal with him. "What do you get from it?" she asked.

He smirked as if already knowing he had won. "My lord and master in my world."

She was at a dead end. If she refused his help, she would have to figure the rest out alone. Havoc was wise beyond his years, but he was ruthless. People thought she was terrible. She had nothing on him.

The water churned, and she closed her eyes. To end this curse would be lovely. If she could find a pure magikal bloodline, she could finish it.

Angel clicked her tongue and nodded before sticking out her hand. "Very well, I'll work with you. If you disappoint me, I'll find a new ally," she said.

He chuckled under his breath and clasped her hand in his icy grip. "I look forward to it."

Operation Tutor is a Go

KARA

"**D**ID YOU HEAR ABOUT the massacre downtown?"

"I know it was horrible. All those kids." Chattering women passed her on the street, and Kara turned.

Angel shouldn't have even known about the party. The seniors were talking about how hidden it was. Someone obviously spilled the beans. She watched the two women disappear into a clothing shop. Sometimes, the older kids organized parties, but they weren't usually caught.

Last night, Angel had a surprise for all of them. She killed every person in attendance: man, woman, and child. She didn't understand why the ruler would decide to take such a drastic measure, but it made her strengthen her resolve.

If Kara didn't pass her final, she would be sent to reform school, and the same fate awaited her. Today was the day. She was going to ask for help.

She scrunched her nose and stopped outside a café. A small brick shop where most of the goods came from Rochester Homestead.

Angel often brought trade goods from the surrounding towns and villages to keep the people content. She imported sweet food, fruits, vegetables, and anything to simulate an actual city. Yorklyn could grow independently, but the work would detract from Angel's vision, so she kept nature out.

Kara saw it as a form of control. If they had to depend on Angel for food and clothes, they would do anything to keep her happy. Her eyes flicked to the window, and she spotted Ryan. He sat at one of the round tables and stirred a wooden stick in a white porcelain cup.

People filtered in and out, holding cupcakes and donuts.

She would bring Dawson home a donut once a week, at the end of each week. They would share a sweet and read a book, curled up on the living room couch. Kara swallowed the lump in her throat. She wasn't ready for that to end.

"Okay, I can do this. I'm going to ask for help," she whispered. Someone pushed past her on the street, and she stumbled with a grunt. She almost hit the window but pivoted on the ball of her foot.

Ryan looked innocent through the thick glass windows. A smile lit up his features, and Kara nodded. Asking for help was no big deal. She had this under control. Or so she thought, until his eyes flicked toward her, and he raised an eyebrow.

Kara all but threw herself to the ground. The stone wall scratched her forehead, and pain spread across her brow. A droplet of blood seeped from the minor cut, and she dabbed it with her sleeve.

The shop bell tingled beautifully, and a shadow fell over her. Kara huffed at herself and peered up at the sandy blonde staring down at her. The sun behind him nearly blinded her and softened his typical gruff features. For a moment, he looked sweet. He shoved his hands in his pockets and chuckled under his breath. "Well, good mornin' Princess," Ryan said, a soft lilt to his voice.

She pushed herself off the ground and grunted. Her mind had already started conjuring a believable lie.

Ryan opened the door and gestured inside without asking. It was like he was expecting her.

Kara slipped past him and tried to ignore how her heart leaped to her throat. It was just Ryan. She wouldn't lose her cool.

The small cafe's fake wood floors shone under the dangling lights. Cobwebs decorated the uppermost corners of the ten-foot vaulted ceilings. The room was as large as her living room, and the lights were dimmed, creating a soft darkness. There was enough light to see where she was going but not enough to determine who was sitting across the way.

Honestly, she was a bit upset for recognizing Ryan so quickly from the outside.

He steered her around the corner, and she froze. Killian sat at the table, tapping his foot and fiddling with crumbs on the wood top. He refused to meet her gaze.

Kara cursed, and Ryan practically shoved her into the third seat between theirs.

"Killian told me you two had a tiff yesterday," Ryan said, "Dawson said you were coming, by the way."

Kara bit her tongue. Her little sneak of a brother. *How dare he betray me?* She almost couldn't believe it. Almost. "We didn't get into anything. Just had a normal conversation," Kara said.

Ryan nodded. "A friendly conversation about murdering each other."

"No one ever said murder," Kara argued.

Ryan smirked; his gaze lingered too long. Her cheeks burned under his scrutiny, and she almost sighed in relief when he looked away.

"What did you need, Kara?" Killian asked. He seemed to be done with their level of "flirting," as Dawson would call it.

Kara nearly forgot why she was there. She cleared her throat and folded her hands in her lap. Asking for a favor was no big deal. It wasn't like she wouldn't pay Ryan back. There could be an equal exchange. "I would like to conduct a... trade of sorts," Kara said, remembering what her teacher said about motivation.

"Sure, what kind of trade?" Ryan asked.

He flicked a crumb of bread off the table at his brother. The morsel pelted Killian in the forehead and landed in his lap. A small smile stained Ryan's lips, and he gave a look that dared Killian to retaliate.

Kara sighed and shook her head. She wouldn't believe Ryan was at the top of the class if their teacher hadn't confirmed it. "I'mfailingmathand-needatutor." The words slipped past her lips in a single sentence. Kara squeezed her eyes shut and waited for the laughter. When none came, she cracked an eye.

He wouldn't make eye contact and rubbed the back of his neck. "That's all?" Ryan asked.

She puffed her cheeks out in frustration. It wasn't like she was going to profess her love or anything. If he was expecting something more exciting, he didn't know the first thing about her.

 Killian leaned back in his chair and sank down. He closed his eyes and hummed a tune that Kara didn't recognize.

"I'm sorry. Did you say you were failing math?" Ryan asked.
She nodded.

He chewed on his bottom lip and shot his brother a stare. An invisible conversation passed between them before Ryan's eyes returned to her. In thirty seconds, he seemed to have decided. "I'd love to help, but what makes you think I can?"

"The teacher told me you have the highest grades. If you don't want to, just say so," she muttered.

"Okay, I don't want to."

Kara scowled and pushed away from the table. Her chair screeched across the floor, leaving behind black marks on the shiny brown floor.

Ryan's shoulders shook with amusement at her frustration, but he had the wisdom to hide his smile behind his hand.

"Well, too bad. I'm not giving you an option. We all know what happens to people who don't pass their program evaluations. I need you," she snapped. Venom colored her words, but it only made him smile more.

"What's in it for me?" Ryan asked.

She bit her tongue and thought for a moment. Ryan and Killian didn't have many friends, which meant their private lives stayed private. If they were out for something, she didn't know what. "What do you want?" she asked after contemplating.

Killian clicked his tongue and shook his head. "She's desperate if she's giving you *that* much freedom."

"No one asked you, psycho," Kara said, shooting him a dark glare. She didn't have the time for his input or sarcasm.

Ryan pushed his coffee out of the way and folded his hands on the table. His emerald eyes narrowed ever so slightly as he thought about his terms. He was going to torture her. "Alright, I'll make sure you pass the program evaluation. And, when you do, you owe me a date," he said.

She cocked her head. It took a while for his words to sink in so she could process what was happening.

He wanted to take her on a date. Of all the things he could ask for, that was missing from the list of possibilities in her head.

"Wait, what?" she asked.

Killian huffed in frustration and slapped his knees. "I gotta go. Homework to do and whatnot. See ya back at the house," he said, leaving them alone.

Kara still stood at the table with her chair toppled behind her. She stared at the other twin, the one who had practically asked her out. And, the scary part was, she couldn't figure out why. Did he ever show interest before, or did he and she just not notice?

"A date. You owe me the worst date ever," Ryan said.

She scowled. She didn't even know what a proper date looked like. There hadn't been much chance for dating. "Alright, you know what, fine. I'll give you the worst date if you help me pass," Kara said.

"Promise?" he asked.

"Absolutely. I'll make you spend all your money and complain about it the next day. Then I won't call."

He stuck out his hand, and Kara straightened. His eyes glimmered, full of amusement. "I'll see what I can do."

She hesitated before reaching out and grasped his hand. His skin was on fire, and his fingers were rough and calloused, like someone who worked in the factories. Kara turned his hand over in wonder. She couldn't figure out why his skin was so hot. It was the same yesterday, too.

He pulled away before she could focus too much on it. "What chapters do you need help with?" Ryan asked. He picked up his cup and sipped. His eyes didn't leave hers.

She fidgeted and twiddled her thumbs before exhaling sharply. He was going to regret agreeing to help. "The whole thing," she murmured.

"I'm sorry, what?"

"If I was doing great, I wouldn't need help," Kara snapped defensively, crossing her arms against her chest.

He shook his head again, and a small sigh escaped his lips. "Alright, here's the deal. We have a ten o'clock curfew thanks to the amazing ruler. School is in session until three. When do you expect me to have the time to help and get home?"

"That's at least five hours a day," Kara said.

"We're down to five or six days. You honestly think maybe thirty hours of studying will cut it?" he asked.

"What choice do I have?" Kara bit back a whine. She was already desperate; she wouldn't act like a crybaby.

Ryan pursed his lips and stared at the table for a bit. His eyes traced the lines of the differing woods that made up the top. He lost himself in whatever thought he had before he looked back. "Would your parents let you stay at our place?" he asked.

Kara laughed until she realized he was serious. "Gods, no, are you joking? My mom would kill me for asking."

"What if she let me stay at your place?"

"No," Kara sighed, "because then I'd have to tell her I'm failing."

Ryan shook his head and slapped the table. "Your parents don't even know. Nope, I'm out. Kara, you can't, not tell your mom about this."

"Watch me," she said, jutting her chin out.

"What're you gonna tell them when I'm over?" he asked.

"I dunno," Kara said.

"Sorry, I'm not gonna go behind your mother's back. That woman's terrifying enough as is," he said.

"She won't do anything to you."

Ryan stood and left a few silver coins on the table as he shook his head.

She was losing him. Kara grabbed his bicep, and he shot her a level stare.

His hands clenched at his side, and he pulled back.

"Ryan, please. I'm desperate. My mom can't find out. If she did, she'd put me six feet in the ground. Plus, I can't stress my dad out. He doesn't sleep enough as is," Kara said.

"It's a bad idea. Your mom can help, can't she?"

"We just discussed why I don't want to tell my parents anything," Kara hissed.

Ryan looked up at the sound of clicking heels. She opened her mouth to say something else when a woman cleared her throat behind them.

Kara whirled around and winced at the sight of sharp blue eyes and blunt-cut black hair. She stood behind them with her hands on her hips, and her eyes narrowed into slits. Kara knew she was dead. "Oh, hey, Mom. Didn't see you there," she said.

Her mom crossed her arms and gestured to them.

Kara looked at Ryan and pushed him away with a startled shout. "No, this isn't what it looks like. I don't even like him. He's a friend, helping me," Kara all but yelled. Her cheeks were burning. This didn't look good.

Ryan rubbed the back of his neck before sticking his hand out. "Afternoon, ma'am. Just meetin' up with Kara for coffee. How you doin'?" he asked.

Her steely gaze didn't move from Kara. "You weren't going to tell me you were failing?" She ignored Ryan. "How could you not tell me you were failing?"

Kara puffed out her cheeks in exasperation. Her mom was the last person she wanted to find out.

"Were you spying on me again? I thought you said you wouldn't do that anymore," Kara said.

"Let's go. Now," her mom demanded and pointed to the cafe door.

Kara's shoulders slouched, and she glared daggers at her mother. She quickly said goodbye to Ryan and stormed past the woman who made her life a living Helwe.

Unknown Number

"Y OU DIDN'T SPEND AS long flirting as I thought," Killian said when Ryan walked through the door. "You realize you asked her on a date?"

Ryan shrugged and ran his hand through his hair. "It was a joke. Plus, she hadn't told her parents about the whole failing thing. Kinda ruined it when mommy dearest turned up all pissed."

Killian smirked but said nothing. It was easy to read between the lines. No parent would want Ryan dating their child. He knew little about the McKenzies, but one thing he knew was how strict their mom was.

Samantha McKenzie was the director of the surveillance team. Nothing happened in the city without her knowing. It was rather foolish of Kara to think she could get it past her mom.

"Did you guys work something out?" Killian asked.

Ryan shot him a glare and shook his head.

Killian shrugged and finished prepping the meal over their rusted, breaking stove. Honestly, there was nothing to figure out. Kara's parents would make sure she got the tutoring she needed. It was the most logical approach.

Ryan's phone rang when they were in the middle of dinner. Killian looked up, and Ryan answered his cell. He listened half-heartedly for a moment.

"Ryan, oh, let me get him. Give me just a moment," Ryan said, holding the phone out to Killian.

Killian swallowed his bite of cream-soaked noodles and shook his head. He hadn't pretended to be Ryan since they were twelve, and he threw a spelling bee. "No."

"Dude, it's her mom. She hates me. You're better at the polite thing," Ryan whispered, covering the phone with his hand.

Killian shook his head again. "No, Helwe, no. She's terrifying. I can't pretend to be you. Everyone knows you have piercings."

"Talk on the phone. She can't see you, moron," Ryan hissed.

"She's the director of surveillance. She can see whatever she damn well wants to see," Killian said.

"Take the phone."

Killian huffed and set his fork down. He wouldn't win the argument, and the longer he made Ms. McKenzie wait, the worse it would be. "Hello. Ryan, speaking."

"Is this the boy that was hanging on my daughter in the coffee shop?" Samantha asked. Her voice was clipped and tight.

Oh Gods, what was he doing hanging on Kara? Killian gulped. "That doesn't sound like something I'd do. Does it?" He eyed Ryan, and his brother shook his head furiously. "But for argument's sake, sure."

"You know my position in the government?" she asked.

"Um, yes, yes I do."

"Good, so let's not beat around the bush. You're an outsider but one with outstanding work in mathematics. I require your help. You'll be compensated." Samantha didn't hesitate to cut to the chase. "Kara needs tutoring, and she insists that you're the best. Is she wrong?"

Killian cleared his throat to buy himself some time. Ryan couldn't be that good in his classes. He didn't know his brother's grades. "I excel in my program, sure. To say I'm the best, that might be exaggerating."

Samantha hummed into the phone. He could almost see her scowl. "This isn't Ryan. You're the other one."

Killian's eyes widened, and he choked on his spit. She was watching them. He knew she was watching. "Sorry?"

"Your brother is obnoxious and arrogant. Why isn't he talking to me?" she demanded.

Because he's a chickenshit. Killian didn't know how to say that without getting hit later, so he made a sound between a gurgle and a choke.

"Whatever the reason, you will report to our house after school tomorrow. That gives Ryan five days to work with Kara. During that time, you'll stay in our guest room. If you leave that room between the hours of ten pm and six am, I will castrate you both. Is that understood?" she asked.

Killian hummed in agreement. Why was he being dragged into it? He wasn't even in the science program.

"Good. See you tomorrow."

The line went dead, and Killian threw the phone at Ryan's chest.

His brother yelped in surprise and almost ducked under the flying piece of tech. "What's that for?"

"Apparently, we're invited to stay as guests for the rest of the week," Killian snarled. "And she knew I wasn't you, so never ask me to do that again."

"Wait, what? I'm not staying at their place the entire week." Ryan said.

"She's not giving us a choice. It happens, or you lose your balls," Killian said.

Ryan shook his head again. It was like he just couldn't believe something like this would backfire. "Why is she threatening my manhood? I didn't even touch her daughter."

They were in trouble. Killian wasn't too keen on being forced to stay at Casa de la McKenzie. It sounded like a nightmare. He was sure Kara's parents would kill them. Not only that but how long would Ryan be able to stay in control?

"We can't stay at their house," Killian said. "Oh man, we can't stay at their house. What if I lose control? They'll put us before Angel." he grabbed his face.

Ryan patted him on the back. "It's gonna be fine. Stop stressing. I stress when you stress, and we need to be calm."

There was no being calm. Killian didn't associate with people on good days, and now he had to stay with some family he didn't know for five. He was going to kill someone, literally.

Ryan chuckled under his breath and tossed his cell onto the coffee table. "So much for a relaxing week, huh?"

"And she said you were hanging all over her daughter. She's going to eat us alive," Killian whined. He let his forehead hit the table in defeat. His shoulders slumped, and the wood bit into his skin.

Samantha never would've invited them if she knew what they were. Killian was half tempted to call her back, tell her they were Descendants, and let it be over with. It wasn't like she wasn't about to find out, anyway.

"You're overthinking," Ryan said. "I can feel you. Stop and eat." He popped another forkful of noodles and vegetables into his mouth.

Killian lost his appetite. He stared duly at his food as if it offended him. How did he go from trying to get rid of Kara and her annoying little brother to spending time with the entire family? He needed help understanding where he went wrong.

"I shouldn't have talked to her," he whispered. "This is retribution for threatening her brother."

Ryan raised his eyebrow and slurped a noodle. "You talkin' to yourself now, buddy? All good there?"

"This is what happens to mean people. If I get out of this, I'll change my ways. I really will." Killian ignored Ryan.

Even when his brother started snapping his fingers in his face. A small puff of smoke circled the air as Ryan snapped repeatedly.

Killian's eye twitched, and he waved the smoke away, scowling. "We're going to die, you stupid son of a-"

"Calm down, Kill. I know how to control my magik. I won't let anything happen. Shut up and eat." Ryan cut him off.

He didn't want to eat. He wanted to sulk. A soft pain in his head made him flinch, and he closed his eyes.

He was dropped in the middle of a black room in his mind. A shadow loomed over a grand piano with crimson and violet keys. Claws danced across them, making the instrument sing.

Killian whirled around as laughter filled the air, matching the dank, gloomy tune of the song. *No, I can't be here. Not back here.*

"We're going to have some fun, kid. Why not smile more?" the shadow cracked a huge smile, showing off sharp teeth.

No, we're not having fun. Don't start. I don't want this. Killian always spoke telepathically with the shadow. He knew little about it, just that it was tied to his magik.

"Your brother will find some way to mess up, then you'll beg me to help."

You're wrong. Ryan said nothing bad will happen.

The music stopped, and the shadow slid across the oily back floor, dragging an elongated claw down his cheek. It was cold, like ice. *"Such a dumb boy."*

Killian trembled and jerked his head away. Crimson half-moon slits stared into his soul, making his legs weak. *I won't be what you want.*

"You already are."

Ryan threw a cup of water in his face.

Killian scowled and cut his gaze to him. If looks could kill. "What the Helwe is wrong with you?"

"You were talking to that voice again. Stop." Ryan stuffed more food into his mouth.

Killian wiped the water off his face and pushed himself to his feet. He wouldn't lose control.

Teach a Man to Fish

JUSTIN

"Cody, I need to go out. Do you think you can avoid blowing anything up?" Justin called from the front door. There was a shout of affirmation from somewhere down the hall, and he sighed. He put a coat on and walked out of the house. He hadn't stopped thinking about the message Nicholas left.

After a day or two of stewing, he trekked to Rochester to find his brother and figure out what was happening. Descendants were common, so if Nick needed to say he found some, something needed to be fixed.

Justin had a bad habit of speaking out of anger when his brother was concerned, so instead of being rational when he should've been, he pushed the other out the door. Almost literally.

The plan was to go out into the woods and call his name. If Nicholas left a message, he would wait for Justin's reply. If that didn't work, he would go from there.

Justin walked across the barriers protecting his land and stepped into the woods of the mountains. He loved a pleasant nature walk.

Birds chirped in the trees, the wind rustled leaves, and even the sound of crunching foliage and twigs beneath his feet was calming. The world was still and gentle. It didn't take long for the animals to go silent, and the world stopped.

Justin turned. Eyes bore into his back. "I read your message," he said. It was best to let Nick know he wasn't coming from a place of anger.

An unfamiliar voice caught him off guard. "Too bad you didn't wait to hear the rest."

It was the voice of a young man. Perhaps a boy? Justin faced the direction the voice came from and flicked his wrist. A rush of blue energy washed through the gray and brown of nature. *Another Descendant. Is this one of the ones Nick found?* "Who are you?" Justin asked.

"Many people call me The Smuggler." The voice stayed level, but there was bitterness there.

Justin found his interest piqued. If someone was stupid enough to come after him, they wouldn't know who he was. "I'm looking for my brother," he said.

"I'm aware. I'm dating him, and I wasn't too pleased with how he came home the other night." An angry boyfriend.

That wasn't something Justin was accustomed to dealing with. When Nick lived with him, he rarely brought his conquests home, let alone called them boyfriend.

He chuckled. "Are you being protective of my brother?" Justin asked.

"Someone needs to be," the boy said with a huff.

Justin watched the other's energy spaz out in anger before calming. Someone was being trained. "You think I don't care about him because of a fight?"

"Do you know how long we've been together?" the boy asked.

Justin could humor him, but he was running out of patience. He didn't know how the brat found him, but he intended to talk to his brother, not his brother's lackey.

"Nick's never hung out with someone for more than a few months," Justin said, waving a hand. "Are you going to tell me where he is?"

The young man sighed. "He said you were unreasonable."

Justin scowled. He wasn't about to be lectured by what sounded like a school kid. "Tell me, has Nick even told you anything substantial about his life besides favorite food or color?" Justin asked. "Because everything I've done is for him. Whether or not he wants to believe it."

The boy was quiet for a while. If Justin couldn't see his energy, he would've thought he vanished. "I know you tried to kill him."

Justin ran a hand through his hair. The woods returned to life, and he knew the boy was gone. The scampering of tiny paws caught his attention, and he returned home.

Their relationship wasn't perfect, but he loved his brother. Sometimes, people needed tough love to find their own paths. Justin missed the relationship they had, but he wouldn't bend on morals when he did everything he could to help his brother.

The soft tingle of magik running up his arms let him know he made it home without incident. Justin sighed and ran a hand down his face.

"I told him you weren't friendly," Nick said.

Justin jumped and cocked his head toward the voice. He hated that he taught him to hide his energy so well. It was becoming a burden on him.

"Is that the new flavor of the month?" Justin asked, disdain coloring his tone. "I didn't appreciate it."

"He wanted to meet you. I can't very well control what he does," Nick said, a smile in his voice. "We've been together about a year."

A sustained relationship was a good sign. Maybe Nick was growing up. Still, it didn't mean Justin was happy to entertain a snot-nose kid.

"And how old's this one? He sounded like a child." Justin scowled, walking up to the porch.

Nick sighed. "He's nineteen, not a kid. Don't make me out to be some creep."

"I don't care who you screw. Just keep them out of my life." He felt around until he found the porch rail and leaned on it.

Nick sighed and set a hand on Justin's arm. It was his first instinct to recoil, but he kept himself still. "I want to come home," Nick whispered.

"You know my arrangement."

"I've been sober, Jay. I miss you and Cody. Rochester is great. I've got the living alone experience, but it's not what I want," Nick said. His voice rose a bit as he tried to hide the desperation.

Justin rubbed his eyes and pulled his arm away. He could still smell the beer from a few nights ago. "Tell me why you smell like alcohol, then."

Nicholas hesitated, even sniffing his shirt to check. "I don't. I haven't had a drink in a year and a half."

Justin grabbed Nicholas' wrist and felt his pulse. His fingers brushed a patch of rough, raised skin. An old scar from a time they would both love to forget. When Justin found the pulse, he focused on how it thumped under his fingers. Nicholas' heart was steady and robust. It couldn't be detected by heart rate alone if he was lying.

"Is that boy going to be staying with us?" Justin sighed.

Nicholas pulled him into a hug before he knew what was going on.

Justin tensed for a moment. The scent of pine and maple washed over him, and he relaxed, wrapping his arms around Nicholas.

"I'm getting better, Jay."

"We both could stand to do better. But that doesn't answer my previous question," Justin said.

Nicholas sniffed and shook his head. "No, he has his own place. I can't say he won't visit, but I think you'll like him if you give him a chance."

It was easier to just say yes. Justin sighed and shook his head. Life was about to get interesting.

Failing!

KARA

KARA SULKED ON THE leather couch in the living room as her mom yelled. She tuned her out a few minutes ago, so Kara needed to figure out where in the lecture they were.

"How could you not tell us something like this?" her mom asked.

Kara shrugged. "You're the surveillance captain, shouldn't you know?"

Her mom scowled and stopped pacing long enough to shoot her a glare. "Don't give me attitude."

Kara huffed in exasperation and shrugged again. Her mom would return to work in about an hour, so it wouldn't matter. She couldn't enforce any punishment without being there.

"I could kill you for this. My influence won't save you like it does your brother." Her mom sat next to her and ran a hand through her hair. "You're supposed to be the one who's got their life together."

Anger settled in Kara's stomach, and she clenched her fists. She was supposed to be the one who had everything down, wasn't she? She had to cook the meals, clean the house, and make sure Dawson made it home safe and sound.

"I'm a kid too, you know?" she shouted, jumping off the couch.

Her mom blinked, startled at the sudden outburst.

Kara threw her hands in the air. "I do everything. If it wasn't for me, Dawson could never finish his homework. He needs help with seventy-five percent of it. And then I have to figure out my own," Kara snapped.

"Now, wait just a minute."

"No. You're never home. Dad's never home. Who else is supposed to keep this family together?" Kara demanded. "Do you even remember you have kids most of the time? Because I'm always here by myself trying to make sure you have a home to return to."

Her mom stood and grabbed her hands, pulling them to her chest and staring into her eyes. "Sweetie, calm down," she whispered. "I didn't realize we were putting so much on you. I know things have been hard, but-"

Kara's eyes filled with tears, and she jerked her hands away. "Just go back to work. I'll figure it out. Ryan's gonna help me. I don't need you." She ran up to her room and slammed the door behind her. Kara brushed the tears off her cheeks angrily.

When it hit her, what she said and how she acted, she slid to the floor and pressed her back to her bedroom door. Her hands tingled and burned like something was trying to escape.

Kara took a few deep breaths until the sobbing stopped, and her breathing became more manageable. What she said wasn't fair. It didn't mean she wasn't being honest, but it was wrong to have said it.

Her parents worked hard, and Kara was unnecessarily cruel. She knew her mom hated being away from them, but they were growing up. They didn't need Mommy around all the time.

She hiccupped and wiped her eyes when a soft tap against her door made her sigh. Three quick taps brought a smile to her lips, and she stood to open it.

"Heard you yelling." Dawson stared at her with soft eyes. "I'm sorry."

She shook her head and hiccupped again. "I should probably apologize to Mom, huh?" she asked.

Dawson frowned. "She went back to work. Thought you needed some time alone."

"Of course." Kara stepped aside so he could walk in. For once, she wanted her mom to fight for her.

Dawson scrambled to her bed when he had the opportunity and belly-flopped onto it. "Your room smells so much better than mine."

"If you cleaned it, you wouldn't have a problem," Kara said.

He patted the spot next to her. "She called Ryan."

Kara's head snapped up, and she stared. "She did what?"

"Yep, told 'em they were gonna come stay with us until school ends. It's gonna be fun having them around," Dawson said with a smirk.

Anxiety rolled through her stomach, and she groaned. Now would be the best time to throw up. Her heart fluttered an unnatural rhythm, and she clutched her head. "No, no, no. He can't say here. Neither of them can. This is my safe place, my Haven," she whispered.

Dawson patted the spot on the bed again. "Sit."

Kara's room spun, and her head pounded. She dropped to her knees and tried to even her breathing again.

Dawson huffed and got off the bed to kneel in front of her. "Hey, calm down. This isn't a bad thing. They're gonna be in the guest room downstairs. Calm down." His hands ran up and down her arms as if trying to warm her.

"I don't want them here," Kara shouted.

Her bedroom light flickered, and Dawson let her go, shaking his hands. "You shocked me," he muttered.

Kara's chest heaved; she wasn't getting enough air. Her body trembled, and Dawson wrapped her in a hug. She pressed her forehead against his chest, and he tightened his hold.

"Breathe with me," he said. Kara closed her eyes and did what he told her to. When she was calm, he let her go and patted her on the back. "I won't let anything happen. You always protect me, so I'll protect you."

Kara blinked and wiped her face again. "Promise?" she asked.

He nodded and beamed. "I'm your brother. Always."

Kara spent the night tossing and turning, knowing Ryan would go home with them the next day. Not only him, but Killian, too. She didn't understand why they both had to be there.

Dawson woke her up the following day. He tried to make eggs and toast but burned everything. She giggled at the attempt and forced half of it down to not hurt his feelings.

She didn't see her mom or dad before they left for school. The day passed in a blur as she tried not to overthink the end.

When the bell rang for lunch, she gathered her things. She chucked her bag in her locker, shouldered past classmates, and went out the side door to the gravelly field where the runners met for practice. She was too nervous to eat.

Shouting caught her attention as she rounded the corner of the school. Kara peered at a group of her classmates standing around, jeering. Another fight. She supposed Ryan would be in the center of that circle. Not even halfway through the day, and he was causing problems.

"Come on, creep. Do something."

Killian's voice made her frown. "You're going to piss me off. Return my things and move." He stayed unnaturally calm, but his voice carried. A warning lingered.

He stood in the middle of four other boys. She recognized some of them from the medical program and some from the business program. Whatever he did, they all leered and snarled to rile him up.

Killian didn't look concerned. His shoulders were relaxed, and his hands were shoved in his pockets. He looked bored, if anything.

She clapped her hands, and the group turned to face her. "Hey, back off before I get a soldier. You know there's no fighting."

Killian cut her a glare. For a moment, he looked just like his brother, even with his flat, combed hair and button-up shirt.

There was something cold around him, and if she stared long enough, Kara could almost make out a purple wisp. Almost like there was a ribbon wrapped around his waist. She frowned and felt the same pull when she looked at his ring. The desire to reach out and grasp the ribbon almost made her move.

She noticed he wasn't wearing the ring when she looked for it. Kara wasn't sure why she was looking for it. There was a pull that she couldn't ignore. Kara frowned and tried to refocus.

One boy, Kara thinks his name was Scott, threw an arm around Killian's shoulders. "Who's fighting? We're just talkin' to our buddy here. Aren't we?"

"Some friends you are," she scoffed. "Now get lost."

Killian moved before anyone could do anything. He ducked under Scott's bulky bronze arm and slammed his palm into the older boy's nose. A sickening crack made Kara cover her face; all she heard was shouting and thudding. When it was over, she spread her fingers to peer through them.

Killian wiped a spot of blood from his cheek, and his eyes flicked to her. His normal emerald gaze was clouded red. Like something unearthly possessed him.

A dark violet shadow lingered behind him. It resembled a human shadow but had glowing red eyes and long, elongated fingers that looked like claws. That wasn't Killian. He walked towards her, but Kara squeaked in terror and ran.

She didn't look back when she threw the school door open, and it slammed behind her. Kara whipped around the hall and pressed her hands to her chest. Her heart was going to come out of her ribcage.

Students snickered and giggled as she sped by. For once, she ignored the judgmental stares and tried to forget the one Killian gave her. A look colder and more complicated than any she had ever seen. Frozen like ice. It was like he didn't have any feelings or emotions.

Kara squealed when she ran into someone and knocked them off balance. "I'm sorry, so sorry," she sputtered, looking behind her to see if Killian was following.

Strong hands grabbed her shoulders, and she whirled around. Ryan stared down at her, a brow quirked in confusion. "What's wrong with you? You look like you saw a monster."

"Killian was-" was what? She didn't know how to explain the icy chill that swept through her blood. Kara couldn't justify the shadow or red eyes. Ryan would think she lost her mind.

"Killian, what? Did he do something?" Ryan asked. His voice lowered, and he stared her in the eyes. "Where is he?"

Kara shook her head and took a couple of deep breaths. It was a trick of the light. It had to be. There weren't shadows with eyes. Monsters like that didn't exist. The only actual monsters were the ones with magik, and there was no way Killian was one of those.

It had to be the book she read to Dawson last night. "Nothing, I'm sorry. It was nothing," she said after a moment.

Ryan shook his head as if he didn't believe her. "What'd he do?"

"I thought..." she trailed off. The thought never left her lips. She thought she saw a monster. She thought *he* was a monster. There was nothing she could think of to say that made sense. "He got into a fight with some jerks in his class. I got scared."

Ryan eyed her for a long time before nodding. He scanned her face, trying to determine if she was telling him the truth. When he seemed content, he asked, "Where?"

"Out the side doors and around the corner of the school. Just left of the field," she whispered.

Ryan nodded and let her go. "I'll see you after school, huh?" he asked.

Kara forced a shaky smile and hummed in agreement. She watched Ryan hurry past her and down the way she came. She was losing her mind. That was it. Killian wasn't unusually cruel. Of course, it would freak her out. He might have been rude sometimes, but he wasn't aggressive. Seeing him fight must've set her anxiety off and caused a hallucination.

"Calm down, Kara. Nothing is going on. You're being weird," she muttered to herself.

When the bell rang, signaling the end of lunch, she hurried to her next class. The day would end soon. Then, she only had to deal with the twins for a few days.

Halfway through their last class, an alarm went off. A speaker called for a town meeting and required everyone who wasn't working to be at the city square. Kara looked up from her work with confusion before gathering her things.

City meetings meant one thing. Execution. Teachers tried to keep their students in line as they filed out of school. When the streets crowded, she lost track of her schoolmates and fell into the growing throng of adults.

She looked around the street with a huff, hoping to find someone she knew before she ran into someone unpleasant. She could barely turn without elbowing someone. The executions were always in the same place, set in the center of Yorklyn, where the four intersections of each quadrant intersected. The residential district, the downtown district, the factory district, and the military district.

They all came together by a vast steel building acting as a conduit for the electricity. Many called it Yorklyn Tower. In front of it sat a large wooden stage with soldiers lining the sides and front. A podium sat in the middle, set up with a microphone, and Angel stood at it. The woman looked over the crowd in a pencil-thin skirt and a white lace blouse. She pinned her fiery red hair in a business-like bun as she shuffled through papers before her. She wouldn't read off her notes. She never did.

"Good afternoon, my beloved subjects," her voice boomed across the crowd, echoing off the buildings. A hush fell as everyone turned their eyes onto their beloved leader.

Kara scanned the crowd for her brother or parents.

"I know there are a lot of rumors going around about a magik running loose. We have caught the man responsible for these terrifying escapades. He will no longer terrorize you.

"I promised you when I took charge of the city I would uphold only the best qualities of humanity while ridding the world of these abominations. Today, I make good on my promise. Guards, bring him."

Applause erupted as the soldiers dragged an unconscious man to the stage. The soldiers dragged him to the stage, bloodied, bruised, and almost unrecognizable, eliciting applause from the audience. Kara put her hands to her mouth as she stared at the swollen eyes and a bruised face. Lacerations littered his arms, and his lips were so chapped from dehydration they cracked.

Her head throbbed, and she shook away the pain. She hated public executions; they always made her sick. Kara didn't want to see someone die. One day, she was afraid it would be someone she knew on that stage.

"This man has been stealing, performing acts of arson, and killing innocents!" A boo ran through the crowd, and Kara winced. "He will pay for his crimes."

"Kill the monster." Someone screamed. "Kill him before he kills us."

The crowd worked itself into a frenzy. Kara covered her ears as the yelling escalated. One voice broke the tension and quieted people down for a moment: the voice of a young woman, "No, please. That's my husband. He isn't magik."

Kara looked through the crowd until she saw the crying woman. She reached up to the podium and begged for her husband's life. Love was one of the stupidest things.

"He isn't a magik, I swear. We have a family. He couldn't possibly be affected."

The look of victory fell from Angel's features, and her eyes narrowed on the woman. "This demon has children?"

The woman clutched her chest as if forgetting herself and stepped back. People from behind grabbed her shoulders and shoved her forward again. "She's a magik too. Kill her, find the kids."

The scene was too horrible. Kara begged for someone to step in and stop the madness. She covered her eyes with a whimper as Angel stalked to the end of the stage to peer into the woman's eyes. "I asked you a question, traitor. You *will* answer."

Kara had enough. She wanted to go home. She had to find her brother and get out of there.

"Stop." a deep voice boomed across the square, reaching the stage.

Images of red flashed through her head, causing her to fall to her knees and dry heave. The nausea was so intense she was sure she was going to vomit. She held her stomach with closed eyes and took deep breaths as sweat ran down her neck. She wouldn't throw up. Gravel cut into her shins. It helped her breath come easier. She looked up at a straw-haired boy on one of the shop balconies when she was sure she was okay. *Ryan.*

Angel careened her neck to face the boy on the balcony. Her eyes caught fire when she saw him, standing defiant against her rule. Her face morphed into something terrifying for half a second before returning to its usual porcelain smile.

Kara shivered.

"And what have we here? A lost little boy?" Angel asked. Her voice was too sweet for the look in her steel-blue eyes.

Ryan narrowed his gaze but kept quiet. His shoulders hunched up, and he stared down at the scene. He seemed to be at a loss for what to do.

Kara groaned to herself as she shook her head. He was going to get himself killed. There's no way Angel would tolerate such blatant disrespect.

"Cat got your tongue, boy?" Angel asked. Her soldiers loaded their guns and pointed them up at the balcony, waiting for him to make a move.

Don't shoot him, please don't shoot. He doesn't know what he's doing. Kara could speak up and plead for his life, but she would become a target. She chewed on her lip until it was bloody. She was a coward. Her chin hit her chest, and she closed her eyes in silent prayer. What else could she do?

Executions and
Brothers

KILLIAN

KILLIAN SHOULD HAVE KNOWN Kara wouldn't keep her mouth shut. Ryan cornered him when he tried to sneak back to his classroom in one of the back halls no one ever went to.

Sometimes, people heard screaming and swore that the place was haunted. It wasn't haunted. Teachers who didn't stick to the curriculum were tortured in the back hall. They let the haunted rumor stay, so none of the kids investigated.

Ryan swore if Killian ever pulled a stunt like that again, he would kill him. They both knew he was bluffing, but it still earned Killian a black eye when he laughed. That snapped him out of his trance.

When the alarms went off for a meeting, he groaned under his breath and reached for the missing ring on his finger. He forgot it that morning. It was supposed to help channel his energy. No wonder he lost control. Without it, he was a walking time bomb.

The last thing he needed was another situation where he could lose control. Another problem cropped up when Ryan thought he would play hero and called Angel out during the execution.

"Come on, what're you tryin' to do to me?" Killian hissed as he stared at his brother on the balcony. "You know I can't handle anymore." He looked around the cheering crowd and noticed Kara inching her way towards the abandoned shop. He sighed and hurried to her side and caught her elbow.

She jumped when he touched her. Her eyes widened, and her breath caught. Her pulse beat wildly under his fingertips. She hadn't forgotten his fight.

"Do nothing. Focus on Dawson," he whispered and cast his eyes towards her little brother.

Dawson punched the air victoriously and chanted Ryan's name.

Kara's face reddened, and she hurried to control him before he could attract the wrong kind of attention.

Killian scowled and made his way to the abandoned shop. He nudged people aside gently so no one would notice him sneaking by.

Killian opened the door to the shop and took a deep breath as a wave of emotion washed over him. Something stuck in his throat, and Killian leaned on the doorjamb, closing his eyes. His chest ached like someone was sitting on top of him, making it impossible to breathe. Anger and worry flooded his veins and gripped him with an icy hand.

He took deep breaths until the feeling passed and opened his eyes when he could breathe again. *Why is Ryan lost in such despair? It's not like any of this is his fault.*

The shop was dark, and the windows were boarded up. A bit of sun filtered through the cracks in the boards, and he could see the dust particles in the air. A deep, musty scent made him wrinkle his nose. There was a set of creaky stairs in the back, and Killian moved towards it.

They groaned under his weight, so he moved slowly in case they came down. His steps were light, and the railing was split in two. One wrong step, and he could get hurt. He got to the door on the balcony just as Ryan threw it open, stony-faced and silent. The only sign Ryan gave him he saw Killian was the slight widening of his eyes.

"What were you thinking?" Killian asked.

Ryan dropped his chin to his chest and stared at the ground. His gaze remained unfocused. His face was emotionless.

Killian's stomach ached, and he clenched his jaw, trying to separate Ryan's emotions from his own. Ever since they were little, they could feel each other's pain when tensions ran high. Sometimes, he struggled to remember they were their own people. "What's wrong?" he asked.

Ryan's back hit the wall of the old shop when a gun was fired. A cheer rose from the crowd of the corrupt city, and Killian watched Ryan's eyes darken. Another fire of the firearm sent pain through Killian's chest, and he fell to his knees when Ryan took a gasping breath.

Killian didn't understand how Ryan could feel so deeply for someone he didn't know. These deaths were tragic and pointless, but why did Ryan try to bear the responsibility? It wasn't his fault.

"I can't," Ryan whispered.

Killian looked up to ask him what he meant, but he was gone. The sensation of his chest being crushed under a boulder faded the further Ryan got. *Great, he'll lose his mind, and I have to deal with it.* Killian exited the shop and looked around the plaza as the city cheered and roared about the deaths of the married couple.

Kara was on her knees. Her brother stood over her, concerned. Ryan was nowhere to be seen.

Killian walked over to the siblings and knelt next to Kara. She didn't even move when he placed a hand on her shoulder. "Are you okay?" he asked.

She shook her head and held her stomach. "My head hurts. I think I'm gonna throw up."

"If you need to throw up, do it. You might feel better," Killian said.

Dawson sent him a curious look but didn't speak. Killian didn't know the younger McKenzie well; he just idolized Ryan. They crossed paths plenty of times, but it wasn't like Killian ever tried to get to know him. "Can you get her home?" Killian asked.

Dawson nodded and managed to smirk. A smile so close to Ryan's Killian almost hit him. Those two needed to stop hanging out. Too bad Kara didn't heed his warning. Killian helped Kara stand, and she looked around, dazed.

"Is Ryan alright?" she asked, her voice raspy.

Not when I get a hold of him. Killian forced a smile. "He's fine. Go home."

Kara and Dawson stumbled out of the square, and soldiers fired guns into the sky. The cheering stopped as everyone stood at attention and waited to see what was commanded of them.

Killian looked around one last time before gazing at the factory district. If most of Angel's forces were in the square, Ryan would likely be somewhere he shouldn't.

Angel's men dragged the bodies off the stage as Killian hurried off. The skyscrapers thinned the further he got from the middle of the city, and when the crowds were all but gone, he broke into a run.

The sectors of the city weren't far, but Killian's lungs still burned by the time he got to his destination. The factory district was big, empty, and polluted. A thick screen of smog met him as he entered the district. He jumped over a "keep out" barrier.

There were three primary factories: weapons, food, and other intelligence Angel used to mimic the outside world. Killian's eyes watered, and he pressed the back of his hand to his mouth, coughing. He didn't know how Ryan could withstand the black smoke.

Killian hurried through the district, looking for armed guards or patrolmen. His pulse quickened when he heard voices ahead, but he couldn't see who it was. *Shoot. I'm gonna get caught.* He ducked behind an old, broken-down car and pressed his chin to his chest to appear small. Two men in green and black walked past without so much as a glance his way.

"How many more do you think there are?" the man spat on the ground. "I can't believe we got 'em livin' right under our noses."

His partner shrugged. "So long as we find 'em before they find us, I don't care."

Killian held his breath until the two men were out of sight. He scrambled from behind the car and tapped his fingers against his wrist. "Shadows veil my gaze and reveal the unseen: energy vision."

Through the smoggy air, strands of ethereal twine appeared. They were thin, quivering lines that led through the city like a trail. He was the only one who could see them, and if he touched one of the strings, it would lead him to the owner.

Killian picked through the different colors to find the energy that matched his brother's. He hesitated when a vibrant orange and green stood out. They were wrapped around the factories and headed back toward the residential district.

Musta done it wrong. Killian called the spell off and tried again. When the faded lines reappeared, all he could make out was the dark violet smog around the city and Ryan's trail of red. He smiled to himself and nodded. *And Ryan said this spell was worthless.*

Killian touched the red strand, and all the other colors vanished, leaving a mix of red and orange. The piece of twine jumped up and down. It led through the district to an old building.

This one was much smaller than any of the others. It was almost the size of a small house. A hut more like. A black raven was smudged across one of the outside walls of the shelter. The exterior wood was charred and broken down with age. Killian stepped over the splintered wood and into the building. "Ryan?" he hissed.

There was no response at first, but then his brother poked his head from the rafters of the fallen ceiling, eyes wide and uncertain. A cigarette settled in between his fingers, and he stared dumbly. "What're you doing here?" Ryan asked. His voice was hoarse like he had been crying.

Killian scowled, walked across a shattered marble floor, and stopped under his brother. He grabbed the unsteady beam and pulled himself up. A grunt escaped his lips, and the beam trembled as he settled on top of it and exhaled a sigh. "I should be asking you that. They condemned this place."

Ryan shrugged and offered him the cigarette. Killian didn't smoke often, but he figured this was an exception. He took it and inhaled, the smoke burning as it traveled down into his lungs. He handed it back to his brother, and Ryan took a drag.

He looked away from Killian and let his leg dangle over the side of the beam. "It brings me peace. Reminds me of home," Ryan said.

Killian scanned the sooty walls and tipped-over benches with a scowl. Burnt papers were spread across the floor, and the stained-glass windows were nothing but pieces of themselves. Someone boarded up the windows that hadn't been shattered. A house of worship brought to its lowest.

Ryan exhaled a trail of smoke at the same time Killian did. He let his head fall back against the pillar behind him. Killian's chest hurt when he breathed deeply and closed his eyes to ignore the sensation. The smog wasn't doing him any favors.

"Taking a drag on that cigarette didn't do you any favors."
Go away.

The voice in his head hissed with laughter. *"Who are you kidding, child?"*

Gonna lecture me about how smoking will kill me?

"Smoking won't kill you, Descendant. I will."

Like, I don't know.

Killian shook his head until the cackling laughter receded enough for him to think. "We shouldn't be here," he said.

When he opened his eyes again, Ryan nodded. His brother stared at one of the broken windows and played with a silver chain around his neck. It was thin and sparkled red.

Killian looked at the matching chain around his wrist, though his glinted violet. *Will we see her again?*

"I miss her too," Ryan said.

Killian pulled himself out of his thoughts and stared at his brother. "What's going on? That rush of emotion I felt-"

"Nothing."

"Bullshit," Killian muttered.

Ryan paled and stubbed the cigarette out rougher than necessary. "We've been using our magik in the city. Someone must've seen us. We got them killed."

"No, Angel's always looking for a reason to kill," Killian said.

Ryan shook his head and dropped the smoldering cigarette butt.

Killian closed his eyes again and touched his chest. He opened his energy to Ryan's, but instead of trying to feel his emotions, he aimed to remove them. The erratic wavelengths clashed with Killian's gentle, calming energy. Killian absorbed the chaotic bits of energy and expelled as much of his own as he could. It only took a few moments for Ryan's breathing to even out.

"Don't you ever get sick of taking care of me?" Ryan asked.

Someone's gotta do it. Killian opened his eyes when he finished transferring his energy. His brother leaned forward and pulled a strand of Killian's hair with a small smile. Killian's breath caught, and he furrowed his brow.

Ryan hadn't done that since they were little. Ryan's smile grew, and Killian rolled his eyes.

Whatever, if it makes him happy. "Someone needs to watch out for you. Ready to go?" he asked.

Ryan shrugged, dropped to the floor, and shoved his hands in his pockets.

Killian hurried after him, grateful to get out of the polluted air. For now, it was the best he could do.

"We don't get to go home," Ryan muttered when they left the old building.

"We're supposed to be at the McKenzie's, right?" Killian asked.

"Something like that. Should we go get stuff from home and get over there?" Ryan asked.

Killian sighed and ran his hand through his hair. "I guess we could get a change of clothes or something."

Ryan tapped his temple. "Wanna race?" They were just talking about lying low; he didn't want to risk that. As if reading his mind, Ryan chuckled. "Joking."

This guy was going to be the death of him.

To Be Or Not?

JUSTIN

"**H**OW MANY DESCENDANTS HAVE you found?" Justin asked.

Nicholas cleared his throat. "Two in the city and Tory."

In the city. Why are there Descendants in the city? I thought all of them cleared out when Angel executed them. Justin pursed his lips and tapped his fingers on his knee. They sat in the living room while Cody did something in the basement. He always played with his technology.

"You said you wanted to fix my past mistakes. What did you mean?" Justin asked.

"Angel is planning something. I don't know the specifics, but there's a growing mass of chaos. She uses it to control adults. The kids don't seem to be affected."

Justin smirked. "Kids are less affected by that specific branch. Don't you remember our fight?" Nick went silent, and Justin rubbed his eyes. Even if Nick didn't, Justin did.

"You were young too," Nick said, his voice nearly a whisper.

"I was in my twenties. You were twelve."

Chaos was a magik in its own class. Justin hoped to never deal with it again. He didn't want to drag Cody into that mess.

"Do you remember that day?" Nick asked.

Justin had a hard time reading him. He wasn't sure where this conversation was going, but he didn't like it. "I do. What do you remember?"

"Pain."

"You want to talk about it." It wasn't a question.

Nick moved across the room and sat next to him. "I need to know what went wrong. I have to avoid the same mistakes, and I know I'm not as strong as you, Jay, but I have to do something."

"You won't fall into the same trap I did." Justin's voice softened. He should have thought further ahead. He could've done a lot differently that would've led to their success. Or, at the very least, kept most of their friends alive. Justin wasn't the only reason the rebellion failed, but his arrogant attitude didn't help.

Nick scoffed to himself. His foot bounced up and down in agitation. The couch shifted under Justin's thigh. "How could you possibly know that?"

Because you were right. I was arrogant. I thought nothing could take me down, and Angel used that to bring me to my knees. Angel's laughter rang somewhere in Justin's memories, and he clenched his fists. It wasn't like he thought he was invincible. He just thought he was stronger.

"Because you have no self-confidence. There's nothing to turn against you." Justin blew a strand of his hair out of his face. He slapped his knees and stood. The house needed deep cleaning and laundry awaited him. Cody was running out of shirts for school.

Nick grabbed Justin's arm and held him still. "You aren't that arrogant."

Justin turned his head and watched the soft green swirls of his brother's energy shield him. They created a bubble around his heart, and thorny vine-looking tendrils wrapped around his arms and legs. The power pulsed lightly, waiting to be called upon as it mixed with Nick's anxiety and discomfort. Black pulses ran like a vein through the green, right down the middle.

"You know, Angel was the first person to beat me in combat. When I faced her, I was overconfident. Everyone tried to warn me. Samantha was seconds from murdering me, but I knew best. That's why people followed me, right?" Justin tried not to sound too far away, but it was hard not to get lost in his thoughts.

"You don't have to do this alone. Let me come with you. We'll destroy her together."

"Hey, are you alright?" Nicholas touched his shoulder, and Justin was startled out of his thoughts. "You spaced out," he said.

"I'm fine," Justin said. He smiled sadly and swept his gaze across the thin gray lines of the inanimate objects in his home. There were a few piles of clothes, the table in front of him, and another sofa on the other side of the table. "You should rearrange things. This place is getting dull."

Nicholas chuckled under his breath. "You used to hate it when I changed things. Why would I do it now?"

Justin shrugged. He wanted things to be different. If they were to be a family again, maybe some change would do good. "You would move the couch in front of the hall when I first lost my sight. Now, I have some semblance of sight, so your tricks won't work." He stepped around the coffee table and slammed his shin against something curved and round. A slew of curses slipped past his lips, and he doubled over to soothe the welting spot.

"Right. My tricks won't work." Nicholas chuckled.

Justin scowled and reached around on the floor for whatever he kicked. There weren't any silver or gray lines drawn out for him. There shouldn't have been anything in front of him. If this was one of Nick's displays of strength, Justin didn't want to see another.

Nicholas grabbed Justin's wrist and pulled him back up. "It's gone. Vanished the moment you ran into it."

"I'll get you back later. You know I will. It's beyond me why you pull such stupid stunts," Justin growled. He headed for the front hall and stopped when the ground vibrated under his feet. He cocked his head to the side and waited to see.

"Tory's coming over, by the way," Nicholas said.

Justin ran his hand down his face. It's not that he didn't like Nick's new boyfriend - oh wait, yes, it was. He couldn't stand him. Their one encounter in the forest was enough that Justin never wanted to have another one. "You can't go to his place?" Justin asked.

Nicholas walked past Justin. His voice was colored with amusement. "No, I can't. I like this place. It would be nice if you tried to get along with someone outside the family."

Justin hummed to himself. He was okay with how he was. He didn't need to pretend to like someone. It's not like he was back in high school. "I'll be busy doing chores. Keep him out of my way."

"And what about the Descendants I found in the city?" Nick asked.

Back to this conversation. I hoped I dragged him off it. Justin forced his face to remain neutral. "What do you mean?"

"Jay, they're kids. They can't stay. I've been monitoring them on SHARLA, and they're in serious trouble. They used their disguise spells in front of cameras. There's no way they know anything about magik," Nicholas muttered.

Justin frowned. If they didn't do something, the kids would die. That was a given. Then again, did he care? It wasn't like he was responsible for kids outside of his own. He had to focus on keeping Cody alive.

"Jay, please help me," Nick whispered. A plea so soft, so tender, they both knew he wouldn't say no.

Justin never told his little brother no when he used that voice. Not since they were children. He closed his eyes and nodded curtly. If he had to do something, it wouldn't be something that could get him killed. He had a lot to figure out if they would help these kids. One of the main things was what magik they held, how strong they were, and what he could do to use them in his new game.

Anxiety Times Ten

KARA

K ARA TWISTED HER HANDS together as she sat on the couch and watched the clock in the living room. Her murky green sofa sat facing the fireplace and back wall of the step-down living room. The walls were an ugly beige her mom insisted on, and then she decided she didn't like the color. The thing was, her parents were too busy to repaint it.

A loveseat was to the right, pushed against the windows that looked out to the fenced backyard. A space with nothing but rocks, gravel, and pavement.

Dawson plopped next to her on the sofa and elbowed her. "Are you feeling better?" he asked.

Nothing was going to make her feel better. The twins were about to infiltrate her home.

Dawson pulled out his phone, a thin rectangular device. He double-tapped the screen, and it flickered to life. "What do ya wanna watch?" he asked.

"Nothing," she muttered. Kara rested her head against the back of the couch and closed her eyes. She wanted to torment herself.

"There's some good stuff on here. I just got this new upgrade that-"

"Is it illegal?" Kara asked.

Dawson sighed. "You know it is. Why ask?"

"Because I don't want anything to do with it if it isn't legal. You put mom in danger."

"Oh, don't act like mom doesn't know. That woman knows everything," Dawson said. He shoved the phone back in his pocket. "It's temporary. Stop freaking out."

She would have intruders in her house. She didn't want any of it. "They'll just leave," she whispered after a while.

"Well, yeah, when finals are over. They're supposed to." Dawson cracked a smile. It was strained, and she knew he understood what she meant. He touched the back of her hand and rested his head on her shoulder. "You can't shut everyone out because of loss," he said.

Kara smirked and ruffled his hair. "When did you get so smart?" she asked.

"I had to when Tory left. Someone has to watch you now," Dawson teased. It was light-hearted.

She hadn't made new friends since they lost him. When the fire happened, he ran back in to save a little girl. She came out, but he didn't. It destroyed Kara. Took her apart from the inside out, and she didn't let herself reconnect with people.

Tory had been their childhood friend. They grew up together, and he always kept her safe. Dawson too. It was too painful without him.

"We'll manage. We always do, right?" she asked.

Dawson nodded and hummed in agreement.

Kara couldn't believe her mom was allowing the twins to stay at their home. What parents let teenage boys remain in a house alone with their teenage daughter? It seemed irresponsible.

It was just after four when someone knocked on the front door. Kara's heart jumped to her throat, and she ejected herself off the couch and rushed to the bathroom next to the guest room. She was going to throw up. Her stomach rolled as she emptied her lunch and breakfast into the toilet bowl with a groan.

Voices filled the living room, and her heart thudded in her ears. *Gods, I can't do this.* She squeezed her eyes shut, and sweat broke across her forehead and the back of her neck.

She vomited again when Dawson knocked on the door. "You okay?" he asked.

No, I'm anything but. Let me die in here. Kara flushed the bowl and wiped her mouth with her hand. "Gimme a minute."

Dawson murmured something and walked away. His footsteps padded until the hall went silent. She could hear the twins talking, and then their voices stopped. He must have taken them to their room.

Kara pushed herself off the cold tile floor and rinsed her mouth in the sink faucet. She couldn't stay in the bathroom forever. Kara splashed cold water on her face until the pink in her cheeks disappeared. She opened the bathroom door, and Dawson nearly tumbled in.

"What are you doing?" she asked. Her energy was all but gone. She didn't want to study, and now she had no choice.

Dawson grinned as he righted himself and grabbed her wrist. "The twins are getting their room set up. Let's get your stuff on the kitchen table."

She knew he was trying to help, but it aggravated her just the same. Still, Kara let Dawson drag her down the hall and up the two stairs in the living area that led up to the vast dining room and connected kitchen. They set up her textbooks, notepads, and some pencils.

Kara's hands shook, and she tried to quell her nerves.

She felt trapped between Ryan's fighting and Killian's intimidating behavior. There was no way she could act like nothing happened. What would Killian do? Was he going to be normal around her? He did kind of act normal when she had a meltdown during the execution.

"Are your parents home?" Ryan asked.

Kara jumped and whirled around at the sound of his voice. She couldn't help the squeak that slipped from her lips. She slapped her hands over her mouth, and his gaze softened.

"I'm not gonna bite," he said, smiling gently. He rubbed the back of his neck.

"No, no, no, I know." She shook her head and waved her hands. "It's not a big deal, not at all. I'm sorry. You startled me, that's it. Nothing more than a startled squeak. You know me, I'm a big scaredy cat." Her laugh was much too loud and way too forced.

Ryan winced and looked at Dawson for help. When her little brother shrugged, Ryan looked back at her. "I get anxious, too. Everyone does."

Kara laughed again, this time for real. "You're joking. You, nervous?"

"Yeah, and I also have these weird little breakdowns. I break stuff and take things apart. Sometimes I talk nonsense and can't remember it." Ryan said. His gaze flicked towards the floor, and he scuffed his shoe against the carpet.

"You're lying," she said, trying not to sound accusatory.

"Actually, he's not." Killian came up behind them and crossed his arms against his chest.

Kara jumped again and took a few steps away. If either of them noticed, they said nothing. She squinted at Killian, trying to see the dark shadow from before, but it was gone. There wasn't a weird violet ribbon around his waist anymore.

The violet and black ring glinted on his finger, and her lips turned down in a frown. He wasn't wearing the ring when the shadow was with him earlier.

"I gotta get some work done," Dawson said, pulling her out of her thoughts. He snagged his bag from beside the island. "You gonna be good?"

She couldn't believe he was already going to break his promise. There's no way she could let him leave to break the rules after an execution. Kara scowled. "You said no spray painting for two weeks."

He opened his bag and revealed nothing but books. "Seriously, I got finals too, Kara. I'm going to study. We have a group project."

She sighed and waved a hand. Dawson might have been dumb, but he wasn't that dumb. She wished he wouldn't leave her to fend for herself, though. Kara watched him disappear down the hall, and the front door clicked behind him.

Ryan beckoned to the table. "Since I'm ninety percent sure your mom's got this place bugged, should we study?"

She nodded and took a seat at the table. Ryan sat across from her, and Killian stood awkwardly in the middle of the dining room. Ryan beckoned him over. "Get over here. We both know I'm going to suck at this teaching thing."

Killian made a face, and they exchanged a silent conversation with their eyes.

It annoyed Kara when they did that. She felt left out.

"I think I'm going to take a walk. I don't know shit about math," Killian grunted and walked out.

"I don't think he likes me," she whispered.

Ryan chuckled under his breath. "He doesn't like anyone. Try not to take it personally. Open your book. We gotta lot of ground to cover."

Another Dead End

ANGEL

ANGEL SNEERED DOWN AT the two sniveling brats. The offspring of a Descendant and a normal human, but not a flicker of magik, passed between them. Her General found the kids with ease, mainly after their parents were shot and killed.

They were two little boys, both under the age of five. Re-homing them wouldn't be a big deal, and she wasn't that heartless to put them to death for their parent's mistake.

She brushed her fingers across the soft brown hair and tried to smile. "It's alright. Mommy and Daddy went to a special place to work. You're going to be in good hands," she said, gulping down a snarl.

The little boys cried and grabbed each other, clinging like they were trying to stay afloat in a raging sea. Children this age were too young to understand the complexities of life. Even if she said the parents were dead, they wouldn't understand.

If their father had magik, she would keep an eye on them and ensure they did nothing to cause problems. For now, she would let them go.

Angel snapped her fingers. "Take them to the home. Make sure they get good care."

Her General nodded and set his hands on both boys' shoulders. They walked out with him, whimpering and crying. Big globby tears with snot running down their faces.

Children. Angel retired to her quarters and poured herself a glass of wine. She needed some serious rest and relaxation. Her day had been Helwe. As she sat and stared at the roaring fire in her hearth, her knuckles whitened around the wine cup. She couldn't stop thinking of the boy who stood up to her.

How dare that insolent child show me up? I'll show him exactly who he's dealing with. I allowed him in this city, and this is how he repays my kindness?

Angel sipped the wine and left red lipstick on the rim of the crystal cup. Her right-hand man was already looking into the boy and his brother to make sure they weren't up to anything behind her back.

She flicked her wrist, and a screen appeared in front of her. It glitched in and out of focus before stabilizing and turning on.

"Ryan Wilson." The screen pulled up a record of the blonde-haired nuisance, and she scrolled through the information.

He was at the top of his class and a part of the physics and engineering programs. He never missed school, but he was always fighting. There were at least ten points on his record for stupid stuff, but he never made waves. He lived in the government apartments downtown with his twin brother.

Angel clicked her tongue. "Killian Wilson."

The screen went black and then returned to life with information on the next boy. This one had no points. He never fought, never talked back, and he didn't miss assignments.

They were night and day, even though they were identical. There were video surveillance videos of them walking to and from school, buying groceries, and attending class. For two boys who never stood out, why would Ryan suddenly take an interest in politics? Angel didn't like not knowing someone and couldn't get a read on either boy. Not from their files.

"Pull up the entrance exams."

The next video started with the two boys in a white room in the tower. They were only about ten years old, nothing but children. The two sat at desks with cards in front of them with their names in bold letters. Ryan sat straight with a fierce gaze and trembling hands. Killian was half asleep in his chair before the exam even began.

Angel tapped her chin and took another sip of the wine. They switched personalities. She went through their early school videos and found nothing of consequence. They lived alone for the last seven years. Angel set the wine glass on a small table beside her and tapped her fingers.

In the most recent video, they were at school. Killian's back was rigid as he took proper notes and stared at his teacher. He was in the medical program studying to be an immunologist. His grades weren't even close to his brother's, but he worked harder.

Slumped over his desk, Ryan slept. He never turned assignments in, but he aced every quiz, written test, and oral exam. The kid never took notes and did every math problem in his head.

A soft knock on her room door brought her out of her thoughts. She stood, and the screen vanished when she swiped it away. Angel opened the door; her General handed her a file with a nod.

"This is their old home. I found some information," he grunted.

She took the file with a pleasant smile. "Import it into the system."

"It's been done."

She waved him off, and he walked down the hall. Angel closed the door and opened the thick yellow envelope. There were endless papers about their childhood.

They were raised by a grandparent and grew up in Rochester. A no-name woman with barely enough money to feed herself, let alone two children.

After a string of fires and deaths, the boys were kicked out of the homestead and left to fend for themselves. She narrowed her eyes. There was no way two ten-year-olds could trek from Rochester to Yorklyn. That trip took days. Not to mention all the beasts and bandits.

"Now, how did you two come to be here?" she asked quietly. "What motivation could you possibly have to come to my city?"

And why didn't she ask before? When the boys came, she didn't so much as bat an eye. Someone raised these children with care and attention. They were intelligent, civilized, and calculated.

Could they have the pure blood she was looking for? Angel tossed the papers into the fire with a noise of disgust. She didn't want to leave a trail that she was onto them. She didn't need hard copies if the system had the newest information.

Angel cracked her neck and pulled her hair tie free. Her hair cascaded down her shoulders, and she walked past her four-poster bed to her window. The city was doused in dark purple energy.

Two little boys with the surname Wilson came from Rochester Homestead. Only one other person found her before with that name, and she was more of a pain in the ass than the children. Angel wasn't a woman who believed in coincidences, but when one stared her in the face, she had a hard time denying it.

They can't know about her, can they?

A figure appeared outside her window, floating hundreds of feet above the city. "Evening, Angel."

She pursed her lips as Havoc bowed his head. He always popped up when she didn't want to see him. "What do you want?"

"I saw your little show today. Were you hoping to draw out more Descendants?" he asked.

Angel smirked despite her annoyance. "Does it matter? No one can teleport in or out of this city, and I hold the keys to the gates. Those doors haven't opened in ten years."

"The child who stood up to you. Do you know him?" Havoc asked, checking his fingernails. His gray mask hid most of his expression, but she could see the intrigue lingering in his cold silver eyes.

"Ryan Wilson. Nothing but a nuisance," she hissed at what he was implying.

He smirked, his lips twisted and chapped. "You know what he is. Why do you question your instincts?"

She crossed her arms against her chest. Her blouse pulled down a bit, revealing the top of a Descendant's mark before she covered it back up. "I'm not questioning anything."

"Then act. Our master doesn't have time to waste, and you want to deny the existence of two pure Descendants. Do you know how far back the Wilson line goes?" he asked.

She tried to hide her surprise. Havoc knew more than he was letting on, and she wanted to know how much more. Angel sucked her teeth with a loud pop and turned away from him. "I don't recall ever hearing that surname," she said.

"The woman you've had in your dungeon for the last ten years is what, then? Fun?" Havoc asked.

Angel dug her nails into her arms and bristled at the accusation. Someone who knew more than her. "They can't possibly know I have her. No one else does."

"If I know, they will. Your secrets aren't as safe as you think," the man taunted. He knew she would want more information, and he withheld it.

She scowled deeply at the floor, hoping he would take the hint and leave. She didn't want to lose control and ruin her image. Her spell would be destroyed, and her hopes of taking over would be crushed if anyone found out she was a Descendant.

"Justin knows everything." Havoc's voice whispered through the air.

The name washed over her and set every ounce of her being on fire. Angel whirled around and slammed her fist towards Havoc's face.

He caught her wrist and shook his head, tsking. "Such an uncontrolled Descendant you are. Someone needs training."

She wrenched away from him and smoothed out her shirt. "I need you to leave. Now."

"When he joins the fight, your reign will end. Don't let anger cloud your judgment. That man will return," Havoc said.

Before she could snarl a reply, he vanished in a wisp of purple smoke. Angel stared at the space outside her window and shut it with shaking hands. If Justin ever returned to her city, he'd lose more than just his sight.

Dinner With Devil(s)

RYAN LOOKED OVER KARA'S shoulder as she stirred some noodles and sauce in a skillet. A creamy sweetness brushed his nose.

She bristled under his stare and whirled around. "I need you to leave."

"What, I'm not doing anything," he said.

She shook her head. "You're hovering, so please leave. Go find your brother."

"Psh, I live with him. I don't need to find him." Ryan shrugged. "This is funner."

"Why are you watching me? There has to be something else you can do," she snapped.

"Don't put meat in it," he said, pointing to the chicken on the counter.

"You have something against processed animals?" she asked with a smile.

"Vegetarian," he said.

Kara's smile vanished, and she blinked. "Are you serious?"

He nodded. "It's a personal thing. You can cook it, just don't mix it all together," he said.

"But..." she trailed off. There was a question in her eyes, and she chewed her lip.

"What?" he asked.

Kara set the spatula down and turned. "There are rumors about you," she said.

"Uh-huh, lots of them." He was aware of what people said. Ryan figured it was best to let people think what they wanted. It would keep them away.

"People say you and Killian... are you from outside the walls?" she asked. Her cheeks were pink, and she refused to meet his eyes.

Ryan chuckled and leaned on the counter. "Yeah, we're from a small town outside. We came here when we were ten," he said.

"Then... I mean." She stopped to gather her thoughts.

Ryan knew where this was going. It wasn't the first time he had gotten that confused stare or bewildered question. "YOu want to know how I managed to survive outside the walls without meat?" he asked.

"People outside have to hunt and grow their own food. What did you eat?" she asked.

He shrugged. The marble was cold against his palms. "Berries, oats, bread, nuts, anything I didn't have to kill. Lots of vegetables and fruit. Meat isn't the only protein out there."

Kara hummed and went back to cooking. She was a lot more relaxed than before, and a slight smile was on her face. "I guess we're not eating meat tonight."

He smirked and wandered around the house for a bit, bored. It was nice. White carpets, beige walls, and huge vaulted ceilings. The place was spotless, with pictures hanging on the walls and vases filling every corner. Someone was an art buff.

Ryan studied the family pictures and stopped when he saw a familiar chestnut-haired boy. He reached up and touched the photo, the cool glass smudging a little. Hazel-green eyes and a toothy grin with olive skin.

"Tory Lawson." He looked at the front door as Dawson walked in. "He was like a brother to us. You remember him?"

Ryan narrowed his eyes and tried to think. "We used to fight. Never could beat him. He threw a mean right hook."

Dawson smirked. "Yeah, you guys acted a lot like fire and water."

"What happened?" Ryan recalled someone saying he had been killed, but the details were never released. He never thought to ask Dawson about it. Honestly, it was never something he really thought about.

Dawson shrugged. "Died in the library fire."

The boy walked past him and called for Kara to let her know he was there. Ryan dropped his hand and clenched his fist until his nails bit into his palm. A library fire. He winced and tried to forget it.

He lost control that day. No matter how hard he tried to remember why, he couldn't. It just happened. The old books went up so fast that there was nothing he could do to stem it without being obvious, so they got out.

Ryan cleared his throat when the front door opened again, and a man with curly red hair walked in. He stepped away from the wall and bowed his head.

"Good evening, sir. I'm-"

The man walked past him without acknowledgment. He was tall with thin, wiry arms and stick legs. Thick-rimmed glasses covered most of his face, but Ryan could see loads of freckles and a short squash nose under them.

"Daddy!" Kara squealed from the kitchen and hugged her father.

Ryan didn't know what to do. The man wanted nothing to do with him, and Ryan wasn't about to push his luck.

It was one thing to avoid the mother, but a dad was an entirely different deal. Being the only daughter, Kara was bound to be a no-go. Plus, she fought with anxiety, so Ryan was sure her parents did everything to make sure she was comfortable, aside from inviting teenage boys into the house.

"I didn't know they would already be here. Didn't your mother take the day off to welcome them?" The man's voice was deep, gruff. "I thought there were supposed to be two of them. Where's the other?"

Ryan walked into the dining room and grabbed the back of the chair with a smirk. "He's out checkin' the sights. We haven't gotten to see the residential area much."

Kara's dad turned to face him. He narrowed his eyes into a slight glare as if he were reprimanding Ryan for answering his question.

Ryan bit back his cocky smile and flicked his gaze to where Kara stood behind him.

Kara shrugged and waved her hands at him, gesturing to her dad and telling him to make nice.

"My name is Ryan, sir. It's nice to meet you." Ryan stuck out his hand. He didn't get along with many, but he supposed he should try to get along with the owner of the house he was staying in.

"Arthur. You can call me Mr. McKenzie, though." The man shook his hand and squeezed unnecessarily tight.

It was a challenge Ryan would generally rise to, but this wasn't the time. Arthur didn't look strong, but an intimidating aura surrounded him.

"Why give me your first name at all?" Ryan asked, unable to contain himself.

Arthur quirked a brow. The smallest of smiles flickered across his lips before vanishing. "My house, my rules."

Ryan nodded and gripped the chair tighter. He wouldn't survive.

"What's for dinner tonight?" Arthur clapped his hands and looked at Kara. "I smell something good."

Kara beamed. "Pasta. It's quick and easy. It would be chicken Alfredo, but someone doesn't eat meat, so I had to change the menu."

Ryan felt his ears burn when Arthur side-eyed him. It wasn't his fault. Animals shouldn't have to die to nourish their bodies. That was selfish and arrogant, and not even Ryan was that arrogant.

"Surely you aren't related to Summer. Never met a real carnivore until she came around," Arthur said without missing a beat.

Ryan's heart stuttered, and he snapped his gaze to the man. *No way this dude knows Mom. He's bluffing.*

"Didn't think I knew that, did you?" Arthur asked.

Kara furrowed her brow in confusion. "Who's Summer?"

"Our mom," Killian said, closing the front door with a gentle click. "How did you know her name?" he asked.

Ryan turned and stared at his brother. His eyes were wide, and his thoughts running a mile a minute. They had left no trace of who they were. He didn't think even Samantha knew.

"I've never met anyone with eyes as green as Summer's. Figured you had to be those little boys Kara used to toddle around with."

Kara choked in the background and flung her spatula at her dad. She splattered his back with white sauce and noodles. "Excuse me, what did you just say?" she asked. "I used to hang out with those two?"

Arthur tapped his chin and shrugged. "Yeah, I thought you knew. Oh, well, I'm starved."

Ryan shook his head and chanced a step toward the man. "Wait, how did you know our mom?" he asked.

Arthur gestured to the table and smiled. "Have a seat. We have plenty of time to talk."

Ryan pulled the chair out he had been squeezing and sat. He didn't trust himself to move that far without losing it.

Arthur sat himself after Kara cleaned her mess on the back of his shirt. He sipped from a glass of water and pursed his lips.

Ryan squeezed his thighs to keep his hands from doing anything. He took deep, even breaths and tried to keep his magik in check.

Killian sat next to him, looking more interested than anxious. He was always better at dealing with these things than Ryan.

"I knew her when we were young. I did an internship at the science academy in Rochester," Arthur said when he finally started talking. "She was quite something, but Samantha captivated me. She was born there. They were best friends."

Killian walked up behind Ryan and crossed his arms. "Mom never mentioned you."

Arthur took his glasses off and wiped them on his sooty shirt. "Of course, she hated my guts. Thought I stole her friend. I didn't mean to, but I had to return, and Sam didn't want to stay."

Killian set his elbows on the table and leaned forward. "That math is a bit off. If Kara used to play with us, you said 'toddled,' so she was walking."

Kara hurried to sit next to her dad and blinked eagerly up at him. "Wait, I played in The Wilds? Why don't I remember this?" she demanded.

Ryan struggled to think through the math in his head. Four years before the rebellion, he was seven. When exactly did Arthur leave the homestead? He would've remembered Kara if they were seven.

As if remembering himself, Arthur let out a low chuckle. "Oh right, there is another reason your mom came. You. When we got home, little Kara was one. Four years later, Angel took over."

Ryan shook his head. Five years before the war, he was six. He paled when the math worked itself out in his head. His mom never mentioned Samantha, Kara, or her dad. Then again, he was old enough to remember. Why couldn't he?

"Why do you think Sam doesn't have a problem with you guys staying?" Arthur asked. "Kara was one, which made you guys about two or three. I can't even remember how far apart you are in age."

Ryan put his face in his hands. It still seemed impossible. He looked at Killian, and his brother sighed. It seemed he wasn't the only one in disbelief.

"I'm sorry. Are you telling me I wasn't born in Yorklyn City?" Kara asked. "I'm from The Wilds?"

Arthur nodded. "Kind of exciting, isn't it?" he asked. "We weren't gonna tell you until this stuff with Angel settled, but things happen."

Ryan didn't find it exciting. He felt mortified and angry. He took a deep breath and pushed away from the table. A walk would clear his mind. He needed to walk.

"Sam was wondering why you two came here. We don't have intel outside the walls." Arthur looked right at Ryan. His eyes accused him of something, suspected something he wouldn't say out loud.

"Our mom left Rochester and never came back," Killian said. "We wanted to find her. Didn't expect to find a place so different." It was a nice way of saying they weren't expecting prison.

She disappeared ten years ago. If Ryan chanced a guess, she was helping the McKenzies during the war. If Sam and his mom were that close, she would want to help the one person she loved.

"She was fighting in the war, wasn't she?" he asked, bitterness coating his tongue.

Arthur looked at him and shrugged. "I can't say."

Ryan's knuckles hurt from how tight he squeezed his legs. "Can't or won't?"

"Isn't it the same?" Arthur asked.

Kara shot a petrified look at them. "Your mom was in the war? Was she-I- I mean, only Descendants fought in the war? You come from magik?"

Ryan bit his tongue until he tasted blood. He didn't know enough about the war to make something up. "Many people fought in the war." Sometimes, the best way out of a question was to answer vaguely.

"But was she a Descendant?" Kara asked. She was too smart to be tricked like that. Her electric blue eyes bore into his. Her frizzy black hair was pulled into a ponytail, but a small strand hung in her face. It waved back and forth when she exhaled too sharply.

"Magik is illegal, Kara. Do you want an answer you might have to turn them in for?" Arthur asked.

She dropped her gaze as if thinking through his question. "I guess you're right."

Killian released the breath he had been holding, and just about his head hit the table. "We didn't know Mom had friends in the city. It's kind of nice hearing about her."

Arthur clapped his hands and beckoned to the kitchen. "I smell something burning. Sweetie, would you check dinner?"

Kara yelped and hurried into the kitchen to save her pasta.

Ryan nodded, numb to the world around him. Their mom fought in a war she had no part in for people who didn't leave the city. He knew Kara from childhood. Somehow, their parents knew each other.

Yorklyn would never stop surprising him.

With All Due Respect

KILLIAN

D INNER WITH THE MCKENZIE'S was nice. Plus, Samantha was a lot warmer to their presence than Arthur. She asked many questions about their lives, where they lived, and their grades. It was like they were part of a family they never knew about. Their mother didn't come up again.

Ryan was mostly silent. He sat stony-faced and answered only the questions that were directed at him. He barely touched his food and glared at Kara when she tried interacting.

Killian knew he was in shock. He thought it was great that someone knew their mom. They could get information about her, hear about her life. Since she went missing, Ryan never talked about her. When Killian brought it up, Ryan changed the conversation. These people wanted to talk about her. He couldn't pass that up.

"How did tutoring go today?" Samantha asked.

Killian elbowed his brother. "Yeah, did you get anything done?"

Ryan nodded and shoved a steamed carrot with his fork. "We did the first three chapters. She has a good understanding of the basics."

The dinner was savory and sweet. Steamed vegetables dribbled with butter and creamy pasta that melted on Killian's tongue. He hadn't had a meal this delicious in ages.

Dinner went without incident, and an hour later, they sent Kara and Dawson to bed. Killian was confused when they didn't whine or complain. They just went upstairs after saying good night.

"We know we aren't your parents, but try not to stay up too late." Samantha smiled and headed for the stairwell.

"Did you really know our mom?" Ryan asked before she could vanish.

Samantha nodded and shot him a curious glance. She wasn't as terrifying outside of her job or the mother role. "I grew up with her. You two look just like her, so I knew who you were when Angel submitted your entrance exams into the system. I'm glad you've been lying low." There was a hint of knowing in her tone.

Killian looked at the table and spread his fingers across the top for lack of better things to do. "You've been watching out," he said, almost in disbelief.

"I promised your mom a long time ago I would." Samantha's voice got serious. Her smile flickered away as she studied them. "So long as you two are here, in the city, no harm will come to you. Good night." She walked upstairs and left them alone.

Arthur went to bed shortly before everyone because he had to be up early for work. Apparently, that wasn't an uncommon occurrence. From the way Kara went on about it, he rarely got to come home from The Lab.

The Lab was Angel's pride and joy. A huge factory where the scientists stayed ninety percent of the time. It's where Ryan was headed after graduation. They made many unique and terrible inventions there. Everything that was in Yorklyn was thanks to The Lab. The cars, the tanks, the weapons, the shops, the artificial sky, and the weather. All of it.

Arthur was lucky to go home at all, but Killian figured since he had a family, Angel made an exception. Or maybe it was because his wife was head of surveillance, and Angel wanted to keep her happy.

"I'm going to bed," Ryan said after a while. "Long day."

Killian nodded and waved his hand. Although he wasn't tired, he had a few things to do. He brought some books and clothes, but it was too late to study. He could watch the news on his phone but didn't want to keep anyone else up. Killian looked around the house for a bit, taking in all the photos of the family and the vases.

He went to bed not long after. Except when he walked into the room, Ryan wasn't there. "Oh hell, where's he now?" Killian hissed. He checked the washroom next to their room and shook his head when he found it empty.

Ryan probably never went to bed. When Killian was preoccupied, he must have slipped out the front door. It wasn't unlike his brother going out at night to blow off steam. The only problem was they heavily watched the residential district. It was different from disappearing somewhere down-town.

Killian pulled his phone out of his pocket and dialed his brother. It rang once and then stopped. He tried three more times, all with the same response. Ryan wasn't going to humor him. Killian put his face in his hands and shook his head. Killian should have expected that Ryan was too agitated to remain still.

When Ryan got into one of his moods, he rarely thought about others. He also should have thought about the consequences of his actions, like all the fighting.

When Ryan got into fights, people blamed Killian. They were identical twins; not everyone knew enough about them to see the difference. This meant that when Ryan fought, Killian took the beating after.

After a moment of contemplation, Killian held his hand over the floor. He had to find his brother and bring him back. "Shadows veil my gaze and reveal the unseen: energy vision." The energy cords floated through the air, and he picked through them.

Killian hesitated when he found the odd colors mixed with the dark purple smog that coated the city. He touched a brown cord. It was jagged and rough and went straight up through the ceiling. He stared for a long while and fell back onto the bed.

Kara's parents were Descendants. Alongside the brown cord, there was a red one. It also led straight up into the ceiling. He was willing to bet her parents' room was there.

He sat back up and looked through the remaining mass of cords and twine before him. A golden ball of light was also hovering in the middle of his room. It didn't move; it lit nothing up just sat there. Waiting for something. Killian had never seen anything like it. He stood to touch the glowing ball, but his hand went right through it.

Killian shook the thoughts off and looked for Ryan's red and orange twisted string. It took a few moments to find it, and as soon as he did, he brushed his fingers against it. The heated cord burned through his veins for half a second, and all the other energies disappeared. It went through the house, out the front door, and down the darkened street of the city. He cursed under his breath. His brother was loose.

It wouldn't be hard to find him. Bringing him back was another story. Plus, if Killian got caught, he would be in serious trouble. Ryan was a Descendant of Fire and could move as quickly as his energy allowed.

Killian didn't have that. His abilities revolved around sneakier tactics. It could take him forever to get to his brother without a teleportation spell, and that took so much energy.

"You're dead to me after this," Killian muttered as he stepped onto the porch and looked around. He was going to have to find his brother. There was no question.

Using magik in the open streets was a horrible idea, but at least he didn't risk waking up Samantha or Arthur.

He pressed his hand to his hip, where a black birthmark rested against his skin. A mark that told the world he was magik. If he used his transformation spell, no one would recognize him. When he was thirteen, the spell came to him in a dream, but Ryan made him swear never to use it.

Their mom told them long ago that transformation spells were unpredictable and dangerous. It was also the only way he could use magik without being seen as himself.

He looked back towards the house as if Ryan would turn up. When nothing happened, he whispered the almost forgotten spell. "Shadows coat the ground, veil me in the peace of darkness: darkness transformation."

Nothing happened, and he wondered if he read it wrong. Killian turned the paper around, and then he felt it. A gentle tug in the pit of his stomach that turned to something fiercer. Pain engulfed his hands first and slithered up his arms, burning like a trail of fire. He collapsed with a low groan and slapped his hands over his mouth to stay quiet.

A hammer began slamming away at his temple, and Killian took deep breaths, squeezing his eyes shut, trying to block out the pain. His energy poured out of him in a burst of darkness, and the light bulb on the porch shattered.

Just when he thought he couldn't take anymore, everything stopped. The pain vanished, and the ringing in his ears dulled to nothing. Sweat dripped down his back and arms as he took breath after breath.

He fell off balance when he tried to stand and crashed to the floor. Killian muttered a curse under his breath and pulled the white shirt up with a snarl. *Chain mail. What? Who uses this shit anymore?* He let this shirt fall into place and pulled himself into a standing position, using the rough exterior of the house as support. Heavy. He could barely move.

The outfit was weird. It didn't cover his entire body as he thought, and an odd chain belt wrapped around his waist. When he touched it, to see if it was just a simple illusion, he cut his finger on a blade hidden in one of the chain links.

"It's real," he said, sticking his finger in his mouth to stop the bleeding.

He found many weapons on his person, hiding in sheaths on his ankles, even a few strapped to his hips under his shirt. He felt like a one-man army. Killian waddled off the porch and into the front yard, panting with effort.

The chain mail covered his chest, down to his hips, but stopped at his shoulders. He was in a white tank top with violet markings all up and down the sides of the shirt, with no protection on his arms. *That makes a lot of sense.*

At least he had pants covering his legs and boots protecting his feet. *No close combat for me. It's too bad all I have at my disposal are daggers.* There was always the summoning spell. If something went wrong, he could start there.

Killian reached up and touched his face. He was curious about how this protected his identity. A mask rested across his cheekbones and covered most of his forehead.

The line of Ryan's energy still floated in front of him, and he nodded. He would risk it. Killian grabbed the trail and snapped his fingers. "Darkness unite: teleportation." A black and violet door opened before him, and he directed the red line inside it. The door glowed red for a moment, and Killian stepped through. He ended up on a sidewalk in the factory district, in the middle of nowhere.

"What are you doing here?" Ryan hissed seconds later.

Killian whirled around and stared at his brother.

He wore an outfit similar to Killian's, but his shirt was black with red markings and flames printed instead of weapons. He also had twin short swords sheathed at either hip with golden hilts and red jewels encrusted in each. A red and gold mask rested against his cheekbones, and his eyes weren't their usual green but closer to blue.

Even with the changes to his appearance, Killian could tell it was him. The way his energy bounced around was a sure sign.

"Good, you're alive. Time to go back."

"Why did you use the spell?" Ryan asked. He crossed his arms against his chest.

Killian gestured to Ryan's opposite attire. "Are you kidding me?"

"I've been using it. You've never used it."

"That doesn't make it okay," Killian whispered. A bolt of pain spasmed behind his eyes, and he took a breath. He rubbed his eyes until the pain vanished and shook his head. "I don't want to lead anyone to the house."

"I can tell it's you." Ryan deadpanned. "How can I tell it's you? This thing is supposed to make us practically invisible."

Killian scowled and pulled on an old memory. "The spell doesn't hide us from other Descendants."

Ryan hummed to himself and was quiet for a moment. He seemed to contemplate something, and Killian couldn't even guess what. "What do you think of it?" he asked.

Think of what, the spell? There were more important things to discuss, definitely not geeking out about magik.

"It's heavy. Who uses chain mail?" he said with a half smile. It was too hard to stop himself from answering. The nagging in his mind returned, and he shook his head once to calm it down.

Ryan let out a breathy chuckle and spoke, "Right? I seriously thought I was going to die when I first used it. It's not practical."

"Not even close," Killian said, unable to contain his smile. "I mean, how is anyone supposed to move in this?"

Ryan laughed about the same time a bitter laugh resounded in Killian's mind.

"Good to see you again."

Not you. Go away, I don't have time.

"You're the one who called me."

It wasn't intentional.

"The soldiers are coming. Can't you hear them parading? It won't be long."

Ryan touched his shoulder, jolting Killian out of his mind. He forced a smile and stepped back, holding his hands up.

"You're gonna lose it, aren't you?" Ryan asked, "How much energy did you use to get here?"

A shout caught their attention, and they turned to face four soldiers behind them. Each holding a bright white shield.

"Watch the weapons and shields. They repel magik. I can't wait to hear you scream."

Not gonna happen this time, psychopath.

Killian bit his lip until he tasted blood. The voice faded, and he grabbed Ryan's arm. "They can repel magik. We gotta go."

"Wait, how do you know they repel magik?" Ryan asked. He didn't resist, but his eyes were full of questions.

Killian didn't want to get into it. "It's a hunch. A nagging in my head," he said. It wasn't like he often conversed with the shadow, but it quickly became more regular.

Ryan didn't argue, and they fled into the darkness. The soldiers gave chase, shouting their whereabouts into radio devices attached to their shirts.

Killian turned and snapped his fingers before they could catch up. "Mother of Shadows, hear my call, grant the protection I seek: black wall." A black screen rose between them and the soldiers.

The men stopped in their tracks. They tested the wall with the butt of their guns and shields, but it didn't budge.

Ryan ran down an alley in front of them, and Killian followed. His legs burned from the effort it took to keep moving.

"You're going to regret that," Ryan said breathlessly.

They reached a chain fence with barbed wire over the top at the end of the alley. Killian watched Ryan scramble to the top and grab the wire. It incinerated under his touch. Killian doubled over, wheezing. His chest tore in two, and he let out a scream. He attempted to fall to his knees, but Ryan grabbed the front of his shirt to keep him upright.

His fingers trembled, and Killian figured he felt the aftershock, too. "Lesson one: we don't use shield spells while we run," Ryan snapped. "Move it."

Killian struggled to stay standing and grabbed.

Guns fired behind them, and Ryan threw up a red shield before the bullets reached them. The wall cracked but didn't fall. "Get your ass moving," Ryan shouted. Sweat beaded his brow, and he shoved Killian again.

Killian scrambled up the fence, forgetting how tired he was at the sense of urgency in Ryan's tone.

When he was over, Ryan let the spell fade and followed. They ran further down the alley, and Ryan dragged him to the right through a broken window.

They crouched silently within the boarded-up shop, and Killian buried his face in his hands. His heart hammered in his chest, and he gagged when his stomach rolled.

"Don't you dare puke," Ryan warned softly.

Like I have control of that. Killian took deep breaths and watched the shadows streak across their hiding spot. Ryan elbowed him in the side, and they crept out the front door. It slid open easily, but as they stepped out, Killian slammed his shin into a bunch of wood crates, and they toppled with a bang.

He winced and mouthed an apology as Ryan shot him a murderous look. "When we get back, you're dead," Ryan promised. He grabbed Killian's bicep and pulled him the opposite way of Kara's house.

The moment they turned the corner, they froze. At least ten men stood before them, holding up guns and calling for their surrender.

"We're screwed," Ryan murmured, holding up his hands.

Killian took a breath and heard the breathy laugh in his ear. He had an option, but Ryan wouldn't like it. "I could-"

Ryan shook his head and cut him off. "Don't even think about it. I don't want you doing anything."

"We don't have many options." Killian closed his eyes and retreated to the dark spot in his mind.

He went to the room with walls of crimson and a shadow with no face but an ugly, gleaming smile. *His* shadow.

"To what do I owe the pleasure?"

I need help. The words were bitter in Killian's head.

"Ah, alas, the little boy comes to the master. What are you going to grant me if I save you?"

Save my brother, too.

"That will cost extra."

Whatever you want.

The shadow smiled at him, the wide thing taking over the space where its face should be. *"Then you will let me have control. You don't do as I say, so you'll let me do what must be done."*

Killian bowed his head and closed his eyes. Death, murder, destruction. He would be no better than Angel and her men if he agreed to that.

I grant you control. If you promise to save Ryan.

"Take off the ring, then."

His fingers slipped across the cool metal of the only thing that controlled that other side of him. If he took it off now...

He slipped the ring off without thinking and put it in his pocket. There weren't any options.

"Surrender, now," the soldiers screamed.

"Killian, get down!"

A black wave crashed through Killian's body, and he froze. The logical side of his mind shut down, and he slipped into the abyss.

Put Your Hands Up!

KILLIAN

WHEN THEY WERE SURROUNDED, Killian froze. Ryan held up his hands and elbowed his brother to get him to comply. There was no fighting their way out. It was best to live in a dungeon and fight another day.

The soldiers shouted for compliance, and Ryan scowled. Killian had a faraway look in his eyes as he stared at the ground. Ryan couldn't afford to throw another shield up without knocking himself out. *Just listen to them. Put your hands up.*

"You have two seconds to comply. One, two."

"Killian, get down." Ryan grabbed his brother's arm.

Killian's chest shook, reverberating through his body. Ryan froze when a disdainful laugh escaped his brother's lips. *No, not now. You can't lose control now!* A black screen fell over the group of soldiers, shrouding everything in darkness. Ryan could barely see two feet in front of his face. He snapped his fingers and conjured a flame to bring light to the blackout. He had never seen Killian use a spell like this.

The soldiers screamed in terror, one by one, and guns went off in every direction. Ryan kept his head low and scanned the abyss for his brother. He could barely make out a large shape moving through the dark, with no problem. It was too fast to be a soldier.

Ryan rubbed his eyes when the darkness faded and the streetlights returned. Splotches of bright light clouded his vision, and he stood. Blood ran through the streets, splattered against buildings and Ryan's skin.

Death everywhere. The soldiers' bodies littered the ground. Ryan took a step back, eyes wide at the destruction. His heart stuttered in his chest, and he released a shaky breath. His hands trembled. Killian stood in the middle of the massacre, wiping blood from his face.

"What did you do?" Ryan asked, trying to maintain a level voice.

Killian turned and smirked. "Oh, you survived. I wasn't sure about that last attack."

"You killed them."

"That was the point," Killian said. He sounded surprised by the anger in Ryan's voice. "They would've killed us."

"They didn't deserve to die." Ryan walked towards Killian, hands balled into fists.

Killian smirked, but the slow clapping stopped Ryan's advance. They looked at a light post and saw a young man clothed in a blue half-robe and silver chain mail. A sword was slung across his back. *Great, another Descendant.*

"Quite the show, shadow user. I'm impressed." His voice was like silk.

Ryan gripped his weapons tighter as he stared at the stranger. "Who the Helwe are you?"

"I'm no one of concern. I'm interested in trying my abilities on a Descendant of Fire."

The boy waved his hand over a bottle on his belt. Water rose from it, and Ryan winced. Killian laughed. It was good to know one of them was amused. Getting wet would wipe out his ability to use magik.

Killian smirked. "I can't wait to see this play out."

"I wish you could stay, but-" The figure vanished from the lamp and appeared just behind Killian, "I can't have you causing problems."

A needle-thin weapon made of ice appeared in his palm, and he slammed it into Killian's back. Killian cried as the weapon went through the rings in the chain mail.

Ryan reached out to grab his brother, but a violet portal appeared behind Killian and whisked him away. Ryan stared openmouthed at the spot his brother stood seconds before. It took him a moment, but once he realized Killian was out of reach and possibly dying, his anger flared.

The stranger circled him at a safe distance, eyes dancing behind a blue and white mask textured like the waves of the ocean.

"Who are you?" Ryan snapped, "What do you want?"

The boy shrugged and waved his hand in the air. The water circled around the water user's body like a ribbon. "Consider this my warning to you. Get out of the McKenzie house before you destroy it." The stranger was an olive-skinned, chestnut brown-haired teen. He was a year or two older than Ryan. His hazel-green eyes stood out behind the light blue mask that rested against his face. A silver chain wrapped around his wrist. It ran up his arm, forming a diamond around the blue mark wrapped around his forearm.

That someone would care about that family told Ryan all he needed to know. Ryan furrowed his brow. "Tory?"

The Descendant of Water froze. It took him a moment to gather his composure, but he laughed at the end and bowed. "You recognized me. I never would've pegged you to be a Descendant."

Just his luck. Ryan couldn't beat Tory on a good day, and now that he was using magik, he was less likely to win. He didn't want to fight, but something told him there wasn't a way around it. "Kara needs help. All I'm doing is tutoring her."

"I don't want you there. You're a danger." Tory's voice was stern. He wasn't leaving a lot of room for negotiating.

If Ryan thought he could win, he wouldn't try to talk Tory out of it. He didn't have time to run around while Killian was bleeding out. "Can we do this later? You stabbed my brother."

"You have all the time in the world. I didn't hit anything vital," Tory said. He pulled the sword off his back, swung it over his head, and drove it into the concrete. Pebbles flew into the air, and the sound of metal grating on rock made Ryan wince.

"I told you I'm tutoring her. If I don't, she could fail," Ryan hissed.

"Find someone else. I know there's someone else with good grades. Tell her you can't do it."

Ryan planted his heels. "What kind of game are you playing? You let them think you died, then try to control her? That's messed up, man."

"I'm not controlling anything. I'm keeping them safe." Tory's voice cut through him like ice.

Who am I kidding? This wasn't going to just go away because he wanted it to. Ryan checked his escape options but needed to find out where Killian was. Escape was useless if he couldn't get a hold of his brother. "Let me help, Killian. We can do this later," Ryan said.

"I told you; my aim is impeccable," Tory smirked. "He's fine.

"You stabbed him. I should check him out. I feel like I shouldn't have to say that."

"All you have to do is leave their house, and you're free to go," Tory said.

Ryan clenched the hilt of his sword and scowled. A part of him didn't want to let Kara go. "I can't promise that," he said.

Tory chuckled and waved a hand in the air. Ryan knew it was coming. He could tell by how Tory tensed his muscles and put his weight on his heels if he needed to dash to the side. Tory's eyes flashed dangerously.

A surge of fire swept across Ryan's blades. At the same time, Tory withdrew his sword and charged. Ryan ducked under the great sword and slashed up with his right hand, cutting through the body.

It fell to the floor with a splash before turning into a puddle of water. *That's not supposed to happen.* Ryan hesitated, and his enemy chose that moment to strike.

Tory ran out of the shadows. Dark blue waves were etched onto the silver steel of the blade's dull edge. Tory ducked to the right when Ryan slashed with his left. The boy pulled his sword up and surged forward, aiming to cut Ryan in two.

Ryan barely jumped out of the way. The wind rushed by as the great sword narrowly missed. He flinched back to reassess the situation.

Tory knew how to wield it, which meant he had been training. He was leaps and bounds ahead of Ryan in that regard. He knew nothing about swordplay and couldn't win by skill alone.

Tory was slower if he had to use two hands to wield the weapon. A disadvantage that could play to his strengths. Ryan sheathed his weapons and ran around his enemy, picking up speed. He never pushed himself so hard, but he was trying to survive.

Dust and smog swirled around Tory like a tornado, and he brought up his arms to shield his eyes from flying debris. His sword drooped in his hands, the blade angled toward the concrete.

When he saw an opening and balls of fire shot from his fingertips like bullets, Ryan snapped his fingers and went straight for Tory. His enemy was ready and blocked the attacks, slinging the sword left and right like a stick. The water at his feet shot at the fire, but he didn't stop.

Ryan watched the boy falter after a minute of their game. Drawing one of his swords, he changed direction and slashed at Tory's stomach.

The boy was ready and recited a spell. The water jumped to his call and swarmed around him, spitting at Ryan and forcing him to back off.

So close.

The water rose in spikes and lashed out at Ryan once more, but he held his blades up, steering the water another way as he jumped out of the way to avoid impact. The spikes veered away and slammed into the nearest building, shattering windows and sending chunks of brick into the air.

Ryan swung his sword and channeled his energy through it, sending a wave of fire towards the boy. He was out of energy. *Draw him in.* He let his sword hang at his side and pretended to pant.

Tory fell for it and charged, raising his sword. When the sword crashed, Ryan raised his weapons in an x above his head. The swords clashed, and Ryan's biceps burned as he struggled to hold off the giant sword. When he felt he could control the situation, he gathered his energy and pushed back, digging his heels into the ground.

Tory's eyes widened for a fraction of a second as he fell off balance. He dropped the sword, and his arms pinwheeled as he tried to stand.

Ryan dropped his left sword and swung the right, using both hands to cut through the air.

Tory cursed and threw himself into a backflip to avoid the blade. A trail of blood snaked down his right cheek, and he panted, staring Ryan down. He dabbed his cheek and put his free hand in the air. "This isn't over."

Ryan was more irritated than Tory saw through his attack. He should have been faster, so why the Helwe couldn't he hit him? A Descendant of Water couldn't match a Descendant of Fire's speed.

Tory threw his hands before him, creating a slide out of the water. He stepped onto it, and it turned to ice, and he whizzed off without another word.

Ryan cursed and looked around, searching for Killian's energy. He tapped his fingers against his thigh, and his vision swam. His stomach rolled, and nausea took over. Ryan took deep breaths as his Descendant's disguise melted, leaving him in his black t-shirt and ratty jeans. He needed to get off the street, away from the cameras, but he wasn't sure he could move.

Deep breaths. Be calm. You've been through worse. He shook the spots out of his vision. Through relaxed breathing, he managed to control the nausea. When he was sure he wouldn't throw up, he stepped into the shadows and looked around. It was time to find his brother.

A Helping Hand

KARA STOOD OUTSIDE HER parents' bedroom door and twisted her hands together. It had been a couple of days since her fight with her mom, and she still felt rotten about it. Her mom acted like everything was fine between them, but Kara could see the lingering sadness when they spoke.

Her mom kept appearances in front of the twins, but now that everyone was in bed, they could talk. Like they should have the day it happened.

She reached out to knock and stopped. Kara always had to reach out. For once, she wanted someone to reach out to her. She knew her parents worked hard, but that didn't excuse their constant absence, did it? Her eyes stared at the door as if she could see through it, but no sound came from the other side. They were probably asleep.

She groaned to herself and slumped back to her room without doing what she intended. Her mom had to be the one to do it. Kara wasn't going to break first this time. If her mom wanted an apology, she would have to say it first.

Kara sat at her desk with a small sigh and tried to review the exercises Ryan created. Some of it was getting easier, but many things still made little sense. The lights in her bedroom flickered, making her look up from the notebook.

She closed her work, and a surge of pain ran through her head. A flash of violet splashed across her vision, turning the world purple for two seconds. She ducked her head and groaned. *I will not be sick.* She looked up to take her mind off the paralyzing wave of nausea and stared at the lights of the city.

Yorklyn shone in the darkness of the artificial night. The moon shimmered in the sky, occasionally glitching. Something was going on. As the nausea subsided, the lights stopped flickering, and she gathered herself.

Her hair was plastered to her forehead when she finally sat upright. She grabbed her curtains to close them, and a figure in the driveway caught her attention. Someone in a white shirt was sprawled on the concrete. Her blood whooshed in her ears, and she pushed away from her desk to see what was wrong. Kara opened her bedroom door and flew down the stairs before stopping at the front door. She didn't want to wake her parents, so she gently turned the knob and slipped outside, running across the concrete. Her bare feet slapped against it, burning the soles. "Are you ok?" she asked, stopping before the body.

The person didn't move and blood soaked the fabric. It dried in some places, making it look darker than the rest. She rolled the body over and looked at the blurred face of a young boy. She was staring right at him, but it was impossible to determine who it was. A violet and black mask rested on his cheekbones, and she took quick breaths.

This is a Descendant. Kara reached out with a shaking hand and pressed her fingers to his neck to check for a pulse. If he was dead, she would figure out what to do. If he wasn't, she would call her parents. Her fingers registered a heartbeat when the boy jolted and grabbed her wrist.

He jumped to his feet, pulling her with him.

Kara opened her mouth to apologize, but he twisted her arm behind her back, and she winced in pain.

He leaned in, chuckling. "Didn't your parents tell you not to talk to strangers?" his breath brushed against her ear, and she shivered.

They set a piece of cold steel against her throat, and she panicked internally. This guy was going to kill her. *This is why people don't help others.*

"Talk above a whisper, and you die," he said.

"I'm sorry," her voice cracked, "I thought you needed help."

"And as a human, what do you think you could have done?" he pulled her fingers up closer to her shoulder blades, wrenching a startled cry of pain from her lips.

Tears stung her eyes, blurring her vision. "Anyone can help anyone."

His grip loosened for a moment as he thought over her words. Eventually, he laughed and let her go.

She hurried away from him and clutched her hands to her chest. Pain ran down her arm and into her shoulder, but she was safe.

The boy winced and doubled over as fresh blood pooled on his left side. He could die if she left him. Then again, he tried to tear her arm off so she should let him.

Kara looked back at her house and then at him. Would he attack her if she ran? "What are you doing out here?" she asked, ignoring every signal in her body that screamed run.

The boy blinked, his eyes going in and out of focus. "I dunno. Magik sent me here."

"Sent here? Can you not control it?"

He waved a hand and leaned against her father's truck, leaving behind a red handprint. "It's not like I have a teacher. My abilities are illegal." red surrounded his irises, and she narrowed her eyes.

They were almost familiar. An unsettled feeling in her stomach told her to help. There was more to the story than she could see. Her dad would tell her to read between the lines in a situation like this.

"Why use your magik at all?" she asked. Anything to keep him talking, to keep him conscious.

The boy turned his head up to admire the sky. The moon's light shone on his face, illuminating his softer features beneath the fuzz. He was a kid, barely older than her. Her wrist throbbed from where he grabbed her, and she ran her fingers along the welting skin. *That's going to bruise.*

"It isn't your business."

Kara shook her head. "You're on my property. I think it is."

"You want to help?"

She nodded. "I said that already."

The boy was hesitant. He still rested against her dad's truck, but his legs shook. He was losing too much blood. Something shimmered in the air like a failing hologram, and she squinted, hoping to force herself to see past it.

"I have to go. My spell's gonna fail," he said.

"Spell?"

He gestured to his clothes. "It hides my real identity."

"If you leave, you'll die," she said.

"And if I don't, you'll turn me in."

"No, I won't," Kara replied. He scoffed, and she interrupted before he could say anything, "I won't. You have my word."

He looked ready to argue, but his skin went pale, and he fell. His face screwed up in pain as he clutched his stomach, eyes unfocused.

She rushed to his side when a purple light exploded around him. She shielded her eyes with a wince. When it was gone, her eyes widened.

He lay stretched out below her, eyes squeezed in pain, short gasps slipping past his lips. Sandy blonde hair and freckles across his cheeks.

"Killian..." she stopped, unable to finish her thought.

The surrounding ribbon and the shadow with eyes. It was all magik. He was the monster she had been seeing, but why? Was he toying with her? It seemed like a shitty secret to let her in on.

He blinked at her, confusion clouding his features. "Kara?"

She put her hands to her mouth, and her eyes filled with tears. How? He was a normal boy, so he shouldn't be bleeding out in her driveway. She knelt beside him and brushed her hand through his sweat-soaked hair. The wetter strands clung to her fingers.

He winced and tried to move. "I didn't hurt you, did I?" His voice was raspy and weak. Even on the verge of passing out, and he was concerned about her.

She wouldn't let him die. Even if he had magik. "Mom, Dad." she started screaming. "Daddy, help!"

The lights turned on in the house.

Killian's skin went cold a few seconds later. His sun-kissed skin turned gray, and she brushed hair from his face.

"Stay awake. Stay with me, Killian." she said, shaking his shoulders. "Wake up, please wake up."

He had to say something.

Her parents rushed out in a panic. Her mom was in a fuzzy bathrobe, and her dad had a tank top and shorts. They stared at her and Killian in absolute shock.

"Help him." she demanded.

Her father was at her side a second later and had Killian in his arms as if he were a small child. "Get inside."

Her mother held the front door open and ushered her husband in. Kara didn't know if her parents had medical training, but she imagined wound care was a normal thing for any parent to know. Perhaps not to this extent, but hopefully, enough.

They hurried through the house and into the dining room, where her father set Killian on his stomach on the table. "I'm going to need water, needle, thread, towels. Anything we have to stop the bleeding." Her dad said, taking charge.

Her mother tapped her on the shoulder. "I'll get my sewing kit; you get the water and towels."

Kara nodded and rushed into the kitchen. She flicked on the tap and grabbed a gray bowl to fill. Then she threw open a couple of drawers until she remembered where the towels were and grabbed a couple for her dad. Her hands shook so badly she almost dropped the water, carrying it back.

Her dad murmured a thanks as he lifted Killian's shirt and prodded a circular wound in his back. "We're going to need to suture that wound." Her dad's voice was calm as he analyzed the damage.

Dawson stood on the stairs, looking down at the scene.

Kara noticed him clinging to the banister. She gestured towards the upstairs hall. "It's ok. You don't have to see this. Go get Ryan." She stayed out of her parent's way as they wiped the blood up and debrided the wound. Kara knew she had to stay calm. It wouldn't help to panic.

Her father was stoic as he and her mom tried to stop the bleeding. "It's just inches above his kidney. He got lucky."

Kara listened to them talk back and forth, wondering how they knew this much about the human body. From what she knew, they never worked in medical. Then again, she also didn't know her mom was from outside the city. There were a lot of secrets in her family.

Her mother prodded the wound, and more blood poured out. "Hand me the needle and thread. I'll close it while you finish cleaning."

Her dad threaded a needle and handed it to her.

She set to work, sticking the needle in his back on one side of the wound and pulling it through.

Killian's eyes shot open, and he struggled against the growing pain.

Arthur set his hand in the middle of Killian's back, pinning him. "I know it hurts." Her dad said, firmly.

Kara stroked the boy's cheek as he squeezed his eyes shut. Sweat drenched his body. "It's going to be ok," she promised.

Dawson reappeared in the dining room and shook his head. "Ryan is gone," he mouthed. The boy kept averting his eyes and bounced from foot to foot as he waited for Kara to tell him to do something.

"What do you mean he's gone?" their dad asked, eyes narrowing. "Where did he go?"

"I don't know." Dawson muttered.

Killian whimpered and his eyes flickered open, moving back and forth across the room as he tried to gather his bearings. He jolted when the needle went into his skin again. "Is Ryan alright?" he asked in a thick voice, wincing every time the needle went through.

Kara shushed him. "We don't know where he is, but I'm sure he's fine."

Killian grunted and tried to push himself up, but her dad pushed him back down with a grunt.

"Stay as still as possible," her mom said in as sweet a voice as she could manage. "I'm almost done."

"I've gotta find Ryan, we were..." he trailed off and his eyes widened. "No, I've gotta find him."

Her dad growled and dropped what he was doing to grab both of Killian's arms to prevent him from moving. "If you don't stop, I'll knock you out. You're losing a lot of blood."

Killian gasped in pain and stopped moving. Kara grabbed his hand when her dad let him go once he was sure the boy wouldn't move again. She couldn't believe how calm her parents were.

"Mom and Dad will patch you up. We'll find Ryan." she said, "if it helps, squeeze my hand."

He squeezed until her fingers were purple, but she didn't make a noise. It wasn't long before he passed out. Whether it was from pain or blood loss, she couldn't be sure.

Her mom finished suturing him up a few seconds later.

The front door slammed, and Ryan appeared in the dining room entrance. "How did he get here? I've been looking everywhere."

She noticed fresh blood on his hands and t-shirt but kept quiet when her parents barred him from getting to his brother. They were trying to talk to him, but he kept yelling.

Her father grabbed Ryan's shoulders to hold him still when the blonde tried to shove his way past. "We need to talk about this."

"Shut up." Ryan screamed.

Her parents exchanged glances before letting him go, and Ryan rushed into the dining room. He checked Killian's pulse and took a deep breath. His lip quivered a little, and Kara watched him fight to keep from breaking down. He clutched his brother's other hand and pressed his forehead to Killian's. "Don't you dare die, asshole. If I'm not allowed to leave you, you're not allowed to either," he whispered.

It took Kara a moment to realize tears were streaming down his cheeks. She watched him cry as he tried his best to keep his composure in front of them. For the first time since knowing him, she saw the real Ryan. The scared boy trying to keep his family together. They weren't that different.

Her father cleaned his hands, not taking his eyes off the boys. "He's stable."

Ryan looked up. "This is my fault." He stopped himself from saying anything else and wiped his eyes.

"Did you do it?" her mother asked.

"No," Ryan croaked in disbelief. "I left the house; he came looking for me." He didn't lift his eyes to look at them.

Samantha waved at Kara and Dawson. "You two go to bed." Kara opened her mouth to argue, but her mom shot her a dangerous look that said, don't argue.

Kara pulled Dawson out of the room and headed up to her room, trying not to be upset by her mother's decision. They were going to do something to Ryan. She almost felt bad. They were Descendants. If her parents found out, they would turn the twins over to Angel. She didn't know what to do.

The Truth Comes Out

"WE'RE DESCENDANTS." RYAN DIDN'T care if Dawson and Kara weren't out of earshot yet. Her parents thought he tried to kill Killian. "Killian and I are Descendants, and I was upset about hearing about our mom, so I left. He followed, and then some other Descendant showed and stuck an icicle in his back."

Samantha shot her husband a look and rubbed Ryan's back. She shook her head. "I figured you were Descendants. I'm not concerned about that. What I am concerned about is you throwing our safety away. What if someone tracked you?"

"I used my disguise. She wouldn't know it was me. Plus, I'm super-fast. I'm a Descendant of Fire," Ryan muttered.

"Of course, they can track you," Samantha said, whacking him upside down.

"What do you know?" Ryan asked. He collapsed in a chair beside the table and pressed his forehead against Killian's arm. His brother breathed steadily, but Ryan's chest cinched in worry.

"I know more than you think. Arthur and I spent a lot of time protecting ourselves," Samantha said.

Ryan furrowed his brow in confusion. They had nothing to hide aside from protecting their kids. She couldn't possibly understand the complexities of... *Wait a minute.* She accepted that too quickly. Ryan looked at Arthur as he wiped his bloody hands on a towel and readjusted his glasses.

"You're Descendants," he said.

"Of course."

Ryan closed his eyes and shook his head. His mom had a lot to explain when they found her. "You've got to stop dropping surprises on me. Do your kids know? Are they Descendants, too?"

"No, they aren't, and they don't know. We'd like to keep it that way. Our son is unpredictable, and Kara worries over the smallest things," Arthur said.

Ryan groaned. Another secret from someone else. They knew what he was now, so they would be watching. He would be lucky if he was allowed to leave the house again.

"I'm gonna get Killian to the room. You both need sleep," Arthur said after a while. He lifted the boy without a problem and entered the living room. He disappeared around the corner, and the bedroom door clicked shut.

Ryan didn't feel like sleeping. There was too much going on in his head. "I'm sorry. I don't think before I act, it's just-"

She shook her head and patted him on the back. "No need to explain." She snapped her fingers, and a small flame appeared. "Try to sleep."

He stood without a word and headed for the bedroom. When he stopped to look over his shoulder, she already vanished. Another Descendant of Fire. He never met someone else with his abilities. It wasn't like he had a thousand questions or anything.

Ryan closed the bedroom door behind him and slid to the floor. He put his face in his hands and hummed softly to calm his nerves.

"I'm alive and well," Killian said.

Ryan looked up and brushed the angry tears from his eyes. "Good, I'd hate to kill you again."

Killian chuckled and pushed himself up on the bed. He winced and grabbed his side, shaking his head. "Kara knows we're magik."

"Her and everyone else," Ryan said. He got up and sat on the end of the bed. No one was keeping secrets. "But I don't think they'll turn us in."

"What's the point in chain mail if anything can pierce it?" Killian asked.

Ryan shrugged. "It was an icicle. Guess it slipped through the cracks."

Killian fell onto his back and frowned at the ceiling. "Her parents are Descendants too."

"When did you find out?" Ryan asked, feeling left out. That seemed like a big deal and something Killian should've shared sooner.

"I searched for your energy and found theirs," Killian smirked, and his smile fell a second later. "When did you?"

"They told me when I told them."

Killian pursed his lips, and his eyes darted across the stucco ceiling. "There's another weird energy here. One I can't figure out," he said.

Ryan cocked his head to the side and waved his hand in the air. The world melted away to reveal the strands of energy through the house. Aside from the parents, he saw nothing unusual. "What're you talking about?" he asked.

Killian whispered his spell and frowned when he didn't see what he was looking for. "It was a golden ball in the middle of the room."

Ryan squeezed in between him and the wall and stared, too. It's possible they were just tired. "Do you remember anything?" Ryan asked, changing the subject. He side-eyed his brother.

Killian clicked his tongue and grabbed his head. He let his spell fall and sighed. "I remember chasing you down and getting shot at. They have poor aim." He uncovered his face.

"That's not a bad thing. It saved our butts," Ryan muttered. He would take poor aim over sniper-grade shooters any day.

The night passed in silence. Both fought sleep until they could no longer stand it. Ryan was afraid of the dreams he would have after his semi-productive night, and every time he looked at Killian, he saw the same flicker of fear. Neither one of them wanted to risk the wrath of whatever was coming.

Hours later, the morning announcements turned on, and Ryan touched the hologram, making it vanish.

A red X appeared seconds later, and an automated voice ribboned around the room. "You broke a rule by not watching the announcements at 8 am. You will earn a point on your record. Any further points will lead to disciplinary action." The voice vanished, and Ryan closed his eyes against the slight thump in his head.

He would be surprised if he could make it through the day. Killian grunted next to him, and Ryan rolled out of the bed. Spending hours crammed between his brother and a wall was not an excellent way to spend the night.

He walked to the door and opened it. Kara and Dawson whispered to each other from the little dining room.

"You gotta check this out. Angel announced stuff about magik people running around," Dawson whispered. Something clattered on the table, and pages of a book flipped in the moment of silence.

"Do you do anything aside from spying?" Kara asked. Her voice was flat. Like she really couldn't care less.

"You know I don't. Be quiet so you don't wake mom and dad."

"They left for work, some sort of emergency at the factory," she said.

Dawson huffed; slight annoyance colored his tone. "Are you going to humor me and watch this?" The book slammed shut, and a chair scooted across the floor.

Angel's voice filled the room. "Good morning, soldiers. We have a problem in the city. Descendants are running loose. There have been many reports about them. I consider our state a crisis and expect things to be handled discreetly. It would be unwise for the citizens to discover their lives could be in danger.

"Anyone who spots these magik beings should kill them on sight. We will no longer offer surrender. There are two. They appear male, but their demonic illusions are hard to see. Do not take this threat lightly. Use every weapon at your disposal.

"Furthermore, the schools need to be patrolled. Students are bringing contraband, and I want to know who the supplier is. Keep your eyes open and protect our people."

Ryan closed his eyes and hit his head against the door. If Angel was on high alert, it would be impossible to do anything. *No more magik.* He wouldn't let either of them get caught because of a stupid mistake. He forced a smile and walked into the dining room before he could overthink. "Mornin', anyone eat yet?"

Kara screamed and slammed her hands over the illegal phone. She knew they were magik, yet she was worried about some device?

Sometimes, he wondered about her. Ryan raised a brow and sat next to her at the table. He folded his hands and offered a cocky smirk. He had appearances to keep.

Dawson puffed out his cheeks and shoved her hands off his phone, checking the screen for damage. "He already knows. You're gonna break it, woman."

Kara's face heated, and she put her hands in her lap. "Sorry, you scared me."

"I can see that," Ryan said.

"Did you sleep well?" Before he could answer, she jumped out of the chair. "How's Killian? Is he alright?"

Ryan scratched his cheek. "He's fine. Don't have a heart attack."

"Is he alright to go to school?" Kara asked.

"I don't have much of a choice, do I?" Killian walked up behind them, yawning. He rubbed the back of his neck and grumbled, "Gotta go home and get stuff."

Dawson stuffed his phone into his pocket and flashed them a smile. "I gotta meet up with some friends. See ya."

Kara smiled and waved as he ran down the hall and out the front door. He was going to get into trouble. She closed her textbook, and Ryan stared at his brother.

It was easy to communicate with a simple look. Killian raised his eyebrows, and his eyes flicked to Kara.

Ryan barely shook his head and narrowed his eyes. *She doesn't need to come.*

Killian frowned and crossed his arms, clearing his throat. He wanted to talk to Kara more but didn't want to do it in her home. Ryan was under the impression that it should be left alone.

Ryan huffed and crossed his arms against his chest when he realized he wouldn't win. "You wanna come?" he asked Kara.

Her breath caught. She hesitated in replying, and a strained smile was glued to her face. "Oh, no, that's fine. I'm sure you don't need me to-."

"I want to talk to you," Killian blurted.

Ryan sighed. "Good job, Kill. That's gonna make her want to come."

"Oh, did I do something wrong?" her eyes watered. "Are you going to take me somewhere and kill me? My mom would know. She's head of surveillance."

Ryan scoffed and stormed down the hall. "Consider your invitation revoked." He couldn't believe she would even think such a thing.

He walked out the front door and paced the walkway for a moment. It was the magik. He knew it was. Now that she knew, she was going to assume they were evil.

"You need to calm down." Killian walked out a few moments later. "She wants to come."

"She doesn't need to be involved. We should stick to ourselves and leave."

Killian eyed him. Ryan didn't want to know what thoughts lurked behind that glare. As much as he wished he wasn't intimidated, he couldn't help but feel it.

"What's your problem?" Killian asked.

Ryan shook his head and put his face in his hands. She thought we were going to hurt her. "I don't want to be here. Can't we leave? Why can't we go home?"

"We've tried. It's impossible. What's going on with you? Is this about what Kara said? She's freaked out," Killian said. He kept his voice low, so Ryan strained to hear him.

The front door slammed shut, and Kara walked out in a long, white, flowy top and tight blue jeans. She shouldered her backpack and stopped to stare when they both looked up. "Everything alright?" she asked.

Ryan scowled and turned away. "Whatever, come on."

Her eye twitched, but she followed, saying nothing. Ryan walked ahead, and Killian fell into step beside Kara. Ryan shoved his hands in his pockets and stayed silent while his brother and Kara talked. He wished he could tune them out.

"About last night," Killian began.

Kara cut him off. "Is it safe to talk about this in the open?"

Ryan shook his head and scoffed internally. He didn't want to be angry, but that wasn't in his nature. "Scared?" he asked. He pulled his shoulders back and stood straight. Besides a snide comment here or there, Ryan tried not to involve himself in their conversation.

Killian glared at his back and shook his head. At least one of them was semi-rational. "It's fine. We talk about this all the time. No one pays any mind." Killian smiled. "I just want you to know that what Angel says about Descendants isn't true."

She nodded and looked at the ground.

"We didn't make a pact with the devil or whatever. We're normal people who can die just as easily as you." Killian kept trying to catch her eye as he spoke.

He was being awfully nice for someone who had not wanted to associate with her.

Ryan was going to ask him about that later.

"And we don't want you to get hurt, so I think it's best if you don't get too attached," Killian said. His words dripped with a hidden pain; Ryan knew only too well.

Kara looked at him. "You don't want to be friends anymore?" she asked. She blinked her big blue eyes and clasped her hands together.

Ryan kicked a rock to keep from saying anything. It wasn't his place.

Killian rubbed the back of his neck. "I don't want to put you at risk." That was a big step for him. Since he didn't like people.

They walked the rest of the way in silence. The rundown apartment building was thirteen stories tall, with dingy black brick and dim lighting.

Some windows on the bottom floors were boarded up from being broken out. Angel didn't care enough about their building to keep it up to date like the others. It was old and shabby, but at least it had a roof.

"I'm gonna change," Ryan muttered once he let them in. He hurried to their shared room and threw on a change of clothes. If he moved fast enough, he could be out before Kara could say anything.

Killian and she spoke in quiet voices in the living room before his brother walked in. "Can you try to be normal?"

Ryan didn't answer as he pulled a belt through his loose-fitting jeans and shrugged. He was acting normal. Everyone knew him as the delinquent, the problem child. "I am."

"No, you're not. You're being cold. We just talked about this. She isn't-"

Ryan cut him off. "Look, say whatever you want. I don't care. I'm going to school."

"Wait a minute."

Ryan walked out and down the hall, shaking his head. He didn't want to have another argument.

Kara looked up and opened her mouth when she saw him. Her eyes dropped a little, and her cheeks went pink. "I was thinking-"

"Killian's gonna walk you to school," he muttered. He opened the front door and stopped when she tugged the back of his shirt. Anger boiled under his skin, and he whirled around with a snarl. Ryan caught Kara's wrist and shoved her back. "Watch it, Princess." He drew the last word out bitterly.

Before he could react, she reached out again and caught the hem of his shirt. Her knuckles whitened as she gripped the fabric and stared at him like a petulant child. He slammed the front door, and Killian hurried out to ensure he wasn't throwing punches.

"What. Do you. Want?" Ryan ground out. He clenched his jaw.

"If Killian's got magik, you do too." Her words were soft, so soft he almost missed what she said.

He scoffed and pressed his back against the door. A burst of energy surged from his body, and the apartment sweltered like a sauna. "We are identical twins. What's that tell you?"

Her grip tightened, and she dropped her chin to her chest. Eyes watering with unshed tears. "I'm sorry." Her hand trembled in his shirt, and she took a breath.

"Stop clinging to me like a petrified toddler. I gotta get to school." Ryan scowled.

"I won't!" her eyes widened in surprise.

Killian walked towards them, and Ryan shot him a death-defying glare. His brother hesitated, and Ryan pried Kara's fingers from his clothes. He didn't have time for this. Or the energy. "You're being ridiculous. Let go."

Kara lurched forward just when he freed himself from her claws. She wrapped her arms around his middle and squeezed her eyes shut. "I'm scared, alright?" He froze under her touch as she spoke through broken sobs. "I'm terrified. My entire life, I've been told you are monsters." Her free-falling tears soaked through his shirt and left a wet spot on his stomach. "I don't want to be. You're my friend, and I want to stay that way."

Ryan stopped breathing for a moment. She already thought so much of them. He didn't understand. "We've never been friends," Ryan said, grabbing her shoulders and pushing her off.

Kara wiped her face, and her cheeks turned splotchy. Her eyes rimmed red, and she scowled. "We are, though. You're always sarcastic, and I've been mean, but that's how we are."

"Friends hang out and do stuff together," he said.

"You're living with me. Doesn't that count?"

Somewhere in the middle of their conversation, Ryan's energy calmed. He could reason again and barely remember why he got angry.

As if sensing the danger pass, Killian returned to the bedroom to finish getting ready. The smallest of smiles flickered across his lips.

"You're different," Ryan muttered. And he wasn't sure how yet, but he would figure it out.

Kara smiled weakly. "You'll walk to school with us?"

And even though he wanted to, he couldn't say no.

Old Acquaintances

ANGEL

ANGEL'S EYES FLICKED UP from the paperwork she was trying to focus on. His presence floated through the city and tainted everything it touched. She whirled around in her black leather chair to stare out the long windows that made up the back wall of her office.

She could see a thin silver trail amid the violet streaks and lines of energy if she squinted. *What does he think he's doing?* She stood and walked out of the Oval Office and down the hall to her room. She slammed the door so no one would think of bothering her and crossed to a dresser.

A large, antique piece of wood that held outfits she no longer wore. She opened the top drawer and pulled out an old photo, still in its frame. Angel stared at the three teens in the picture and clenched her jaw.

A boy with thick black hair, a girl with dark skin and curled hair, and herself. Angel was in the middle of the other two, her hands clutched her chest, and she smiled nervously into the camera. The boy rested his elbow on her head, and the other girl had an arm around her shoulders.

When did simple get complicated? She couldn't remember when she started resenting those times. *Ten years.* She hadn't seen that boy in ten years, and when they last met, he was fierce and cold. Nothing like the boy she grew up with.

"You took me for granted." She scowled at the black girl in the photo. "I welcomed you as a sister. You broke us."

Angel tossed the photo back in the drawer and shut it. The dresser shook, and she hung her head. She wouldn't take it lying down. Justin had to know who he was messing with.

She opened her bedroom window and stepped out into the open air. Instead of plummeting to her death, she walked across the sky like one would on concrete or grass. Angel waved her hands, and a gust of wind carried her high into the sky, away from prying eyes and civilian life.

The considerable steel walls that once protected the city now kept them prisoners. She perched herself atop the wall and closed her eyes. A stream of energy poured from her chest and disappeared on the winds she summoned with a whisper.

Angel stood still until she felt his presence. It washed over her like a burning furnace, and she clutched her hands to her chest without thinking. *Ten years.*

She turned when he appeared behind her. He wore a button-up shirt and a pair of jeans. The man was slimmer than she remembered, with less muscle and more weariness. Dark bags hung under his eyes, and gray streaked his black hair. He was only three years older than she was. How could so little time make him look haggard?

Her eyes brushed the scar running horizontally across his eyes. The milky white pupils haunted her. They were orange once, weren't they? Or maybe it was amber. She couldn't remember.

"Well, Rebecca. It isn't often you're at a loss for words." Justin smiled.

She could've hissed at the name. Angel scoffed. "What business do you have?"

He laughed. "Oh, do I make you nervous?"

"You? Don't be serious," she snapped. Her cheeks burned, and her heart fluttered at the sarcasm in his voice. She was thankful he couldn't see her.

Justin reached out to touch her cheek, and she slapped his hand. Even when he couldn't see, he could still make her feel so small. It's like he saw right through her. He always had a bad habit of making people feel inferior.

"If you're here for the Descendants, you can let it go. I'm not giving them up," Angel said.

"Oh, and you think you're going to find them?" Justin asked.

Angel's heart thudded against her ribcage. Her blood boiled, and her stomach fluttered. There were so many conflicting emotions she didn't know which to lead with.

"I know I will. They can't avoid me forever. I rule all," she said, sounding more confident than she felt.

Justin tsked and shook his head as if he were lecturing a child. "No one is that arrogant. Not since the chaos users who attacked the schools of magik. If you think you're stronger than those previously defeated, that's just something, ain't it?"

Angel pursed her lips. She knew the two she was looking for were kids. The little she had seen of them, they were reckless, wild, and charged in without thinking. Those weren't the actions of someone with experience. She didn't have the time to seek them further. Not with all the covering up she had to do.

"Too flustered to argue with me?" he asked.

"I won't give up. My mission is to destroy you. And when that's done, I'll be free," she said.

He laughed again. It was a giant, roaring laugh that made her flinch. She drowned in memories of that laugh, and her throat closed. *No, I'm not that person anymore.*

"How funny, a Descendant who can't even face what she is. You use it to twist the minds of people close to you but refuse to accept what you are."

"I know what I am, but I will soon rectify that," Angel said with a scowl. "First, I need one of pure blood. Why don't I use you, huh? I miss my little puppet." She brushed his cheek with the flair and bravado of a woman with nothing to lose.

Justin grabbed her wrist and squeezed. She winced as pain shot through her arm, and he gave a cruel smile. "If you ever think of doing such a thing, I'll kill you. How little do you value your life?"

She was at a loss for words. Fear squeezed her heart, and her breath caught. She had never experienced such malice. Not from him.

"Good, now that that's cleared up. I have a brother to get home to. Looks like we're repeating history, aren't we?" he asked his voice light again.

Angel frowned and shook her head. "I don't understand."

"Chaos against light. Just like always," Justin said, his voice far away. "This time, we won't lose."

Before she could respond, he vanished in a whirlwind of leaves and flowers. Angel stared at the spot where he had been standing. It took ages for her heart to calm and her energy to subdue.

He was different. The war changed him. For once, she could admit that he terrified her. Because that look in his eyes was that of someone who had nothing to lose. Someone like her.

The Smuggler

RYAN

Tʜᴇʏ ɢᴏᴛ ᴛᴏ sᴄʜᴏᴏʟ well before the first bell was due to ring. Ryan didn't know that was possible.

Kara happily chattered the entire way. She even held his hand. It was unfamiliar. She was way more affectionate than anyone else he knew. She even grabbed Killian's hand twice when she got excited. He

Ryan rolled his eyes when Dawson stopped them at the entrance. He stared at Ryan with a slight smirk and beckoned to him. *Marvelous, what does he want? Can't anyone see I'm not in the mood to deal with people?* He slipped his hand out of Kara's and followed Dawson to the side of the school.

"This better be good, kid. If it's gossip, I'll punch you," Ryan growled.

"Janie told Spencer that she-" Dawson groaned when Ryan punched him in the stomach. "Ow, that hurt more than I thought. Someone's grumpy."

"I'm going to class."

Dawson grabbed his arm. "Wait. I was joking. We don't have anyone at this school named Janie."

"How am I supposed to know that?" Ryan asked.

"Uh, be more social, duh. This is about something else. I need you to come with me to see The Smuggler."

Ryan stopped. "Why?"

"I need something. You get smokes from him, and others get alcohol-the ones still alive, anyway. Otherwise, I'll walk the factory district alone."

Ryan crossed his arms against his chest. "Not gonna happen."

Dawson sighed. "I'm going. I just thought I'd extend the offer."

"What could you need from outside the city that would lead you to do something so dumb?" Ryan asked with a huff.

"Nothing, I just need backup."

"I'm not going," Ryan said.

The boy shrugged and called his bluff. "Fine."

"Dawson, if you get yourself killed, Imma tell Kara I tried to stop you."

"Go for it. She'll be madder that you didn't come."

He was right. Ryan let out a frustrated sigh and stalked away. He would have to keep an eye on the brat because he would get blamed if anything happened to him. The first bell rang, and he groaned. He should have skipped. Ryan waited until the halls cleared before heading inside the school. There was no point in fighting the crowd.

Dawson's words weighed heavily on his mind, and he sat through class, tapping his fingers against his thigh and staring out the windows. His mind wasn't in math, but he didn't need to pay attention. He finished the rest of the textbook about a week ago so he could focus on other things.

When the last bell rang, Ryan packed his bag and hurried out of the classroom. He wouldn't let the kid go alone.

Kara caught him in the hall before he could go after Dawson. She waved him down and smiled when he stopped to see what she needed. She was weird. Even though she was afraid, she acted normal around him.

"Are you coming?" she asked.

Dawson walked towards the back of the school. There was a small skip to his step, and nobody paid attention as he passed.

"Head to the house with Killian. I'll catch up." He hurried off when Dawson slipped out the school's side door.

Kara stared after him.

Dawson climbed through a hole in the back fence and took off towards the factory district.

Yes, these kids have a death wish. Good to know. Ryan sighed before following.

Dawson didn't notice Ryan but was careful as he walked through restricted territory. He kept his eyes on everything around him and didn't make too much noise.

The smog of the large weapons plants filled the deserted streets, making it hard to see. Of all the buildings in the city, the vast factories downtown were the only source of weapons manufacturing. It was also the most polluted area and smelt like a skunk's ass.

Dawson pressed his sleeve to his mouth and kept moving.

Just turn around and go home. You're killing me.

When the kid made it to the old worship building, Ryan watched him hesitate. After deliberation, he entered the burned-out building, and Ryan cursed. He crept towards the building and studied some old art on the walls. They faded with the fire, but most were still there. His gaze landed on a tribal painting of Raven, and he bowed his head in respect.

"If you got some trick up your sleeve, Spirit now is your chance," Ryan whispered. He looked through the busted-down doors and spotted Dawson in the middle of the room.

The fire had charred and knocked aside the tables and pews, but everything else was still. Ryan stood just outside the door and watched. If Dawson needed help, it would only take a second for him to get to him.

Dawson looked left and right, trying to figure out what to do, and then the streetlights flickered. Ryan cursed again when he realized the man

Dawson was looking for would show. When the flickering stopped, The Smuggler stood before Dawson, his face hidden behind a black mask.

"You shouldn't be out alone," he said.

"I'm looking for someone." Dawson puffed out his chest. "I know what I'm doing."

The figure waved his hand, and a series of objects appeared before Dawson, glimmering in the sunlight.

Ryan tensed, poised to strike.

"I'm aware. You want something special for your sister, correct?"

Dawson looked at the floating objects. Ryan couldn't see what they were from his position. It wasn't anything to worry about if they were just gifts. "None of these fit my needs, Sir. I'm sorry, but I need something specific."

"What is it you want?"

"Books." Dawson didn't hesitate.

Ryan smiled. When The Smuggler chuckled, Ryan remembered why he was there. He tensed again and kept his eyes on the man. The Smuggler waved his hand again, and a series of books replaced the original items.

Dawson pulled a wad of cash out of his pocket. "How much? I've been saving all year."

Ryan grumbled, "Where the Helwe did you get that kind of money? How many phones did you make that?"

The man shook his head. "Take them, Dawson. Consider it a present from both of us."

Dawson looked confused for a moment.

Ryan stood and took a step forward, nearly crossing the threshold of the shrine, but then The Smuggler removed his hood.

A young man with chestnut brown hair stood before the boy, smiling widely. He let out a booming laugh and held out his arms.

Dawson stepped back in confusion and clenched his fists. "Wait, what are you-you're supposed to be dead."

Ryan's blood boiled, and he stormed into the building. *Tory.*

The man rubbed the back of his neck and laughed again. His voice was deep. "I know this is probably a shock, but I heard you were looking for me. I couldn't let the opportunity pass."

Dawson sniffled and wiped his nose with his shoulder. "How are you alive?" he shouted, his voice broke.

"Hey." Ryan stopped a few feet back, grabbing their attention. "You stabbed my brother."

Tory waved a hand, and a ribbon of water surrounded him. "Back for more?" he asked.

Ryan's fingers curled into fists. "You ran off last time. I woulda beat you," he snarled.

Dawson stared at the water and reached out to touch it. It spread apart before his fingers could interfere with the spell. "You're magik," the boy whispered.

Tory winced and looked at him. "This is why I had to go," he said. "Angel was onto me."

Ryan scowled and walked forward.

Dawson stepped in front of him, eyes wide and uncertain. "Don't hurt him. Please," he whispered.

Ryan wanted blood. He bit his lip until he tasted copper and stepped back. If he fought the person Dawson idolized as a brother, he would be the bad guy. He couldn't do that to the kid. Ryan jabbed a finger in Tory's direction. "We aren't done. The only reason I'm not gonna do anything is because of him," he growled.

The water fell, and Dawson ran to Tory. He clung to him, and soft sobs wracked his body.

Tory knelt to hug him back.

"I can't believe you're The Smuggler." Dawson cried.

"It's only been four years. You'd think it had been an eternity since you last saw me." Tory laughed nervously. His eyes didn't leave Ryan like he expected him not to follow through on his word.

"You were *dead*. No one expected to see you again."

Ryan turned away and walked out before he did something awful. He leaned against the building with a small sigh when he got outside. Ryan pulled his last cigarette from his back pocket and lit it with a snap of his fingers.

When Dawson was done, he would walk him home and finish tutoring. If he found something else to focus on, the anger would subside.

After a few minutes, Dawson came out, wiping his eyes and sniffing. "Thanks," he whispered.

Ryan exhaled smoke and shrugged. "Let's just get out of here before I change my mind," he said.

Dawson tossed Ryan a pack of cigarettes. "He didn't mean to hurt anyone. It was an accident if that makes it better."

Ryan didn't want to talk about it. "Did you get what you needed?" he asked, catching and pocketing the new pack.

"How did you get into a fight like that with Tory? What were you doing?" Dawson asked.

"Nothing. Don't worry about it." Ryan still didn't want to talk about it.

"Yeah."

Ryan threw his arm around the boy's shoulders. "Cool. Time to teach some math."

"Killian yells less. I'm sure she's learning a lot," Dawson said, reading his mind.

Ryan smirked. He was sure Killian had everything under control.

When they got to the home, Killian had his head on the table, and Kara was yelling. They both looked up at him, their faces relieved as he sat down.

"So, how's it going?" he asked. His words were slow.

"Horrible," they shouted at the same time.

Kara jabbed a finger at Killian, a storm brewing in her eyes. "I can't understand a single word he's saying. It's all technical bullshit."

"Alright, where are you guys working from?" Ryan asked.

Killian had yet to take his head off the table. He turned his head to stare at his brother with sad puppy-dog eyes.

Kara pushed her book at him and spouted off three questions. He drew out some pictures and tried to come up with an explanation. Apparently, Killian didn't have everything under control.

By the end of the afternoon, they almost caught Kara up. Killian stopped sulking after they entered the seventh chapter and stuck to keeping Ryan from shouting when he lost his temper. The three of them were a good team.

The front door opened and closed just as they called it a night. Kara looked up when her parents walked in with a cake and brightly wrapped gifts.

"Happy birthday," they said in unison.

Ryan sunk in his chair and shot Killian a panicked look. *Birthday.* Why was this the first time he heard about it?

Killian barely shook his head, eyes wide. He didn't know either. They had one of their silent conversations before Killian's hand dropped to the chain around his wrist.

Ryan narrowed his eyes and listened to the gleeful celebration in the background. They hadn't taken those chains off since they got them.

Kara giggled. "I can't believe you guys did all this," she said. "Thank you. I didn't need a celebration."

"Of course you did," her mom said, "and it's our job to ensure it happens."

Ryan undid the chain around his neck, and his eyes flicked to his brother. He nodded, just barely. An action for Killian alone.

They stood when Kara and her parents made it to the table. Ryan smiled weakly. He didn't like big celebrations. Hopefully, they didn't plan on inviting a bunch of people.

"Happy birthday," he said, holding out the chain.

Kara blinked at it, and her cheeks went pink. She brushed her fingers across it and shook her head. "It's magik."

He grabbed her wrist and pulled her forward. He looped the thin chain around her wrist twice and clasped it with a sigh. "Right, it's a protection spell. Look at it closer," he said.

Kara squinted at the tiny links. "It's red and orange, but it's not. Clearly, it's silver."

He chuckled. "Uh-huh. It's connected to my magik. It'll protect you from anyone who intends harm," he said.

She blinked at it, and her eyes flicked to her parents. The chain was loose on her skin despite being wrapped twice. "You always wear this. Are you sure you can give it up?" she asked.

Ryan rubbed the back of his neck. If he was being honest, he wasn't sure it worked, anyway. "Yeah, it's mostly superstition anyway," he said.

Kara beamed at him with that smile that made his stomach tighten. She held up her hand to show her parents and little brother.

"Isn't that pretty?" Samantha asked.

Ryan hoped she didn't know what it was. He moved back to his brother so the family could have their moment.

Killian tapped his fingers on the table. "You sure you wanna give that up?" he asked.

The last remnant of a mother he could barely remember. Ryan nodded, a small smile crossing his lips as he stared at Kara.

She had a huge smile, and her cheeks were pink with excitement. She spoke with her hands; her eyes were so bright they were like the sky on a beautiful sunny day. If she was happy, he didn't mind giving it up.

"You like her," Killian whispered.

Ryan shook his head. His cheeks warmed. "I have no clue what you're talking about," he said. He tore his gaze away from Kara and cleared his throat. "She's a good friend."

"Right, that's why I'm all warm and fuzzy right now." His brother shivered. "Disgusting."

"Get over it."

They set everything on the table, and Ryan cleared their tutoring stuff. If everyone was going to celebrate, he didn't want to dampen the mood by reminding Kara of the bad stuff.

"How was everyone's day?" Arthur asked, shooting a glance at them.

Ryan shrugged. "Nothing unusual. All good," he muttered.

Kara grinned.

He tried to read into that smile, which said she had a secret, but he couldn't tell what she was saying. Maybe he didn't want to know.

Samantha made dinner that night. Strong, meaty smells filled the house, and Ryan wrinkled his nose.

Angel kept her higher-ups happy. That thought shouldn't have surprised him. Without them, the city wouldn't run like it was supposed to. A little special treatment was an excellent incentive, a wise move in the long run.

"How's it feel being sixteen?" Dawson asked.

Kara shrugged as she set the table. "No different from fifteen, I suppose."

"Are you gonna be moodier now?"

She slapped him upside the head, and Ryan set some cups in front of each plate. He was trying to learn how ordinary families did things. There wasn't a time when his family sat down to eat like this. These moments confused him.

Kara talked to her parents about work and how things were going.

Ryan half-listened as he pushed food around on his plate. His anger thrummed in his veins, and he shook his head. He got irritated because of the family thing, even though he tried not to. He felt confined amid the laughing, giggling, and conversation. Ryan set his fork down and excused himself. He hadn't eaten, merely pushed some salted vegetables around.

"Are you alright?" Killian asked.

Ryan forced a smile and a curt nod. "Not feeling super well." He walked out of the dining room and entered the living room. *Weird. It's weird. Why do they act so casually? They don't know us, they claim to, but they don't.*

He closed the bedroom door after he walked in and leaned against it. The room was quiet and dark. Something he was used to dealing with.

A soft knock made his chest tighten. *Don't be Kara. For the love of-don't be her.* If she faced him now, he would snap. He knew he would. When he opened the door and peeked out, his eyes widened when he saw Samantha.

She smiled and gestured to be let in. "I think we need to talk."

"No, I don't think we do."

She leveled him with a stare that could only be described as pure mother. A look that commanded authority and told him she wasn't asking.

His fingers itched to slam the door in her face, to deny that authority, but he didn't.

"You're going to let me in," she said. It wasn't a question.

Ryan took a breath and opened the door, letting her by.

Samantha swept in and kicked the door shut, a childish motion that made him smile. "Gotcha, don't think I didn't see it," she said, pointing at the quirked-up corners of his lips.

He crossed his arms against his chest and stared at her. "Sorry, I know I'm no fun."

Samantha clicked her tongue and sat on the bed, where he and Killian took turns sleeping. She patted the spot next to her. "Come on, sit," she said with a sweet smile.

It was a smile that made his heart ache. She wasn't expecting anything from him, not trying to manipulate him. He only sometimes understood how this worked.

Ryan shuffled over to her and sat with a soft thud. He stared hard at the floor, refusing to look at her. If he did, she might sway him with her motherly charm.

"You don't trust people," she said.

Ryan shrugged. It didn't matter. "I trust enough," he said.

"It'll stop you from connecting to those who care."

He couldn't help the bitter laugh that slipped past his lips. Perhaps he was too cynical for his own good. "Like you?" he snapped. His voice was tight and cold.

The bed creaked when Samantha leaned back on her palms. "If I didn't care about you, you wouldn't be in my house."

Ryan scoffed despite not wanting to. They were Descendants. They could take care of themselves. He didn't need a fake mom doing that for him.

"You don't believe me?" she asked.

Ryan shrugged. He didn't want to talk. If she wanted to, he would listen, but she shouldn't expect much of a conversation.

"If I didn't care, you two wouldn't have survived this long," Samantha said.

He blinked at the plush white carpet. He liked how it felt on his feet. It wasn't cold like everything back home. This place was lived in and cared for.

"Do you remember a lot about your mom?" she asked.

"Mommy loves you. I want you all to myself," a voice whispered. She hugged him, something cold and rigid. "You don't need to go out and play."

Ryan pulled himself from the memory before it could hurt. He shrugged again, keeping his face emotionless. His eyes burned. "No," he whispered.

"Are you sure?"

Ryan's fingers curled into the blankets. "I don't remember, alright?"

Samantha touched his shoulder, and he jerked out of her touch. Her hand hesitated, but she reached for him again. He didn't move the second time. "Can I tell you something I remember?"

He looked at her, still blinking back the tears threatening to give him away. "About my mom?" he asked.

"No, about you."

His head throbbed just behind his eyes. He nodded, forgetting to breathe for a moment. "Sure."

"I remember a small boy who always had dirt on him," she said. "He didn't get to leave the hut much, but when he did, he always found something new."

The pain got stronger as he tried not to remember the things she said.

"He was sweet and caring until his mom came around," Samantha whispered. "When she was, he was quiet, scared. Ryan, I don't know what your mom did, but maybe it isn't the worst-"

He jumped off the bed before she could finish. "My mom loves me. I don't need you telling me anything about her."

Dainty arms encircled him, and Ryan stopped breathing. He froze as Samantha pulled him close and ran a hand through his hair. She hummed a soft tune. She smelt like cinnamon and lavender. Overall, it was an odd combination, but okay.

Ryan trembled. His mind was a raging storm of emotions. *Is this what a mom is supposed to be?* He reached up, wondering what it would be like to return to that. His pride stopped him, and he dropped his arms, making them useless at his sides.

"You're allowed to hug me," she whispered.

He shook his head. "There's no point."

"Doesn't have to have one. It's a hug."

Ryan chewed his lip until it was bloody. A hug from someone other than his brother. He wrapped his arms around her and squeezed his eyes shut, letting the tears fall.

They wet her shirt, but she didn't seem to mind. If she noticed them, Samantha didn't say a word.

When he stopped crying, Samantha held him at arm's length and smiled. "How do you feel?"

Guilty. "Better."

This wasn't something he should be enjoying. Every moment he spent with them was another moment they were in danger.

"I'm sorry," he whispered.

She brushed her thumbs across his cheeks and beamed. For a moment, he could see Kara in her. The girl was a lot more like her mom than she knew.

"You're not a bad kid, and I'm sorry I couldn't protect you from the person you needed it from," Samantha whispered.

Ryan wiped his eyes. He couldn't believe he cried. "That was weird."

"That was normal for any teenager," Samantha said with a grin. "Join us for cake or stay in here. Not gonna lie, it's damn good."

Ryan smirked and nodded. He wiped his eyes and tried to make it look like he hadn't just sobbed into Samantha's shoulder.

"Don't stand here and primp. Come on, I want cake." Samantha dragged him out of the room and back into the joyous laughter of the kitchen.

After dinner, Ryan opted to help Kara clean so her parents could relax. She did the dishes while he cleared the table and put leftovers in the fridge.

"Tonight was outstanding. Are you feeling better?" she asked.

Ryan looked up from shoving a bunch of leftovers in the fridge. The containers wobbled on top of each other, but he shut the door before they could fall. That would be someone else's problem. "Sorry, what?" he asked.

She smirked. "You said you weren't feeling well earlier."

"Yeah, I'm fine. This is all weird," he said. It was overwhelming. That was a better word.

Kara smiled, though something sad lingered in her eyes. Kara said nothing. She just went back to scrubbing the dishes.

He was finishing his job when she whirled around and flicked water at him. He jumped back, startled. His heart thundered in his ears as he stared at the droplets on his shirt, wondering if it touched his skin.

Kara apologized and lunged forward. "I didn't mean to scare you. I'm sorry."

He moved away and shoved her. "Don't touch me," he snapped.

"I'm sorry, I didn't mean to," she whispered.

Ryan hissed in anger and looked away.

She didn't understand. She wasn't like him. The kicked-puppy look was physically painful.

Ryan took a couple of breaths. "Water," he said, "I'm-my magik is fire, so water is different with me. It burns, and I can't use it if I get wet."

Kara wiped her hands on her pants frantically. "I'm so sorry. I didn't know. I just figured you were being-oh my god. Can I do anything?"

He forced a chuckle. "After our day, it's not that big a deal."

"How do you shower? Or drink?" she asked.

Ryan shrugged. "Quickly. Warm water and doesn't seem to bother me."

"So, you drink warm water?" she asked.

He shrugged again. People did weirder things. "I mean, it's water."

Kara sighed, and her parents shouted for bedtime.

Ryan smirked. "Good night, Kara."

She nodded and wiped her hands on her pants before waving. "Night."

A Favor

KILLIAN DIDN'T SLEEP WELL that night. He tossed and turned. It was his turn on the floor, and the carpet was harder than it looked.

Ryan snored lightly in the bed. It seemed he spent most of his energy in his heart-to-heart with Samantha. His brother didn't tell them what they talked about, just that she made him feel welcome. That was a feat.

He noticed the change after dinner when a warm surge ran through his body instead of the cold anxiousness. Neither of them did well with people, but Ryan was surprisingly worse. Especially when things happened that he didn't expect.

A soft knock made him sit up. *Kara?* She wouldn't try to get on her mom's bad side, would she? At the very least, she had to know this would get them killed. He opened the door, and Arthur stood on the other side.

He smiled weakly and gestured to the living room. "I was wondering if we could talk?" he asked.

Killian looked at Ryan and frowned. His brother snored away, his leg dangled off the side of the bed, and his arm was thrown across his eyes. "He's asleep. Could you just talk to me and-"

"No." Arthur cut him off.

Killian sighed, walked to the bed, and shook Ryan's shoulder. He hated waking him. Sometimes, he came up swinging.

Ryan jolted and swung his fist with a grumble.

Killian caught his wrist, narrowly avoiding being hit in the nose. "Arthur and Samantha want to talk to us."

Ryan blinked and stretched. "Oh, just you. Morning?"

"No," Killian muttered. "Her parents want to talk to us."

Ryan flopped back down on the bed and groaned. "Ten more minutes."

Arthur peeked in with a raised brow. His glasses rode up on his face, and he looked more irritated than nervous.

Killian forced a smile. He held up a finger. "Just a sec." He leaned to whisper in Ryan's ear, "Get up, or I'm throwing the coldest glass of water on you."

"You wouldn't," Ryan whined. His voice was thick with sleep.

"Try me."

Ryan popped back up in bed and swung his legs over the side. "Fine."

Arthur walked into the living room with them, where Samantha was on the couch.

Killian gulped. He didn't think this was going to be a delightful conversation. The twins sat on the other couch when Arthur sat beside his wife.

"Kara and Dawson are asleep, so we figured this was a good time to talk in private," Arthur said.

Ryan yawned and scratched the back of his head. "Sure."

"This is about your magik," Samantha said.

Killian went rigid and refused to look at Ryan. He knew this talk was coming. Since he came back injured, they had been a little stiff around him.

"What about it?" Ryan asked.

When one of them couldn't make conversation, the other could. Whoever said they didn't work well together was insane.

"You've gotta stop using it. Angel's going to see through those disguises," Arthur said.

Killian winced. "I suppose we could benefit from not using magik," he said.

"*Could* is an understatement." Samantha chuckled. "But I like how you try."

Ryan sighed and ran a hand down his face. "Cool, we done? I'm exhausted."

"No, we have one more thing to ask," Samantha said. "A favor of sorts."

"We kind of owe you, so sure?" Ryan sounded less sure than he looked.

"When we get you an escape, take Kara and Dawson," Arthur said.

Killian frowned. Taking people with them would slow them down. They hadn't been outside the walls in seven years. Finding a suitable home would take time, and reacclimating would take more. There's no way he planned on caring for two kids on top of that. Especially one as reckless as Dawson. That was asking for instant death.

"We can do that," Ryan agreed. His stupid brother didn't stop to think about anything that went with that.

"No, we can't!" Everyone looked at him. Killian turned to Ryan. "They'll get us killed." He stared hard at his brother, begging him to pick up on his emotions for once.

Ryan shrugged and leaned back, closing his eyes. "What's two more people?"

"Ryan, this is going too far. You're pushing yourself too much as is, and watching them would be a nightmare," Killian said.

Samantha pursed her lips. "Those *are* my children you're talking about."

Killian barely heard her over the roaring panic in his head. He planned on going home to live a semi-normal life again.

"Shut up, you don't know what you're talking about," Ryan snapped.

"I do. You can't lie to me; I feel how exhausted you are. The world is dangerous, and those two know nothing about self-preservation."

"Killian, shut up! I'm fine," Ryan shouted.

This was seconds from turning into one of their famous fistfights. Killian ground his teeth in frustration. "You're *not* fine."

Ryan threw his hands in the air. "For god's sake, what do you want from me?"

I want you to stop killing yourself for people we barely know. It's supposed to be us, not us and them. Killian scowled and crossed his arms against his chest. "I want you not to be responsible for once."

"Oh, oh, that's rich." Ryan laughed bitterly. "You want to lecture me on responsibility? Should we talk about the people you murdered the other night?"

Samantha stood and grabbed both their ears. They hissed in pain and went quiet. "Now, there's no need for all this ruckus. At this rate, you'll wake the whole house."

"You're not our mom, so stop acting like it," Ryan said. There was some bite in his voice, but he stopped yelling.

"You're in my house, and I won't have this fighting. I know we're asking a lot, but we are out of options. Something is coming, and I don't want my kids here for it," Samantha said.

"We can protect them," Ryan said. He looked back at his brother. "*I* can protect them. I protect you, don't I?"

Killian clenched his jaw. "*Stop* protecting me. I'm tired of you acting like-"

"Are you quite done?" Ryan snapped. His eyes darkened. "You're my brother, but I will hurt you if you say another word."

Arthur sighed and ran a hand down his face. "We only need you to get the kids to someone in Rochester who will help. After that, you can do whatever you want."

Samantha let their ears go when they calmed.

Killian shot Arthur a look mixed with frustration and anxiety. "Do you know how long it takes to get to Rochester?" he asked. "This isn't an easy trip with magik, let alone without."

"Who?" Ryan asked, ignoring him. He was past their argument and moving on. Whether Killian agreed or not, he would escort the McKenzie kids.

"We know how far it is, but we have faith that you two can do this," Samantha said. "Don't forget, I've been watching you for a while."

"His name is Nicholas. He can train you and teach you about your magik. He will protect all of you," Arthur said.

Killian obviously didn't get a say in things. He kept his mouth shut to avoid angering anyone, but he wouldn't forget this. When things went south, he would get to say so.

"Your kids won't leave you," Ryan said.

"They will. We'll talk with them before it happens," Arthur said.

"Do you accept?" Samantha asked.

Ryan nodded. "Yes."

Killian bit his tongue and nodded. Ryan was going to do whatever he wanted. He just had to stick around and ensure things didn't go wrong. This was bad, though. There was a feeling he couldn't shake like things were about to change.

"No more magik," Arthur repeated. "Lie low until we tell you. For now, act like nothing's changed."

Ryan ran a hand through his hair and beckoned to the bedroom. "I'm going back to bed if we're done."

Killian sat on the couch and listened to the door click shut.

Samantha's eyes were on him, and a small smile played on her lips.

He tried to ignore her, but after a while, he caved. "What?" he asked.

"I thought he was the difficult one, but he's not. Once you figure him out, he's simple, but you... you're something different," she said.

"That's new. Most just tell me I'm a dick instead of going around the bush," he said.

"I don't think you're a dick. You're scared. It shows differently in different people." Samantha sounded impressed, or maybe she was pleased with herself.

Killian snorted and stood. "You got me down, don't you? Good-night."

"When did you switch?" she asked.

Killian hesitated. He wasn't sure he understood the question. His magik was under control right now. To be sure, his fingers ran across the ring on his opposite hand.

"Not magik, dear boy. Your roles. When did you stop protecting him?" Her words made his heart jump a beat.

Killian didn't know what to say, so he shrugged and walked past her. She didn't push the subject, and he tried his best to quell the roll of magik in his veins.

"It's coming, little shadow user. Best be prepared." his shadow purred.

Shut up. No one asked your opinion.

"My price will come. Don't forget you owe me."

How could he possibly forget?

An Unwelcome Stranger

KARA

K ARA CORNERED HER PARENTS when they woke to leave for work. There was a lot she had to figure out.

Her mom took one look at her defiant stare and sighed. "What's up, my dear?" she asked.

Kara threw her hands in the air. "Uh, The Wilds?" she asked.

Her mom chuckled and ruffled her hair. "Your dad told me about that." She acted like it was no big deal.

Kara scowled and crossed her arms against her chest. "Mom, this is kinda a big deal," she said.

Her dad sighed and rubbed his eyes. "Do we have to do this now?"

"Yes, my whole life has been a lie," she almost shouted. It took her a minute to remind herself others were still sleeping.

"Don't be so dramatic. So, you were born somewhere else. You don't even remember," her mom said.

That wasn't the point. Kara could've lived a whole new life. Something different and exciting, but she was stuck in prison.

As if reading her mind, her dad touched her shoulder. "Nothing changes just because you were born elsewhere," he said.

Except there wasn't a tyrant outside the walls. She didn't voice her thoughts but rubbed her forehead. "Are you going to tell Dawson?" she asked.

Her parents exchanged looks. "We don't think that's the best idea. Not until things calm down."

She could almost see it now. He would tear the city apart if he thought he was anything else.

"Now, we've got to go, love. Stay safe and study," her mom said.

Kara opened her mouth to argue, but her parents left without another word. She sat at the kitchen table and grumped to herself. If Kara was from the outside, she wanted to know more. She didn't understand how they could keep this from her and act so nonchalantly.

"Hey, where's Ryan?" Killian asked.

She looked up as he entered the dining room. "He left early this morning. Seemed agitated."

Killian sat across from her. He toyed with a strand of his hair before shrugging. "He didn't sleep well."

"Apparently, you didn't either," Kara said, noticing the bags under his eyes. Whatever problems she had, she didn't need to bring them into it.

Killian rubbed them and yawned. "I slept fine."

The front door opened and closed. Ryan walked in with slumped shoulders and dark bags under his eyes. He froze when he saw her and his brother at the table. "Didn't know you were all up," he muttered.

Kara smiled. "We gotta get ready for school. Do you guys need to stop at home?"

"I'm going to go back and get some stuff. I'll bring it to you at school."

"No, no more magik. We'll walk," Killian said.

Ryan glared but didn't argue. "Fine, then we need to go."

"Is it alright if I tag along?" Kara asked.

She could bond with them. When no one turned her down, she ran to her room to get dressed. When she returned, they were waiting for her at the foot of the stairs.

"Let's go!" she beamed.

Ryan grunted and walked out the front door. Killian smiled and followed her as she talked about her weird dream. He seemed genuinely interested and didn't interrupt as they all but ran to keep up with Ryan.

"It's way too early for you," Ryan growled.

She laughed and grabbed his hand, pulling back to slow him down. "Are you not a morning person?" she asked.

His fingers entwined with hers, and he grunted again. Killian smirked, and she took his hand, standing between them.

When they reached the apartment building, Ryan stopped. He tightened his grip. "Hey, why don't you guys stay out here?"

Killian shook his head. "Not gonna happen. Kara, wait here."

She frowned but nodded, and they went in, whispering amongst themselves. Something was off. She clutched her hands to her chest and waited.

Kara sighed and sat on the steps of the building. It wouldn't take long. It never did. There was a crash, and glass shattered minutes later. She jumped up and ran to their apartment door, stopping just outside.

Ryan shouted something and another crash was accompanied by a pained cry. *Are they fighting?*

She threw open the door and froze. A man was standing in the middle of the living room. He had Killian by the throat, and Ryan was unconscious by the far wall.

"Is that all you got?" the man asked.

Kara pressed her hands to her mouth and trembled. The fighting filled the room with tension and cluttered emotions. Her chest constricted as she tried to breathe. It was like walking into another world.

"Let him go," she shouted before she could stop herself.

The man turned at the sound of her voice but didn't look at her. It was then she noticed a gnarly horizontal scar across his eyes. *He's blind. But, how did he-*

"And what have we here? A little mouse to ruin the fun?" the man asked.

"Kara, run!" Killian gasped for breath, struggling against the man's grip.

The man let Killian go. His body was suspended in the air before flying across the room. Killian slid to the floor unconscious.

Another Descendant. She wanted to run, but the man was in front of her as soon as she stepped back.

He caught her chin with stiff fingers. His skin was freezing, and it sent a bolt of terror through her body. "You're quite interesting, little girl," he mused.

Kara slapped his hand.

He let out a deep laugh.

Her vision clouded with blue and silver streams, and her head pounded. She didn't want to look scared, but something was wrong. The pressure on her chest let up a little, and she took a shaky breath. "You're not going to hurt me," she said.

The man chuckled and asked, "Why do you say that?"

"I don't know, but I know you're not going to."

"Well, you're not wrong. I don't make it a habit to hurt kids."

Then why did you hurt them? She ran past him to Ryan's side and checked for a pulse.

The man watched her, or at least stared in her general direction.

Kara shifted under his gaze and went to check on Killian. He could see her. She didn't know how, but she knew he could see her.

"They will be fine, little mouse. I simply knocked them out."

Kara turned and glared. "Why?"

"I was testing them." His voice was light, almost playful.

Kara stood and beckoned to her friends. "Fix them."

"I can't."

"Yes, you can. I know you can."

As the pressure on her chest vanished, the room filled with dazzling colors. Reds, violets, and gold surrounded her. Colors that held their own meanings, and she somehow knew what they were. A bolt of pain tore through her head, and she whimpered.

Blood trickled from her nose, and the room spun. She stumbled, and the man caught her arm, steadying her. *How can he move so fast?*

"If you keep pushing, little mouse, you're going to get hurt," he whispered. "I will make them better, but calm down." Kara nodded, and he pointed to the couch. "Sit."

The man waved his hand, and a golden light surrounded Killian and Ryan. Kara looked up to thank him, but he was gone. Vanished.

A few seconds later, Ryan's eyes opened, and he jumped to his feet.

"It's alright," Kara whispered.

Ryan ran to her side. "You're bleeding. What happened?"

She wiped the blood from her upper lip and looked away. *I don't know. Something weird.* Tears slipped down her cheeks, and he knelt in front of her and wrapped his arms around her with a sigh. *Why do I feel this crushing sadness?*

Ryan stroked her hair, and she clung to him, sobbing.

Killian woke up a few minutes later, dazed and confused.

She knew they wanted answers, but Kara couldn't tell them. She didn't know what had happened. The only thing that ran through her mind was: *maybe I'm not entirely human.*

His Decision

JUSTIN

JUSTIN APPEARED IN HIS living room and wrung his hands together. He hadn't seen one since Jessica. He didn't know there were any left. His energy tore through the house, and he hurried down the hall, tripping over a towel. *God, why do I even bother cleaning?* He pounded on Nicholas's bedroom door and heard cursing on the other side. *Oh, for the love of-* He opened the door, thankful for once, he couldn't see. "Get your clothes on. I'm going to help."

Nicholas yelped, and someone fell off the bed. By the pained groan, he assumed it was the boy toy. "Privacy! Don't you know you're supposed to wait for someone to open the door after you knock?"

"Not like I can see a damn thing. Get out here," Justin snapped. He shut the door and returned to the living room.

"You must have approved of the boys?" Nick asked.

Justin didn't turn around. "Yes, I approve. I have one stipulation. There's a girl with them. She comes too."

"Girl? What girl are you talking about?" Tory asked. His footsteps were so light they barely made a sound.

Right, he's still here. Justin shook his head. "It doesn't matter."

Nick held his breath.

Justin wouldn't give anything away. He wouldn't do something as stupid as that. All he knew was that whatever this girl was, he wanted her.

Tory made a noncommittal noise behind them.

Justin cut Nicholas off before he could dive into a lecture. "Those are my stipulations. You bring her or no one at all."

Nick sighed. "I mean, if that's the only way for you to agree, fine." The sigh of defeat was enough to tell Justin he had won.

"Good, then we need to draw up a plan."

"I don't even know how to convince them to come," Nick said.

Justin didn't care. They would figure it out. The front door banged open, and he forced a smile as Cody ran into the living room. He threw himself into Nick's arms and giggled like a madman. "Hi, Uncle Nicky! Oh, we have a guest?" Cody noticed Tory.

"That's your uncle's current boy toy," Justin said, waving his hands. The last thing he needed was Cody getting attached to someone who wouldn't stick around.

Nicholas spluttered, "He's my boyfriend!"

"Whatever, same thing," Justin said.

Tory introduced himself, and they talked for a little. Justin tapped his chin and thought.

"What's for a snack, Jay?" Cody asked, tugging his arm. "I'm starving."

"Why doesn't he call you dad?" Tory asked.

Justin shrugged. "Ever since he was little, he called me what Nicholas called me. I always wanted him to be free to use the words he was comfortable with."

"So, he was adopted?" Tory asked.

Nicholas coughed. "Cody, the garden is ready for harvesting. Would you like to help?"

The boy didn't miss a beat. He jumped at the chance to spend some time with his favorite person. As soon as the front door closed, Justin grabbed the front of Tory's shirt. "I'll tolerate you because my brother will tire of you. Be careful what lines you cross. Cody is my son, and that's all you need to know."

Tory put his hands up. "I didn't mean to overstep. He just-he didn't call you dad."

"Mind your own business." Justin shoved him.

Tory grunted. He didn't say a word as Justin walked past.

When put there, Tory was smart enough to know his place. If he didn't, Justin would take care of it in due time.

Curious Questions

RYAN

K ARA REFUSED TO TELL them what happened in the apartment when they were unconscious. Ryan asked multiple times, but all she did was shrug. Even Killian couldn't get her to say anything.

Ryan sat by the rock at the back of the school and smoked a cigarette when lunch came. He hoped it would calm his nerves before anyone else showed. Things didn't help when Killian walked up with a black eye. *Deep breaths. Lay low.*

"You look constipated," Killian muttered.

Ryan elbowed him in the ribs. "You're not helping."

"You're always in a mood these days."

Ryan made a face and resisted the urge to stick out his tongue. He wasn't that childish. "I'm not sleeping well."

Killian leaned back against the boulder and yawned. "Coulda fooled me, you snore like a bear."

Ryan clenched his jaw. "Aside from that. What happened?" he asked.

"I'm not telling you. You're just gonna fly off the handle. Lay low, remember?" Killian said.

"I don't need magik to beat someone. I'm capable without it."

Killian rolled his eyes. "More and more soldiers patrol the school. If you get caught fighting, they'll take you to Angel."

Ryan stuck out his tongue. Killian chuckled and tossed a sandwich into Ryan's lap. Almost offended, Ryan looked at the food before unwrapping it.

"Vegetarian," Killian muttered as he began looking through the bread. "Don't you think I know you by now?" he asked.

He knew his brother would never intentionally give him meat, but Ryan couldn't help his instincts. He had been checking his food for as long as he could remember.

Kara showed up a few minutes later. She sat across from them and didn't say a word. Her moodiness was making him worse.

"How was class?" Killian asked.

She shrugged. "I haven't been focusing well."

"You need to start," Ryan said. "If you don't, you're going to fail."

Unless Samantha and Arthur figure something out and get them outside the walls in the next four days.

"I know my predicament, Wilson. Thank you."

"Chin up, Princess. It isn't so bad," Ryan said.

She shot him a deadly glare, and he shut his mouth. For someone who insisted she wasn't like her mom, she was a lot like her mom. They ate in silence for a while, and Kara huffed. "Do you guys know that man from earlier?" she asked.

"No, but he was a Descendant," Killian replied.

Kara nodded.

Ryan wanted to know what was happening in her head, but she didn't look like she wanted to share. He couldn't force her. Whatever that man did or said had her on edge.

"People are talking about Descendants, you know? It won't be safe for you to go out anymore," Kara said.

Ryan rubbed the back of his neck. "That shouldn't be a problem. We decided not to traverse out." *Traverse. I didn't just use that word, did I?* Ryan shook his head and hoped she wouldn't say anything.

"Did you just-"

Killian grunted and shook his head, and she shut her mouth.

Ryan shot him a grateful stare.

"Why aren't you guys-I mean, I'm not unhappy, but why did you decide that?" she asked.

Killian smirked playfully. "Because I almost died. Is that not a good enough reason?"

Kara scowled at him and bit her lip. She looked two seconds from sticking out her tongue. "That's not what I meant."

"He's messing with you," Ryan said.

She looked at the ground and shrugged. "We're friends, right? Like, I can ask you anything?"

Ryan raised a brow. This didn't sound good.

Killian nodded when he decided Ryan wouldn't say anything. "Of course. What's up?"

Her voice was quiet when she spoke, and she refused to meet their eyes. "I was curious about when you found out about your magik. Like, how did you know you were Descendants?"

Ryan shot Killian a look, and he shrugged back. She didn't think she was a magik, did she? *What did that man say to her?*

"Actually, Ryan found his magik first. It just kind of happened," Killian said.

"Yeah, we were probably about seven or eight. Killian broke his ankle, and I had to save him, so the combination of fear and my desire to help turned into fire. I suppose things had been odd for a few weeks leading up to that moment," Ryan said after some thought. Most of that part of his life was blank.

"Weird, like how?"

Ryan leaned forward and touched her cheek. Her eyes flicked to his, and her cheeks turned red. "Kara, are you worried about something?" he asked, keeping his voice low.

She shook her head and pulled away. "Now that's silly. Why would you say something like that? I think you've been hit one too many times."

"Okay, but you didn't even-you know what, don't worry about it. Before my magik woke, I was having odd dreams and high fevers. I also had a weird aversion to water. The rivers especially scared the Helwe out of me."

The bell rang, signaling the end of lunch, and she groaned. Ryan chuckled. "See you guys later," she said, jumping up. Kara disappeared inside the school with a wave.

Ryan sighed.

"You think she's a Descendant?" Killian asked.

"I don't know, but something happened. She had a bloody nose and was bawling," Ryan said.

"And she has random headaches. I notice they take hold when one of our tempers is out of control."

Ryan noticed that, too. She might have sleeping magik, but most Descendants woke before they were ten. She was sixteen. He didn't know anyone who had magik wake when they were adults. Then again, he knew few people with magik.

"Get to class. We'll keep an eye on her. If anything weird happens, we'll figure it out."

Killian nodded, and they parted ways.

Ryan's stomach churned, and he chewed the inside of his cheek. He had a bad feeling.

Their night was uneventful. After school, Ryan tutored a little more, and Kara asked questions about The Wilds. It surprised him that she waited so long.

He talked about nature, the animals, and the mountains. Things he thought she would like to hear. They ate dinner without Dawson or her parents. Kara's brother was out with friends, and Samantha and her husband had to work late.

Ryan tried to make conversation, but Kara was sullen and quiet. She frowned at her steamed vegetables and flicked them around her plate.

"Are you alright?" he asked after a while.

He ignored Killian's knowing stare. His brother was on this, 'You like her but won't say anything' kick, driving Ryan nuts.

Kara popped leafy greens into her mouth and pointed to it as she chewed. That was her way of telling him to leave her the Helwe alone.

Ryan shrugged and finished his dinner without another word. He thought Killian was bad when he was moody. This was a whole new level of dealing with emotions.

Kara pushed away from the table and gathered her dishes. "Night," she said, disappearing down the hall.

Ryan stared as she went up the stairs with the plate and half-full cup. "You think she's gonna put those where they go?" he asked Killian.

"Probably not. How long you wanna sit and see if she does?"

Ryan wasn't a betting man. He didn't need to turn things into challenges to beat his brother. That was childish and immature. "I bet the bed tonight, she doesn't come back."

"I call for ten minutes," Killian said. They shook hands and stared at the stairwell. Killian had his phone out on the table, and they watched the time as they listened to the shuffling upstairs.

Kara thumped up and down the hall, making a lot of noise for a small girl.

The clock just hit ten minutes when she reappeared. Kara froze like a deer caught in a flashlight, and Ryan cursed.

Killian chuckled and pushed away from the table, ruffling his hair. "Seems I know your girlfriend more than you, buddy. Night." He waved to Kara with a smug smile and headed for the room.

Kara blinked in confusion. Her eyes narrowed in suspicion. "What was that about?" she asked.

"I lost a bet," Ryan said. "You lost me a bet."

Her cheeks went pink, and she puffed out her cheeks. "You were betting on me?" she asked.

"Yeah, well, you're the one who took a dirty plate and cup to your room," he said. "What else am I gonna do with that?"

Kara turned on her heel and went back upstairs. "You're a dick," she said.

He smirked and waited until she was out of sight before exhaling. *I think I'm in trouble with her.* His stomach fluttered, sending his mind into a peaceful buzz. *She didn't freak out when Killian called her my girlfriend. That shouldn't make me happy.* But it did. Tremendously so.

When Ryan tried to get comfortable on the floor, Kara pounded on the bedroom door. He sighed and threw his arm over his eyes. "Killian."

His brother was bundled in a bunch of blankets on his bed. The cocoon barely moved when he spoke, "Nope. Your problem."

Ryan pushed himself off the floor and opened the door. Any semblance of sleep vanished when he saw her.

Kara had tears in her eyes, and the moment the door opened, she grabbed his arm like he was her only lifeline. "Dawson is trapped in an alley. Soldiers tracked his phone. You have to help." The words left her body in one go.

"Whoa, whoa, whoa. I didn't get all of that. Dawson is where?" he asked. If it was a security issue, why wasn't her mother dealing with it?

Killian stepped behind him, peeking out. "Everything okay?" he asked.

Sure, get up for someone else, but when I'm trying to revive you, you're dead for hours. Ryan scrunched his nose but kept his thoughts to himself. "No, something about Dawson and a phone," he murmured.

"He's going to get caught by Angel!" Kara shouted.

Killian shook his head and pushed past Ryan. "We won't let that happen."

Ryan grabbed the back of his brother's shirt, and his eye twitched. "I'll go. You cause problems. Stay with Kara. If he returns, call me."

"You can't go alone," Kara squeaked.

"Don't worry. I've done this loads of times." Ryan tried to sound confident. It was one thing to go after his brother, but trying to track someone else's wasn't on his list.

"Ryan's right, he's faster," Killian said.

"He's somewhere between here and downtown. Near the bakery and coffee shops," Kara whispered.

"Okay, I'll be back." *Hopefully, I mean, I don't think this is a good idea.* It was one of the worst he had. Even if he wanted to, though, he couldn't stop himself after looking at Kara's red eyes and tear-stained face.

She clutched her hands to her chest and fiddled with her fingers that had the cuticles picked and chewed down. Her chest heaved with panicked breaths. Her bright blue eyes were watery and wary as she stared at him, begging him to fix it.

Killian cleared his throat beside him, pulling Ryan out of his thoughts. "Be careful," he warned.

Right, because they didn't have enough going on in their lives. He ran outside and pulled his shirt sleeve up just enough to press his palm to the mark on his bicep. A black ball of fire wrapped around his bicep and trailed toward his elbow.

His mark as a Descendant. It was a black dot when he was younger but had grown considerably. There were rumors that the marks evolved as the Descendant grew, but his had yet to do much aside from growing in size. Keeping it hidden was a pain.

When the disguise spell worked, its magik, Ryan hissed in pain. It was getting more manageable, but he still had trouble with the hammer pounding against his skull.

Alright, let's find the kid.

Ryan tore through the streets as fast as he could manage without draining too much energy. After all, he had no clue what he would need to do when he found Dawson.

Soldiers roamed up and down the residential district, combing for the kid. *Man, he really pissed Angel off, didn't he?* Ryan stopped down the first alley he found and scanned the darkness. There was a puddle of something against the left wall right next to the bright green and blue dumpster with Angel's logo stamped. The symbol resembled a crown and thorns, but Ryan could never quite make it out.

The walls were covered in orange and red paint. Most were Angel or things resembling her that Ryan wasn't comfortable naming. The majority of the pictures were of her with horns or red eyes. In one, she was burning at the stake and laughing wildly. The kid was creative, but man, oh man. He was dark.

I can see why she would be upset. Ryan cleared his throat and stepped into the alley. Something clicked, and he ducked two seconds before a trash bag was hurled overhead. He froze and stared at the slimy green bag before looking back into the darkness.

"Dawson," Ryan hissed. "You almost hit me."

A scruffy mop of black hair appeared from behind the dumpster at the back of the alley. Dawson's blue eyes blinked wide with wonder. "Dude, you're illegal."

Ryan beckoned to the paint on the walls. "I'm not the only one. Do you have a death wish?" he asked. It was great work, but this was treasonous. Nothing would save him if Angel found out who the culprit was.

Dawson chuckled and walked out from behind the trash without hesitation. He pulled his black face mask down, uncovering his freckled face. "I was wondering if I'd get to see your magik," he said.

Ryan frowned. *This kid.* He shook his head and beckoned to the entrance. "Let me get you out of here. I don't need your mom skinning me."

"Aren't you gonna ask me how I figured it out?" Dawson asked. He was obviously proud of himself. He puffed his chest out and jabbed his thumb in the center of it.

He wasn't interested in the back and forth. "No, I don't care. So long as you don't talk to anyone else about it. Now, can we go?" Ryan asked.

"You don't think I've been trying? I need help slipping by. You've gotta have an idea," Dawson said. There was a hopeful twinge in his voice.

Ryan scoffed. *Like Helwe.* There was always a backway. He headed further into the alley and kept his eyes on the walls. Usually, the shops had back entrances. At the very end was a locked steel door and a window.

Not large enough for him to crawl through, but someone smaller could. "Dawson, get your ass over here," Ryan called back. They had a way out if he could hoist the kid into the shop.

The boy showed up behind him. He chewed his lip bloody, and his eyes darted around the narrow space. "Is this safe?" he asked.

"I'm going to boost you. Climb through there and open the door." Ryan ignored the question. They were anything but safe, but it didn't need to be said aloud.

"Cool plan, but I'll cut myself."

This kid better be joking. Ryan clenched his jaw and snapped his fingers. He didn't take his eyes off Dawson. Some of him feared that the boy would run if he did. That was in his particular set of skills that pissed people off. A fireball flew through the window and shattered it.

Dawson beamed. His eyes shone brighter than any Ryan had ever seen. They twinkled like little stars. "That was wicked cool," he said.

A few voices stopped at the entrance to the alley. "Check down there."

Son of a... Ryan knelt and cupped his hands together. "Hurry."

Dawson scrambled up the side of the wall and into the building. His muffled voice didn't take long to whisper through the steel. "Uh, problem."

No, no problems. Ryan put his face in his hands, and footsteps approached from behind. "Figure it out," he snapped.

There was scrambling inside the building, and some heavy stuff scraped across the floor. Ryan flicked his wrist, and a red wall cut him off from the soldiers. He was breaking his own first rule. If they took down that barrier before Dawson could get him inside... he didn't want to think about that.

"I uh-the door is stuck," Dawson called. Panic rose in his voice.

The soldiers raised their weapons and fired into the shield. It cracked like glass, and Ryan grabbed the front of his shirt and doubled over.

Ragged gasps wracked his body as he closed his eyes. *Breathe through it. Replace and manage.* The chips and cracks melted as the wall refreshed. "You still out there, magik boy?"

Ryan looked up, and his muscles trembled with anticipation. They were going to his it again. "Not for much longer," Ryan said.

There was silence, and something heavy thudded against the steel. Ryan groaned again and took stock of his options. He could try to scale the wall.

Another round of bullets hit the shield, and the world darkened. Stars spotted his vision, and he dropped to his butt. Hammers pounded against his temple, making it hard to come up with any sort of plan. *Breathe through it. Manage it.*

"This one won't go down easy. Bring out the big guns." The soldiers talked back and forth like he wasn't there.

These aren't the big guns? Dawson, hurry it up.

"I can't do it, Ryan," Dawson shouted, hitting the door again.

Ryan pressed his back against the door and sighed. "Okay, here's what we're going to do. You sneak out the door and go home," Ryan said. If they were lucky, the paintings would be blamed on him.

"What? No, but what about you?" Dawson asked.

It was easier to lie, even if it ate away at his stomach. Given his options, Ryan didn't know how long he would live to feel guilt. "I'm a Descendant. I got this," Ryan said. If there was weakness in his voice, he sure as Helwe couldn't hear it.

Another round of bullets nearly knocked him unconscious. Ryan bit his tongue until the light returned, and he could see clearly again. Blood dripped off his chin, and he wiped it away. *Killian.*

"Kid, if you can get out and head for home, my brother can get you," Ryan said, straining to raise his voice. "He can get us both, but you have to go now."

"Hit that wall again!"

The guns clicked with the sound of a reload. Ryan reached into his pocket and pulled out his phone. He dialed Killian's number. Ryan waved his hand, and the shield replenished once more.

His hand trembled, and he made a fist to quell the tremors. This wasn't the time to be weak. *Manage it. Come on, manage it.* Ryan's heart thudded an unsteady rhythm, and he tried to count the beats to distract himself.

Shields were connected to his heart. He could train his stamina all he wanted, but if they broke too many, he wouldn't have a chance in Helwe at survival.

Killian, answer the dang phone. Ryan squeezed his eyes shut and took a steadying breath.

"Ryan, did you find him?" Killian asked.

"Track me." Ryan didn't leave the opportunity for a lot of questions. They could take care of that later. The line went dead, and Ryan stared at the shield. He took a deep breath and watched the barrier disintegrate before the last round of bullets could. It was like playing the extreme version of the trust game.

A hand grabbed the back of his neck, submerging him in darkness. When he opened his eyes, he was on Kara's living room floor with Dawson and Killian. Knowing his brother was thoughtful enough to get the kid first was good.

He fell onto his back, and his disguise vanished. Ryan didn't bother trying to hide the relief. "Oh, thank God, I thought I was dead."

Kara peered down at him; concern clouded her eyes. "Are you injured?" "Just my pride," he said with a cheeky grin.

Dawson laughed and sat on the ground next to him. "I can't believe you and Killian are magik. Dude, why didn't you tell me?"

"Because I have no intention of saving your butt every night," Ryan growled. He shot a glare at the child and narrowed his eyes.

Dawson's cheeks had a pinkish tinge, and his eyes were circled in red. He sat with sunken shoulders and a slight dimness in his gaze. He fiddled with his fingers in front of him for lack of anything to do.

"You were crying."

Dawson's back straightened, and he grabbed his legs when he leaned forward. "Not at all."

"He was terrified something happened to you," Killian said. "*I* was worried." He punched Ryan's arm and frowned.

Close to the truth. Ryan laughed and scrubbed his face. "I have no clue what you're talking about. I was doing fine, but just so that you know," Ryan's cheeks heated. "It's not a bad thing to need to cry. I wouldn't have made fun of you."

Dawson's cheeks went pink, and he cleared his throat. "I might've been a little worried."

Ryan smirked and ruffled his hair. "I got you, don't worry about it."

Kara sighed. "It's past ten. We need to go to bed, or no one will get up for school."

Dawson nodded and sniffled a little. "I-thanks, Ryan. I owe you."

Ryan pushed himself into a sitting position. "You can repay me by never doing it again. I didn't get a scratch." This time. He probably wouldn't be so lucky next.

Dawson smiled up at him and nodded.

Ryan walked into the guest bedroom and sighed. His chest throbbed, and his head pounded, but he was alive. That was a plus.

"Are you really alright?" Killian asked. "How many shields did you use?"

"I dunno, two or three. I'm fine," Ryan groaned.

Killian lay on the bed on the floor and smirked. "Take the bed tonight. I'll switch with you. We gotta long day tomorrow, so you gotta be ready to go."

Ryan nodded and collapsed on the bed with a yawn. Sleep. That sounded amazing.

How to Catch Fire

A NGEL WATCHED THE VIDEO with wide eyes. *The twins, of course.* She didn't find the footage surprising, not really. Her General stood behind her with his arms crossed behind his back. All she needed was to bring them to her. She only needed to mark them, and they would have no choice but to come.

Justin was out of time. There was one thing that would draw any child in. The promise of their missing parent.

Angel smiled and hurried from her room. It was time to visit her favorite prisoner. She went down into her dungeons and stopped at the first cell. The door slid open with a wave of her hand, and she stepped inside.

"Good evening, Summer. And how do you fare today?" Angel asked.

A ragged, blonde-haired woman sat in the middle of the cell. Special chains bound her hands and wrists together and hung on her ankles. Her once bright emerald eyes were dull.

The woman didn't look up when Angel spoke. Her skin was pale and streaked with dirt. Her clothes were nothing but tattered rags. The cell stunk of human filth, and Angel couldn't be more delighted to see her like this.

A proud Descendant of Wind brought to nothing. *How delightful is this? She doesn't even talk anymore.* "You know, I found two boys recently. They remind me an awful lot of someone. Identical twins, probably close to seventeen." Angel hummed. This was her moment to gloat. "I can't place who they remind me of."

Summer's eyes widened. Fear rolled off her in erratic waves, and Angel soaked in the energy with pleasure.

"It's interesting because the boys are Descendants. They must come from a long line of magik. Lord Malsumis will be pleased to have them."

Summer looked at Angel then. Her eyes were fierce and protective, the dullness fading. "Only one." Her voice cracked with disuse.

"I'm sorry?"

"You can have one. The Descendant of Fire. You leave the other one, and I'll tell you anything."

Angel scoffed. "You've been an absentee parent for years. What would you know?"

"I know my children."

The Descendant of Fire. Angel pondered what would make a mother surrender one of her children so quickly. Wasn't there supposed to be some sort of bond between parent and child?

"What makes you give one up? I'm not offering a trade."

Summer seethed, clenching her jaw and biting out her words. "He's worse than you." Her mind *must've* been going. Perhaps she didn't know the things her son did. The trouble he got into for others.

Angel didn't think a boy with strong morals could be considered evil. After all, she was the jaded one. She was capable of evil, but that child, he wasn't. "And what makes you say that?" Angel asked. She was genuinely interested.

"Intuition," Summer whispered.

Angel clicked her tongue. Such an answer wasn't satisfying in the least. She should get back to business. "So, if I agree not to harm the other, you'll tell me about the boy of fire?"

Summer nodded and said, "Ryan, the one with fire, is named Ryan."

"Then tell me what you know. I don't have all night."

"He's driven by power and leans too heavily on his brother. Most of the time, he acts before thinking. He uses magik without saying a word since he was a small boy," Summer said. Her last words were more spoken to herself.

Angel laughed and waved her hand. "I'm going to end the world. He'll be nothing but a pawn." It was information she could work with.

A boy who wanted power to protect the ones he loved. That was the oldest story in the book. He couldn't get more basic if he tried.

Angel smirked and left the cell, thanking Summer for her cooperation. Her plan was the same. Capture both and sacrifice them. With their help, she would bring a new era to the world. One with true happiness.

Late Night Escapades

KILLIAN

A SIREN BLARED THROUGH the house, and Killian pushed himself off the floor. He didn't recognize the sound, but it was much too early, and he didn't have the energy to be nice.

As he stormed into the dining area, Kara shouted for Dawson. The boy jumped down the stairs like a deer and stopped beside her, panting.

Angel's image hovered above the phone as they played the most recent broadcast. "Two Descendants were in the city last night, and I fear they have overtaken us. They will not remain loose, so don't fear. In fact, we will hold a special execution in my dungeon tomorrow night where we will destroy the very person drawing all these monsters."

The screen flickered, and a blonde woman's face appeared next to Angel's. She was older, but Killian's anger vanished in a second. Even time couldn't make him forget those almond eyes and thin lips.

Mom.

Ryan slammed his fist into the wall, making them all jump. "That bitch. I'll tear her apart."

Killian didn't know he had been followed. He tried to move toward Ryan to stop him from doing something stupid, but he was stuck. Rooted to the spot as he tried to work through the swirl of emotions going through him. *Mom's here. She's been right here with us the entire time.*

Kara looked at them. "Is everything alright?" she asked. Her attention was no longer on the video.

Angel's voice continued, "Once this woman dies, the others will stop coming. We will film the event live so everyone knows there's no reason to be here."

"That's our mom," Killian whispered.

Kara's eyes widened, and she put her hands to her mouth. "Oh, no."

"Everyone in my city will be safe while we conduct these searches. If an armed guard appears on your doorstep, do not fear. He is there for your protection."

Ryan's anger grew with every word said.

Killian pulled on his shirt collar and shook his head. Heat surged through the house as his brother's anger grew. "Don't lose control," he said. They didn't have the time for a house fire.

"Also, the local high school will have a city-wide assembly tomorrow. We wish to celebrate the lives lost in the tragic misunderstanding downtown. Presence is mandatory."

The image faded, and Killian ran a hand through his hair. Their mom was in the city. He didn't understand how they didn't feel or see her. Her energy was difficult to miss. The woman was a whirlwind.

Ryan scowled and headed for the front hall.

Killian dragged himself out of his thoughts. He grabbed the back of Ryan's shirt and tugged him to a stop. "Where are you going?"

Ryan turned and scowled. "I won't let her kill Mom."

"Think this through. That place will be locked up. At least wait until night. We need coverage." Killian tried to maintain a level voice despite everything running through his thoughts. There had to be something they could do, but this was an obvious trap.

Angel knew their identities and was now trying to lure them out. It was the only thing that made sense. After all, why would she keep their mom a secret all this time only to bring her out now?

"We need to think this through," Killian said. He was the logical one. That was something his brother relied on. They both did.

Ryan ripped out of his hold and whirled around. His face was pinched with anger, and he jabbed Killian in the chest. "We're not letting the witch get away with this. I'm going after her."

Kara and Dawson tiptoed after them. Kara chewed her lip and held Dawson's shoulder to stop him from getting in the middle.

"Don't go, Ryan. It's not safe," Kara whispered.

Killian nodded. If anyone had a chance of talking him down, it was her. Ryan would never admit it, but he was attached to Kara. The more time they spent with her, the warmer and fuzzier Killian felt. It was a gross, obnoxious feeling that made breathing difficult. The only emotions he could share with his brother were intense ones that Ryan didn't know how to manage.

The feelings were evolving from casual interest to something more. An emotion his brother would never willingly express.

Ryan took a breath and closed his eyes. "I'll stay for now."

Killian thought about talking to Kara's parents. Surely, they could figure out some way to help. They were stronger and more experienced. It would be unwise to go alone. He didn't want to see his mother die, but realistically, what could they do?

"I'm going tonight. That's not negotiable," Ryan said.

Killian had until then to figure out what he would do, whether he would take it up with the McKenzies or go out with his brother.

"Why would Angel have your mom here?" Kara asked.

He shook his head. If he knew, they wouldn't be sitting there. Killian was out of ideas. Things never stopped surprising him in Yorklyn.

Ryan returned to the guest room without another word. If their mom really was going to die tomorrow, they had a lot to figure out.

"We'll skip tutoring today." Kara forced a smile. "I don't want to stress him further," she said.

Killian nodded and headed for the back room. Even if they figured something out, it was short notice to develop a plan. They were in trouble.

Killian woke in the dead of night, covered in sweat. He looked around the empty room. *Where the Helwe's Ryan?* He jumped out of bed and tried not to panic. His heart thundered in his ears, and his stomach dropped when he realized his brother wasn't in the house. *No, Ryan wouldn't be stupid enough to go after Angel alone.*

Killian cursed himself for falling asleep. He hurried onto the front lawn and transformed using his Descendant spell. It looked like they would take Angel as a duo.

His heart skipped a beat when he teleported to the tower. The buildings were difficult to recognize in the dark, but he could make out Ryan's red line of energy. It stopped before the tower behind a broken-down car.

Ryan was hunched down, scanning the plaza for movement. His bright red mask flickered like a flame from the streetlights.

Killian grabbed his shoulder as he moved towards the entrance. "What are you doing?" he asked. It was hard keeping the anger from his voice.

Ryan turned on him with fire in his eyes. "She has our mother. I'm getting actual answers, not some vague story Arthur told. Angel is the only one who can tell us what's happening."

Killian held his brother tighter when Ryan tried to move again. "No. Please, Ryan, just think for a moment. There are reasons people don't stand up to her."

Ever since they arrived, Killian knew there was something not right. The people waited on Angel's every word. Even when she killed kids, no one batted an eye. This couldn't be normal behavior. He knew anyone back home would have lost it the moment someone killed their child.

"Her soldiers and weapons don't scare me," Ryan snapped. "Now let go."

Killian knew there was no going back. He hoped Ryan knew that. "I'm going."

Ryan shrugged him off and hurried into the building under the cover of night. Everything was quiet. Not a single soldier was on patrol, and it sent dread through his body.

The boys crept through the tower lobby and peered through the darkness. It was pitch black. Without Killian feeling through the shadows with his magik, they would have never found their way to the elevators.

"Is it wise to take this thing?" he asked. "I mean, won't someone be guarding her floor?"

"I can run faster than they can shoot, and you can jump through shadows," Ryan said, jamming his thumb against the up button. "You act like she's some sort of goddess. She bleeds, too."

Killian resisted the urge to correct his twin as they got into the elevator and hit the button for the top floor. No one had ever seen the woman bleed. It was possible she didn't. His teleportation skills were also far from where

Ryan's were. He couldn't manage his magik as quickly, so getting shot at was not ideal.

The doors closed behind them, and they sat silently as they rode up. The electrical device's hum didn't help ease Killian's nerves. Each floor they passed, the elevator would ding, setting his heart a beat faster. He tensed when the doors swished open again, and there was more darkness. He wouldn't mind everything being black on a good night, but this was not a good night.

Killian whimpered and grabbed Ryan's bicep before he could disembark. He fidgeted from foot to foot as he shook his head. "Dude, this is how every horror story begins and ends. We should go."

"Not a chance." Ryan pulled out of Killian's grasp and walked off the elevator confidently.

Killian took a deep breath and followed. It was a cold, narrow hall with marbled floors like the lobby. There were paintings of Angel hanging on the frozen walls. Their footsteps were too loud in the small space.

About halfway down, sharp laughter made them freeze. Angel, wearing a closely fitted black dress, appeared in the middle of the walkway. "Now, boys, don't you know it's past bedtime?"

Ryan grabbed the twin swords on his hips. "We came for answers." He fumbled with the weapons before dropping one and snarling at himself.

You don't know how to fight. I don't know how to fight. This is stupid. They were going to die. Killian could feel it in his bones.

"Oh, sweet child, I'll answer any question you have. If you can beat me," she cooed.

"We can make that happen," Ryan said, charging.

Killian felt the change in energy too late. The floor shook before he could yell for Ryan to back off, and black spikes shot from the marble. Killian stumbled, managing to catch himself on the wall with a grunt.

Angel was a Descendant.

Killian studied the magik spikes and tried to focus on the energy surrounding them. They dripped black with malice, but he couldn't see anything past that. This was a magik he was unfamiliar with. It was deadlier somehow.

Angel tsked and shook her head. "I missed." She pouted her red lips before breaking into a devious smile. Her eyes were blue-gray, like the color of wet steel, and sparkled. Danced in the few lights that twinkled on the walls.

We are fu-

Ryan shouted in pain, and his blood splashed the floor, staining it red.

Killian gaped at a large gash across the back of his brother's right calf. *So much for speed.* He looked back at Angel. A million things were going through his head, but none were fully formed plans.

She was toying with them. Her lips moved silently, and Killian unwrapped the chain scythe from around his waist. The most he could do was cause a big enough distraction to get them out.

He threw the weapon and tugged on the chain to keep it straight. Killian used too much force, and the chain whipped to the right, slamming into the wall. The blades shredded the wallpaper, but it was nowhere near his target.

Angel held up her hand and threw a violet shell out. The bubble flowered around her, and Killian huffed. His shoulder sagged with defeat. *This isn't going well.*

Ryan moved, ignoring Killian, who was trying to beckon him back. His blades ignited in flames. Fire flew forward, covering the shell in red and orange light before disappearing.

She can absorb magik. "She's toying with us," Killian yelled. "We need to go."

"Not until I get our mother." Ryan dove in again, slashing at the bubble, striking with all his might. Each time his swords fell upon the shell, the hall echoed with clanging metal.

Killian exhaled slowly. One had to be logical at all times. This was his time to shine. He looked up and down the hall as Ryan sprinted the length of it. The shell absorbed the blast and threw him back to the elevator every time he attacked.

Killian wouldn't do the same thing; his weapon was useless if he couldn't use it. There had to be something else.

"Shields are connected to a Descendant's heart." Ryan's voice rang in his ears.

Her heart. Killian studied the shell and dropped the chain scythe. If he could find a weakness in the barrier, it might slow her down. He stepped into the shadows to his right.

The world moved slower around him. Killian walked toward Angel, keeping his eyes on her. He didn't know what she could do and wouldn't let her take him by surprise again.

Killian set his hands on the shell the moment he reached it. He sent his energy zinging across the surface to find a weak point.

Angel must have felt the twinge on her shield because her eyes fell in his direction. "No cheating." And she snapped her fingers, commanding a burst of electricity to shoot from the shield.

Killian was pulled out of the shadows, and he screamed in pain, pulling his hands back. Ryan grabbed the back of his shirt and jerked him away from the shell as a bolt of electricity struck where he had been standing.

Killian slid across the floor a couple of feet and rubbed his hands together. A deep ache set through his body, and he scrunched his nose in discomfort. That couldn't be good for his heart. "We can't beat her; we can't even touch her," he said.

Ryan glared at Angel. The boy had a one-track mind, so Killian knew what was coming before the words left his mouth, "I'm not giving up." He dropped his swords and pressed his hands together, exhaling. "I'm going to break it."

Killian watched Ryan set his hands against the bubble and close his eyes. The hall heated about a thousand degrees, and he pushed himself off the floor. He ran towards his brother, shouting at him to stop before he blew the place up.

Ryan's face contorted with rage. His back was rigid, and he put every ounce of energy into the spell. "You can die for all I care!"

The explosion happened within seconds and rocked the entirety of Yorklyn Towers, shattering Angel's defenses like glass.

She let out a gasp as acidic smoke filled the halls, and Killian ducked to avoid flying shrapnel from the torn floor. He coughed as the black smoke worked its way toward him, and he covered his mouth with his hand.

Through the smoggy, polluted air, he saw Angel fall and stare at Ryan as he held his sword to her throat. The world was going in and out of focus, and he coughed again, trying to call out.

"Tell me where my mother is," Ryan demanded.

Her eyes flicked to Killian when he dropped to get under the smoke. *It's the library all over again.*

"You can stay and learn or save him."

Ryan turned his head, and Killian looked up. He begged his brother to leave, but when Ryan turned back, his heart sank. If he survived, he was kicking Ryan's ass.

Killian squeezed his eyes shut when the smoke burned. In all honesty, he should have thrown a shield up when he knew Ryan was casting it. He caught sight of a statue in the hall, and army crawled towards it. If he could get above the smoke, it might increase his chances of survival. Going under didn't help, so he had one other option. He could make out more of the conversation as he got closer.

"I'm not leaving without answers."

He rolled his eyes, wishing Ryan could feel what he felt. His lungs were clogged, his eyes hurt like hell, and he had no clue how much longer he could handle it. He gave it a good minute, maybe two if he held his breath.

"He's always had it easier than you, hasn't he? He's had the best control over his magik while yours bursts to life. Isn't that what happened at the library? That's how you killed your friend's little boyfriend, isn't it?" Angel's sickly, sweet voice made his skin crawl.

She's kidding, right? He better not even believe that. Killian pushed himself to his knees and looked through the dense smog.

Ryan froze, staring down at Angel. He didn't refute or ignore what she said.

He coughed again and tasted copper. *Running out of time.* Ryan either needed to kill her or get them out.

Angel's voice was like silk, and she brushed her fingers along Ryan's arm. "Perhaps he should die. You'll have nothing holding you back. You can be the Descendant you want."

Killian groaned and opened his mouth to yell but couldn't make a sound. That just caused him to inhale more smoke, and he coughed until tears streamed down his cheeks.

"Come to me, weapons of night and darkness." A dagger appeared in his palm, and he fell on his stomach as the rest of the energy left his body.

"Let him die. Come with me, and we can rule the pathetic people in this world." Angel's voice was low.

He had one shot. Killian lifted his head and threw the dagger, willing Ryan to escape her trance.

The darkness took him before he could tell if the hit landed.

"Wake up! I'm sorry. Come on, Kill, open your eyes."

Killian's eyes flew open, and he threw his fist. The last thing he remembered was they were fighting with Angel. He hit Ryan in the jaw, making his brother yelp. Killian's knees gave out, and he hit the floor, groaning as he sucked in breaths of fresh air.

"You didn't have to hit me," Ryan muttered.

Killian glared, trying not to cough up a lung. "And you didn't have to use that spell."

Ryan shrugged. Apathy crossed his face, making Killian's blood boil. "Can you walk?" he asked.

This was not a moment they could sweep under the rug. There was something wrong, and Killian didn't want to ignore it.

"Ryan, seriously, what the Helwe?" he snapped.

"I should've listened. I'm sorry."

Killian shook his head. That wasn't a response. "Fine, don't talk. Get us home."

That was going to be another problem. Kara's parents were going to kill them. They stumbled back to the McKenzie house. When they arrived, their clothes returned to normal, and Killian could breathe better.

"Our mom's going to die," Ryan said in a monotonous tone. His hold was weak around Killian's waist, and he had been in a trance since they left the tower.

Killian shook his head, and they walked into the living room. He waited for the lecture, anything, but no one was waiting. He almost breathed a sigh of relief when Kara popped up.

Her lips were pulled into a straight, thin line, and her eyes narrowed to angry slits. "Where were you two?" she asked.

Killian jerked his thumb towards Ryan. "Bringing back a moron."

"We're fine, thanks," Ryan said with a low growl.

"You're bleeding. We need to clean and wrap it before my parents get home."

Killian walked into the guest room and closed the door. He let his back hit the wood as he slid to the floor, and his eyes burned with unshed tears. They failed. Angel was a Descendant with magik he had never seen, and they didn't get close to hurting her.

His head throbbed, and he let out a slight whine. Killian forced himself back to his feet and stumbled to the bed. Ryan could fight him all he wanted, but he didn't have the energy to care.

There was a mandatory school meeting for the dead in the morning. Finals were the next day. Soon, he would be outside these walls and free. That was the most he could hope for.

He's Coming

ANGEL

ANGEL LOOKED AT THE night sky from atop the wall with cold indifference. One twin got away. The night went differently than planned. She underestimated them. While the boys were fledgling Descendants, they were stronger than she gave them credit for. That was her bad. A mistake she wouldn't repeat in the morning when she finally brought them down.

"You know he will come." A cold voice brought her back to Earth.

She turned and faced Havoc with a blank look. He always found her. It didn't matter what she did or where she went. "Havoc," she said as politely as she could.

He smirked at her, a look that was all teeth and dark eyes. "I like what you've done with the city."

"When he faces me tomorrow, I have no choice but to use magik. What can you do to prevent the people from turning on me?" she asked.

"I could use a shield of sorts. Maybe it's more of an illusion," Havoc said with a hum.

"I infected one twin tonight. The other will fall tomorrow." It aggravated her how he didn't fear her.

His energy remained minute and tamed; it was nothing like hers. How he held himself made it hard to read his strengths or motivations. "You underestimated them. Don't let it happen again," he said, his voice cold and calculating.

Angel scowled. He was hot one minute, and the next, ice cold. She crossed her arms against her chest and glowered. Angel would never let a man control her again. "Who do you think you are?"

He snapped his fingers, and a suffocating weight crashed against her chest. It was like a large animal had run into her and pressed her against a wall. She gave a strangled cry and fell to her knees.

I've never felt such power.

"I'm the reason you're still alive, or have you forgotten?" Havoc asked. His voice lowered to a dangerous tone, and the weight lifted.

Angel pressed her palms into the top of the steel wall and gulped breaths.

"Don't mistake kindness for weakness. I can put you right back where I found you," Havoc said.

Angel nodded. "You're right, I was wrong."

He sneered but didn't say a word. For a quiet man, he had something dark crawling through him.

Angel wasn't sure he was remotely human. "I'm going to train to strengthen the hold on the one I got. Would you like to help?" she asked. *Keep your friends close but your enemies closer. Don't let him think I'm afraid.*

Havoc blinked in surprise. His eyes widened for a second, and he re-composed himself. "You want my help?"

Angel faked a smile and nodded. "After all, my power has nothing on yours." She lived to see the day she choked the life out of him.

Failure to Protect

RYAN SAT ON THE tub's edge and watched as she cleaned the laceration on the back of his calf. She looked up when he winced, and his fingers gripped where he sat.

"Did I hurt you?" she asked.

He shook his head. "Nah, I just feel dumb. I almost killed my brother."

Kara smiled gently and went back to dabbing the wound. It could've been worse, considering the circumstances. "How did you manage that?"

He shook his head and stayed silent.

She used a roll of gauze to wrap the injury and stood with a smirk at her handiwork. "Well, that will have to do. Get some sleep. We have to deal with the school thing tomorrow."

Ryan nodded, kicking his foot like he was testing it out. "Yeah, thanks."

"I'll ask my parents about your mom. They'll have ideas," she said.

"Thanks." Ryan was quiet. His voice was glum, and his eyes were glued to the floor.

She frowned and began putting the medical supplies away, trying to ignore the pounding headache threatening to surface. She didn't like seeing the people she cared about sad.

"Do you think you're a Descendant?" he asked when she moved to the washroom door.

Kara didn't know how to answer that. For the last 48 hours, she had been trying to maintain her composure. It didn't help the headache that finally broke through. "I don't know. Why ask?"

"Angel is a Descendant. I'm, like, fifty percent sure that's how she makes everyone love her. I want you to be careful," Ryan said.

"What does that have to do with how I think?" Kara asked.

Ryan leveled her with a serious stare. "She will kill you if she thinks you're magik. Don't give her any reason to think that," he said.

She smiled despite the way his lips pulled into a frown. "Thanks, but I'll be alright. I'm not the one using magik."

He shrugged and looked away as if she had slapped him.

Kara returned to her room, and her cheeks heated. Ryan was worried about her. Her heart thumped against her ribcage, and a small smile crossed her lips. Even if it was a horrible reason to worry, she couldn't help the jolt of surprise that lit up her stomach. It was almost a nice feeling.

Kara yawned in the early morning light as students gathered. Dawson rested his head on her arm with closed eyes. She rested her cheek against him and yawned again.

Ryan and Killian stood behind them. They were both tense.

"Are you alright?" she asked without looking back.

"We had a long night." Killian was the first to respond.

She didn't find it as surprising as she did that she could tell them apart without looking now.

Ryan yawned as if to prove his brother's point. "How about you?"

"I'm fine," she said.

Angel held her hand up after everyone stopped arriving. The crowd went quiet. Many dull-eyed teenagers stood close, hoping for the best.

"They attacked me in my home last night." The air went still. "They escaped but are believed to be in high school. I urge them to come forward, and I shall show mercy." Her eyes flicked toward Ryan and Killian

The boys exchanged glances, Kara bit her lip, and Dawson went rigid.

A few students clasped hands and bowed their heads in silent prayer. Kara didn't know who they were praying to, but she felt their prayers would go unanswered. She tried not to look at all the students that trembled around her.

Angel scanned the crowd of adults standing on the other side of the soldiers that surrounded the class of students. A black shroud rested around Angel's shoulders, almost like a shawl. Kara squinted, and the black mass vanished.

"If these two don't surrender, I will start killing their peers." Angel beckoned to her soldiers, and they tightened the wall around the student body.

Parents shouted in concern, but when anyone moved, the soldiers pointed a gun at them.

Kara watched colors shimmer and flicker through the air, but she couldn't capture them. Anytime she got close, they danced out of reach.

Surely, parents wouldn't watch their children being gunned down.

Angel's General, a man with an eyepatch and a buzz cut, stood beside his lady and looked out into the crowd with a cold eye. He never spoke to the people. Facing the one-eyed General was death.

A few girls began crying, and some of the older boys pushed younger teens behind them, hoping to protect them.

Death. Destruction. Chaos. A voice whispered through Kara's head, and she grabbed Dawson's hand. Their fingers entwined, and she squeezed. He had to stay with her. She wouldn't let him go.

"She can't do this," Dawson whispered.

"Say nothing. Stay calm." Her eyes darted to the uneasy group of parents, but she didn't see hers. That meant she had to protect Dawson. It all fell to her.

"We'll start with this one." Angel grabbed a young girl's arm and pulled her up the steps. "She will die in thirty seconds unless I get what I want."

Dawson broke out of Kara's hold and pointed at Angel. "You can't do this."

Kara grabbed his arm. "Stop."

"No. You can't kill innocent people. You're a monster."

Angel scoffed and flicked her wrist like she was bored. "Shoot him," she said.

Kara lurched forward. "No, wait!"

The General pulled his weapon and fired.

All Kara could do was watch in horror as Dawson fell. The world went silent. Everything faded, and all she could see was him.

Dawson clutched his side and curled into a ball, gasping for breath. Pain flashed across his face, and a couple tears slipped down his cheeks.

Kara dropped next to him and took his hands. *This isn't happening.*

Dawson looked at her, his eyes dancing across her face like he was trying to memorize her.

Kara brushed his hair away from his face, and he stared wide-eyed. Tears flowed down her cheeks, but she couldn't remember when she started crying.

He attempted to comfort her with a strained smile, but a few seconds later, it was replaced with a pinched frown.

Kara pressed her hands to the bullet wound and shushed him when he tried to talk. A storm raged in her head, something dark and dangerous. Her hands tingled with an energy she couldn't explain, and when she tried to shake it off, it returned tenfold.

Ryan knelt and took her hands off the wound. "Let me see," he whispered. "Hang on. It's gonna be okay."

Kara put her hands to her cheeks and trembled as she sobbed. Another gunshot tore through the street. *This isn't supposed to happen.* She couldn't breathe. Her heart was pounding painfully against her ribs, and Kara gasped to keep from throwing up.

Killian wrapped an arm around her shoulders as if to shield her.

Dawson coughed, and blood coated his lips. His eyes closed.

"That's not good," Killian whispered.

She pushed him away, and her chest constricted. She tried to take a breath, and her lungs burned with the effort. Her world felt small as she watched the bright light dim around her brother.

"No, I won't let him die!" She screamed. Her voice returned in full force, and she threw herself over her brother, sobbing uncontrollably. "You don't get to die!"

"Fifteen seconds before I kill another one," Angel's voice carried. "Where are you?"

"Don't panic, he's already terrified," Ryan said. He grabbed Dawson's hand and squeezed.

The boy opened his eyes again and blinked at Kara. He trembled, but she couldn't be sure if it was from fear or pain.

She rocked back and forth and tried to stop her tears. She pressed her lips to his forehead and squeezed his other hand. "Don't leave me," she begged. "Please, stay."

Dawson pulled out of her grip and touched her cheek. "You'll win."

Dawson didn't take his eyes off Kara but squeezed Ryan's hand as much as possible.

"I'm sorry." Ryan's voice cracked. "I-this is my fault."

Dawson smiled. Even as he began to leave their world, he smiled and spoke, "Make it up to me by protecting her."

Kara swallowed her sobs. They were going to let him die. Couldn't magik do something? She had so much to tell him. They had much to experience.

His grip loosened, but his eyes didn't leave hers. She could see him fading. "I love you so much," she said before he was gone. "I wanted to be like you. It was always us, you and me. You were supposed to stay with me, don't you remember?"

His body stopped shaking, and his grip loosened. She felt his fingers fall from her cheek, but she tightened hers. "Wherever you go, whatever world you end up in, always fight for the weak. That's what you do best."

Another gun fired, and soldiers had to push students back to keep them from running away. A few of the parents were gunned down when they attempted to fight back. The world filled with screaming of those who lost more.

Kara smiled at Dawson as he gasped one last time, and his eyes went dull. She pressed her cheek to his chest and sobbed like she never had before.

The bubble she placed herself in all those years ago burst. Shattered like a glass cup on a hardwood floor. Adults and kids cried for each other, and those who passed had blank faces. Kara didn't look around. She didn't want to see the victims of those Angel claimed. Not anymore.

Kara stood. Her body was numb, and she turned to face Angel's General. The man's eye fell upon her as she stared daggers at him, wishing he would drop dead. Violet and red swarmed through her vision as Ryan and Killian watched her.

Kara pointed and let the tears stream freely. "You won't get away with this." An enormous swell of energy warmed her being. It pulsed through her body, welling from deep within. Kara would dare say it came from her very essence, but she didn't know enough about it. All she knew was she wanted the man to suffer, to bring blazing ruin down on him and his master.

It happened fast. One minute, Kara stood there, pointing, and the next, a blast of energy reared from her body and shot at the one-eyed man. The pulsing energy left her body in a burst of purple lightning.

Streetlamps shattered at the sporadic surge of energy, and people fell to the floor, screaming in agony. Soldiers dropped their weapons, convulsing as some unknown force tore through their insides, ripping them to shreds. Angel lunged to the side to avoid the blast of lightning as everyone else fell around her.

Ryan threw his hands up as the energy tore past him and Killian, seeking blood. His shield nearly disintegrated at the last blast that materialized. A golden light encompassed her body and flowered until the veil shrouded her.

"She's a magik, get her!" Angel shouted, throwing her hands in the air. Her eyes were wide with horror and anger, but something else flickered through her.

Kara didn't care about her yet. That wasn't her objective. She wanted the man who shot her brother dead.

The man held up his weapon and aimed, but Ryan was faster.

Kara stood over her brother's body as the light tore through innocents, soldiers, and buildings. People dropped, screaming in pain, and she felt it. The light burned away everything inside them, turning them to ash.

Before it could reach Angel, the world went silent once more. This time, the wind wrapped around them, pinning everyone to the middle of a giant storm.

Kara shielded her eyes as rock and debris flew. She looked up and watched a figure descend.

Declarations of War

KARA SHATTERED THE BARRIER, and Ryan collapsed.

Killian shielded his eyes from the bright light and cursed under his breath.

She was a Descendant.

When Angel commanded her men to shoot the girl, Ryan jumped up and slammed his fists into one of the soldier's faces.

Killian bit the side of his hand until he tasted blood. It was going to be a fight, and they were vastly outnumbered. He didn't have the advantage of being picky with his morals.

You want death and destruction. I grant you the freedom you seek.

"Alas, the price will finally be paid."

Killian couldn't be what Ryan wanted. He was nothing more than an expendable tool, but he did have the advantage of not caring about anything else. "Come to me, weapons of the night: summon dagger."

A slew of weapons surrounded him, as red as the blood he exchanged for them. The wound on his hand vanished, and Killian ducked as a stray light beam flew towards him.

Kara was a Descendant, and she was out of control. It was a magik he didn't know how to fight, but one he could avoid easily. So long as he wasn't hit, he could use this out-of-control energy to his advantage.

He threw two daggers and felled the men who had moved to attack his brother. Killian moved on instinct, for once not fearing what his other side would do. He melted into the shadows at his feet when soldiers broke rank to shoot him down. The surviving kids took that moment to flee with their parents.

He resurfaced next to his brother and grabbed two more daggers. They found their marks in the necks of two men who thought to flank them.

Ryan didn't say a word this time as Killian felled their enemies. They fought as one unit, feeding off the other's energy. Killian ducked when Ryan clicked his tongue, and a wave of fire flew over his head and engulfed men behind him.

Killian looked through them and sought the woman responsible for such Helwe.

She was at the school's doors; her eyes didn't leave Ryan's back. No one knew she was a Descendant, so she wouldn't use her magik. Her General stood by her side with his gun poised, ready to defend his ruler.

He stabbed his palm with a dagger and winced as blood gushed from the wound. So long as he bled, he had weapons. He moved forward without a second of hesitation. Killian dove through the soldiers, who looked to end his life, and ignored them.

Ryan had his back; he knew his brother would watch.

When Killian got close, the General raised his weapon and fired three shots. Killian stepped into the shadow of the school building and vanished. The bullets flew past.

The General pulled a stick from his pocket and slammed it against the ground. A bright light filled the air, distorting the shadows, and Killian shielded his eyes.

Ryan pushed him to the ground a second later as Angel's bodyguard took aim. "We can't fight them, not all of them," he said.

"We don't need to fight them; we need to kill Angel," Killian said. It made perfect sense. All they had to do was kill one person.

Ryan jerked him back as more soldiers fired. "They'll kill you. Are you crazy?"

The gunshots stopped, and Killian felt his energy dwindle. Before either could move, the wind whipped around them, walling them off from the world.

Everyone stopped and looked up. The man who attacked them in their apartment descended in a flourish of tree leaves and flower petals. *Well, someone's dramatic.*

As soon as his feet touched the ground, Angel scowled. She stepped past her bodyguard and stared the man down. "Nice of you to join us, Justin," she growled.

So, the man had a name, and Angel didn't like him. That was good enough for Killian. He looked back to where his brother stood but found Ryan gone. His eyes flicked around, and he found Ryan by Kara.

Her energy flew in dangerous sparks around her. Pain flashed across Ryan's face when they hit him, but he still reached for her, trying to calm her anger.

Justin didn't turn, but he snapped his fingers and sighed. "That's enough of that for now, little mouse. I told you before you were going to hurt yourself."

Kara went limp, and Ryan caught her before she fell.

Killian would fight Angel with Justin if he was going to protect her. He took his spot beside the man.

The man didn't look at him when he spoke. "Are you controlled enough to fight?" he asked.

Killian smirked and held up his daggers. "I'm a Descendant of Shadow. You don't want me to control myself."

"Fair enough. Try to keep up." Justin flicked his wrist and moved everyone aside.

The students, parents, and soldiers were all pushed to the edge of the arena he created.

Angel walked toward them, her hips swaying as she snarled. Her General was at her side.

"I told you I made them an offer they couldn't refuse," Justin said.

Angel cackled and crossed her arms against her chest. "Using me to lure them out, aren't you smart?" She didn't sound impressed.

Justin chuckled. "I did nothing of the sort. This isn't our first meeting," he said.

Killian held up his weapons. "Enough talk, you're going to pay." He tried to charge, but his legs refused to move.

Justin ruffled his hair like he was a child. "Play backup. Let me show you how to use your magik properly." He stepped forward and snapped his fingers.

A silver bow appeared in his hands.

Killian frowned and tried to move his leg again but was glued. *What's this guy playing at?* Before, when they fought, he and Ryan didn't stand a chance. That menacing energy wasn't there now.

"You're blind. How do you expect to shoot a bow?" Angel deadpanned.

Killian did a double-take. He didn't get a good enough look at the man before, but sure enough, he was. A horrid, jagged scar ran horizontally across milky white eyes.

Apparently, Justin didn't only surprise him.

"Why can't we move? We should be moving," his shadow roared.

There's a spell or something. I dunno.

"Fix it. We should be spilling blood."

Killian scoffed. Even if he wanted to break the spell, there's no way he would be able to. That man's power exceeded his if the tornado around them spoke to any of his capabilities.

The moment Justin moved, the fight was on. He sped at Angel, and she stepped back, hesitant.

He pulled back on the bowstring, and the wind swirled around him, forming an arrow.

Killian's eyes widened. Wind wasn't a physical object, but what Justin held between his fingers was solid.

He let it fly, and Angel jumped about ten feet into the air. The arrow whizzed under her, and she whispered a spell into her palms. A ball of fire appeared, and she threw it at the man.

Before Killian could open his mouth, Justin looked up and blew as if he were blowing a bubble. The fire went out, and nothing but ash fell upon his shoulders.

"You shouldn't be able to fight," Angel said, landing as nimbly as a cat. "How are you?" she asked.

Justin smirked and put a finger to his lips. "Magicians never tell." He formed another arrow and fired at her chest.

She summoned her own weapon, a spear made of ice, and smacked the projectile off course. Before she could gloat, Justin sent three more.

He was fast. Killian almost couldn't keep up with how quickly he formed his arrows. The man moved on instinct like he was a predator stalking its prey.

Angel dodged the first two, but the third cut across the left side of her neck, drawing a thin line of blood.

Her General stepped in front of her and fired six rounds at Justin. The bullets froze in midair.

Angel roared and shoved her bodyguard aside, brandishing her spear.

Killian attempted to move again, but he remained immobile. What was the point in backup if he couldn't move?

Angel struck out, but Justin stepped to the side, knocking the weapon away. Angel stumbled, and Justin touched her shoulder. At least, that's what Killian thought he did until Angel went flying. The man sent her a good fifteen feet up with a simple brush of his hand.

Her body twisted in the air, and she landed on her feet on the side of the school. Her hair fell in her face, covering red cheeks and a stormy gaze.

Her eyes flicked across the battleground before landing on Ryan and Kara. A bitter smile slipped across her lips, and Killian turned. Before he could say anything, Angel closed her eyes and breathed. It only took two seconds, but a black snake shot from her palm and landed beside his brother.

"Ryan, watch out," Killian shouted.

The snake hissed and snapped at Ryan, its teeth sinking into his arm as he shifted Kara out of harm's way.

Ryan cried in shock and whipped his arm up, sending the snake flying.

Justin frowned and turned his head toward the sound.

Killian surged forward when he saw Angel push off the building and fly towards the man. He slid before Justin and held his daggers up in an x, as he had seen Ryan do with his weapons.

The spear slid across the top of the x, and he dug his heels into the ground and shoved back with all his might. It stopped the weapon's advance, and Killian huffed in barely concealed relief.

Justin grabbed the back of his shirt and threw him at Ryan and Kara, where he landed in a heap next to them. "Cheap trick, Rebecca. I'll be sure to return the favor next time."

Killian squeezed his eyes shut when the world spun into a blended gray and silver mess. *What now?*

A Temporary Setback

ANGEL

ANGEL THREW A VASE against the wall in her room. She couldn't believe there was another Descendant right under her nose. She screamed in frustration at the loss. Not only did Justin get the twins, but he got the girl, too.

It was unlike him to run from a fight. She had a hard time believing it had happened. They left her with a curse that could take months to pay off and the glory of waiting.

He was blind; a blind man bested her. How he moved and used his magik was unlike the man she was used to fighting. It made her blood boil. Not a single Descendant in history suffered a disability like him. Yet, he was better than all of them.

"I swear, when I get my hands on that little brat, she's going to be dead. I can't believe how much Arthur and Samantha got by me," Angel screamed again and threw another vase.

The sound of shattering glass didn't make her feel as good as she hoped. When she got her hands on those bastards, she would make them pay for everything.

First, she needed to get her hands on Ryan, and then she could focus on the others. If the twins were with that girl, she would come for all three simultaneously.

The McKenzie child hadn't seen the last of her, and Angel would be sure to pay her back for making her look like a fool. This gave her time to hone her skills and strengthen her abilities.

Havoc would work with her, and they would become an unstoppable force. And when Angel was finally done with her mission, she would eliminate Havoc. He was a temporary obstacle, though a useful one.

Angel smoothed out her hair and took a deep breath. She had to see the positive side of things. She opened her bedroom door and stepped out to speak with her General. "Clean up the bodies, set up a meeting to apologize, and I'll make sure everyone knows who did this. When I'm done, no one will question my dedication."

Her hands fisted at her sides and trembled.

"Done," her General said.

"I knew I liked you." She headed for her office. There were going to be a lot of consequences for killing kids in front of their parents. Angel brought months of work upon herself if she wanted to retain her power.

First, she needed to calm herself and do damage control. Once everything was normal, she could continue her plan to capture the Descendants.

I will get what I want, boy. I always do.

Haven

KARA'S EYES FLICKERED OPEN, and she blinked at something blue. Puffy white things slid across her vision, taking up a little space in the vast expanse of the sky. *It looks so natural.* Maybe she died.

Her last hour was a blur of emotion and pain. Kara winced as she pushed herself up onto her elbows. Her body ached, and she whimpered a little, touching her temple. She must've been hit by a tank.

"Breathe, little mouse. All is well," a voice whispered beside her.

Kara jumped, and everything rushed back. Angel's meeting, Dawson dying, the screams of those she hurt with that weird energy she didn't want to think about. Her eyes darted around, and she stopped breathing.

Trees taller than her dad waved in the wind, bearing orange and red leaves. Grass, dirt, and vibrant flowers left their sweet, honey-like scent around her. Massive rock formations behind the forest were clad in white like wedding dresses.

Behind her was a tall, crooked house with windows and balconies. It looked more like a hazard than a home. Some sections were oddly shaped and bent in ways that should send it crashing to the ground. It looked about two or three stories tall and was mostly made of brick and log.

There was a white wraparound porch and, to the left of it, a flourishing garden with vegetables. On the other side was a grove of fruit trees bearing many juicy fruits she had never seen before.

Kara forced herself to stand and gaped. She wasn't in Yorklyn anymore.

"Welcome to the rest of the world," the man whispered.

Kara stared at him, almost afraid to take her eyes off the scenery. "You're that man," she said, her voice hushed. "The one in the apartment."

"I'm Justin. I brought you here," he said. "You've been out for quite a while. I was beginning to worry." He patted the ground next to him. "I've been told you're the daughter of Arthur and Samantha McKenzie."

She nodded, and her eyes snapped to the ground. *Dawson, where is he? I can't leave him.* Her heart thudded against her ribcage, and she whirled around, searching for him. "My brother." Her voice shook so badly she almost couldn't talk.

Justin gestured to the wooded area at the edge of a field of flowers. "Buried, put to rest, at peace. I can take you there," he said. "My brother extracted his body during the fight."

They buried him. She didn't get to say goodbye, and they buried him. Tears filled her eyes, and she hid her face in her hands. It couldn't be real. *This has to be fake.*

"Kara." Ryan stepped out of the house upon hearing her voice.

She looked up from her palms, and her lip quivered. "They buried him," she whispered.

Ryan nodded. "He wasn't alone." He held out his arms and walked toward her.

Kara craved an interaction that didn't make her hurt. She wanted the comfort of someone telling her it would be fine while rubbing her head like her mom used to. *Where even would Mom and Dad be? I didn't see them at the school.*

Ryan wrapped his arms around her and rested his cheek on her head. "It's okay," he whispered. "You're safe here."

Kara sobbed into his chest and clung to his shirt when the door opened again. She peeked up, and the tears stopped. Emotion clogged her throat, and Kara stepped away from Ryan, pointing.

He had chestnut brown hair, but it was longer than she remembered. His skin was golden and matched the dark spots in his hair. His eyes were turned down, and his full lips pulled into a frown.

"Wait a minute," she said, taking a step back.

Tory met her gaze, his eyes pleading. It was a wonder she could still read his expressions. "Hey, sweetie," he whispered. His voice was deeper than she remembered.

"You died. You're dead. Can I see ghosts now?" she asked.

"No, you can't see ghosts," Ryan said. "He's not dead."

Kara shook her head and brushed the tears from her cheeks. Her parents were gone, Dawson was dead, and Tory was standing before her. Something was happening in her life, and she didn't understand what.

Justin walked up behind her and set his hands on her shoulders. "There's a lot to take in, but I think now is a good time to-"

Her stomach flipped over itself, and Kara gagged. It was possible she could throw up.

Ryan and Tory backed off, and Kara straightened. She ducked under Justin's hands and tore into the forest without a look back. Kara wanted to be alone. Her mind was so busy and chaotic. There was so much she couldn't think through. Tory shouted behind her, but Kara ignored his cries, no matter how desperate they became.

The forest welcomed her with open arms. Trees blocked the burning sun and swayed in the wind she could feel but couldn't see. Wind. There was never any wind in the city. It was crisp and tasted like she imagined the forest would. Earthy, fresh.

Branches and brambles tugged at her jeans and shirt scratched at her arms, but Kara didn't mind. She ignored the burning in her legs and lungs until she couldn't.

It was dim by the time she stopped running. Sweat and tears coated her face and skin as she dropped to her knees. The smell of moss and dirt was heavy as she took deep, gasping breaths to calm her jumping heart. She gripped her chest and sobbed, letting her screams fill the surrounding quiet.

"You ain't alone," a voice startled her out of her thoughts.

Kara looked up at a young man wearing a black jacket, eyes so dark they looked black. His hair on the sides was shaved, and the tuft on top fell into that coal-colored gaze.

He squatted in front of her and locked eyes with her. Like Ryan's, his skin was tanned by the sun but darker. He cocked his head to the side and flashed a crooked smile. "I hear it inside you. The broken pieces rattlin' around like they can't be fixed." He poked over her heart. "Scream if it makes it hurt less. You ain't alone." His voice was gentle. It was the accent that drew her, though. He didn't scare her or make her want to run. His voice was deep, gravelly. Some words sounded too heavy on his tongue, and others were light and rolled right off.

"Who're you?" she asked.

"A friend," he said. "Your energy is thrummin'. I heard it all the way in the homestead."

Homestead. Kara frowned. She didn't know what that was. She noticed how he dropped certain letters or combined some words when he spoke. It was almost like he didn't know the language, but that couldn't be because Ryan knew her language. So did Killian.

The boy stood and looked through the trees, blinking with his too-dark eyes. He had a bow across his back and a leather guard on his forearm.

He's a hunter.

"You scared my kill," he said, primarily to himself. "Where'd you come from?"

Kara looked back at the way she had come. She wasn't sure. She wasn't sure she would know how even if she tried to return. "I don't know."

"Where ya headed?"

She shrugged again and pulled her knees to her chest. "I dunno."

The boy smirked again and sat next to her. His fingers tapped against his cloth pants in a slow rhythm. If she focused, she could almost hear a tune.

"What happened that's makin' you feel so alone?" he asked.

She didn't want to answer. Kara wondered how often they could go back and forth before one of them caved. "You have an unfamiliar accent. Is it because of the outside?" she asked.

His thick brows went up, almost disappearing under his hair. "Outside. You mean in the forest?" he asked.

Did the people outside the walls call it 'The Wilds,' like the citizens in Yorklyn? She didn't want to give too much away. It was possible the people outside wouldn't like her.

As if reading her mind, he nodded. "You're from the city with those walls," he said. He didn't sound cold or malicious, and his energy didn't flicker in any way that told her she was in danger.

Kara trusted her instincts and nodded back. "Who're you?" she asked again.

A soft shade surrounded him, something like what was always around Killian. A ribbon that she couldn't quite glimpse.

"Name's Avery," he said.

She stared at tiny bugs crossing a leaf. "Kara."

"Nice to meet ya."

She nodded and watched the itty-bitty animals trying to get from one end of their world to the next. She wondered how they would respond if she turned their entire world upside down, like moving that leaf to another part of the forest and seeing how they coped.

"What broke?" he asked.

Kara scoffed. Usually, this situation would have been so exciting. To see the sky and taste the air. It should've exhilarated her, so why couldn't she smile?

"Maybe I'm just broken. Maybe I always have been," she said.

He chuckled and ran a hand through his hair. "You remind me of someone I knew a long time ago. He didn't like sharing either."

"Should I share? I don't even know you."

He cut her a stare and bowed his head. "You found me."

She snarled at him, baring her teeth. Every instinct told her to punch him in his squinty, cheerful face. "I came here to be alone. You dropped in unannounced."

Avery chuckled again, not at all put off by her sudden rage. He flicked a strand of hair away from her face, and his knuckle brushed her cheek.

Electricity ran down her spine, and she pulled away, trying not to look alarmed. Was that her magik or his?

"I told my mom I didn't need her," she whispered. Kara wasn't sure what made her open her mouth, but some of the pressure came off her chest when she did.

Avery's eyes softened, and he let his hand fall.

Pain raged through her, and she shoved him, not sure what to do with all that anger. She wanted to break things, to see how many pieces she could make of the mess that was her life.

The tears started again, and Kara pressed her palms into the ground to keep herself from hitting Avery again. "I told her I didn't need her. I never apologized. Now she's gone. They all are, and I never told her I was sorry."

Avery smiled weakly. He captured her wrists and pulled her hands into his. His skin was warm and rough. "She knew. Moms always do."

"My mom might be dead. She might be gone, and I have to live with this guilt! How am I supposed to act like everything is alright?"

Avery tugged her forward and wrapped his arms around her. He squeezed so tight she felt the breath rush from her lungs. "You don't. It's not alright, and it won't be."

Kara buried her face in his chest and screamed again. A surge of energy tore across the forest. Her mom, her dad, her brother. Angel took everything. Kara didn't want to feel this pain.

Avery rocked back and forth, shushing her gently. His voice soothed those pains like a salve for a burn, and slowly, Kara's energy faded.

When her insides stopped threatening to burst out of her, she pulled away, feeling stupid. "I'm sorry," she whispered.

Twigs snapped in the distance, and Avery tensed. Her eyes flicked up, and he jumped, slapping a hand over her mouth.

Kara's eyes widened as she followed his stare and saw a pale white wolf. It had electric blue eyes. It sniffed the air, whiskers twitching as it stared.

Avery reached for his bow, but she grabbed his wrist. He stared. "It'd kill you without hesitation," he said.

Kara's eyes filled with tears. "No, it won't. Let it be," she said. She couldn't watch another creature die.

He nodded but didn't take his eyes off the animal.

The wolf let out a low melancholic howl. Kara sniffled and watched it. Its beauty broke her heart in a way she couldn't describe.

It padded forward, ignoring Avery, and pressed a cold nose to the back of her hand. Warmth surged through her, and she blinked, wondering what it was trying to tell her.

"I ain't ever seen one do that," Avery whispered. His hand was still half up as if he wanted to grab an arrow and slay it.

Kara ran her fingers through the silky fur on the animal's chest, and her throat constricted. "I see you," she said, speaking only to the animal.

It growled in response and gave its tail a playful wag before bounding into the forest. Kara stared at the spot.

"I ain't seen one of them out here in years. Wonder what brought it back," Avery said.

She smiled a little. *It was here for me.* "I want to keep running, to forget my problems. How far do you think I could go?" she asked.

Avery clicked his tongue and held a hand down to her. "Get up and find out."

Ryan's voice broke through the trees, and she sighed. Even if she ran, she would have someone much faster on her trail.

Avery offered one last smile. "Pain is just a reminder you're alive."

Before she could respond, he was gone. Kara looked at the space he previously occupied and wiped her eyes when Ryan stepped into the dense meadow. Some of her didn't know if Avery was real, but his presence was appreciated.

Ryan's chest heaved as he stared down at her, his brow furrowed with concern. "It's not safe to be out alone," he said.

Kara nodded and pushed herself to her feet. She didn't want to argue. Her body hurt, her head hurt, but her chest felt lighter. "I'm sorry."

He wrapped his arms around her and gave her a squeeze. "We'll figure it out. It's going to be alright," he said.

It didn't feel like it.

New Enemies

Ryan clenched his fists when Kara disappeared. The day's events hit him, and he took a few deep breaths to steady his nerves. He couldn't believe all of this was happening. If he left Angel alone, Kara wouldn't be suffering.

When Tory tried to run after her, Ryan grabbed his bicep and shot him a dark glare. "She wants to be alone. Give her time."

Tory threw a punch without hesitation. "Get off!" he shouted. "This is your fault."

Ryan rubbed the bruise welting along his jaw, and his eyes flashed angrily. He stepped forward, but Killian set a hand on his shoulder.

"Don't you dare stop me," Ryan growled.

"I'll stop you if it's stupid."

"No, you won't. I'm going to kill him this time," Ryan snarled, lunging forward.

A long-haired man wearing shorts and a tank top began to hurry toward them. His name was Nicholas, and Ryan got to speak with him a little when Kara was unconscious. He was Justin's younger brother and the person Arthur wanted the twins to take his kids to.

Ryan curled his fingers into Tory's shirt as he readied to pummel him.

Killian grabbed the back of his shirt and ripped him away.

"I told you not to stop me," Ryan said. He leveled his brother with a burning glare.

Killian growled in reply and held him tight as Nicholas grabbed Tory's arm and pulled him away.

Ryan had a lot of pent-up aggression, and who better to take it out on than some coward?

"You don't need to fight. Come on, what did we talk about? Don't be stupid." Nicholas kept an arm around Tory's chest to keep him from jumping. "I take it you two know each other."

"Is he your boyfriend?" Ryan asked, his question directed at Tory.

Tory's eyes narrowed, and he tried to duck under Nicholas's arm. "What's it matter to you?"

"Because I need to know who to apologize to when I kill you."

Nicholas laughed nervously and looked towards the forest where Kara disappeared. "Alright, we have a lot going on. This would be the perfect time to talk about our feelings. Who wants to go first?"

Ryan slipped out of Killian's grasp with a well-timed elbow to the stomach. Nicholas didn't even know what hit him when the blonde shoved him aside and punched Tory in the nose.

"Okay," Nicholas muttered.

Ryan scoffed and backed up when Tory grabbed the front of his shirt. His eyes were fierce and cold. This is the man who left the McKenzie's. The one who made them suffer and cry.

"You have no idea what you did to that family," Ryan snapped.

Tory laughed and clenched his fist tighter into the fabric. So, that's where Kara got that from. He supposed someone had to teach it to her.

"Don't act like you know me because you two became friends," Tory snapped. "They raised me; I know what it did."

"And you still did it!" Ryan knocked Tory's arms away.

Killian tried to reel him back in. He grabbed Ryan's ear and pulled to keep him from lunging. "This has to stop. We're not here to fight."

"I'm gonna kill him!" Ryan roared.

"Why? Because he made some people cry or because he stabbed me? Ryan, it doesn't matter what happened. If you kill him now, how will Kara feel? Hasn't she been through enough?"

Tory's eyes widened when Killian spoke.

Ryan deflated and let his hands drop to his sides. He didn't want to hurt her. How quickly Killian picked up on Ryan's devotion to Kara was aggravating. When his energy calmed, Killian let his ear go and wiped his hands on his pants.

"You left her first," Tory whispered, "or did you forget all that time in school?"

Ryan scowled. He knew what he did when they were kids, but that's all. Kids being kids.

Tory nodded. "I thought I was protecting her, Ryan, but if you hadn't been there, Kara would be dead too, so thank you." He stuck out his hand.

Ryan blew out the rest of his anger and shook Tory's hand. Just because they were fire and water didn't mean they had to act like dicks. "Truce. If you apologize to my brother for almost killing him."

Tory looked at Killian and nodded. "I regret what I did. I never intended all that when Dawson told me I was upset."

Ryan crossed his arms against his chest and looked around the large yard.

The grass was immaculate. There was a garden along the side of the home and a large pond towards the back of the land.

"How do you guys keep everything so green?" he asked. "The fall and summer are when all this shit dies."

Tory rubbed the back of his neck. He must have felt just as awkward trying to make small talk. "Nicholas is a Descendant of Earth."

Ah, that made sense. Ryan forgot about that.

Killian elbowed him in the side and pointed to Nick. "Didn't Arthur tell us to find him?"

"Yea. Guess they found us first." His brother was oblivious sometimes. Ryan didn't know what Killian would do on his own.

"Why would Samantha and Arthur tell you to look for me? What happened?" Nicholas asked.

Ryan shrugged. He only got a little information from that family. Only if it benefitted them. "Arthur told us to come here and deposit the kids with you."

Nicholas tapped his chin. "After all this time, I thought they'd forgotten about me."

"How did you know them?" Tory asked.

Nicholas shot a charming smile and put a finger to his lips. "That's a story for another time, isn't it? Hey Jay..." he trailed off when he turned and noticed his brother missing.

Ryan's calf burned, and he took the weight off that side with a wince. He probably reopened the wound by attacking Tory. He had to remember to clean it later.

Killian set a hand on his shoulder, and Ryan resisted the urge to shrug him off.

"Are they dead too?" Tory whispered. "Arthur and Sam?"

Ryan stared at the ground. "We don't know."

"I'm sure they're fine," Tory muttered.

Hopefully. His thoughts turned to his mom, and he brushed his hand across his eyes. Their mom would be dead any minute now.

"I guess we should wait for everyone to get back. Do you guys wanna come in?" Tory asked.

Ryan didn't want to miss when Kara came back. Too much going on could make her decide to run for good. He shook his head. "Nah, I think I'm gonna enjoy the wind and the grass." He plopped onto the ground and laid back. He tilted his face towards the sun and inhaled. *Outside.* Gods, he missed the place.

When Tory and the others went inside, he turned his head to stare at the trees. Kara was out there, alone and unprotected. As much as he wanted to give her space, he didn't want her getting eaten by something worse.

Ryan waited until the shadows stretched across the ground before going after her. As he entered the woods, he took a deep breath. Pine, moss and the scent of sap filled his nostrils. It was the most refreshing thing he smelt in a long time.

The woods whispered sweet nothings as he crushed leaves under his feet. The sound of the trees, wind, and critters was a symphony he missed from long ago. He brushed his fingers against the rough bark of an old maple and closed his eyes. It hummed under his touch, and he couldn't stop the grin. *Home.*

He could almost see images of kids playing if he concentrated hard enough. Running and hiding, climbing as fast as their little legs would allow. Long, distant screams of joy and delight reminded him of a lost world.

He wanted to show her this world. How beautiful it could be if she looked past the danger. Ryan dropped his hand and ran into the forest, listening for Kara and any sound she might make telling him where to go.

When he found her, she was sitting alone in a dark enclosure, blanketed by vines and the long branches of some willows. Her dark hair covered her soft face, and she peeked at him with those dazzling blue eyes now rimmed red and slightly swollen.

She stood and smiled. Her rounded face was darkened by the things she witnessed. By the people she hurt and the lives that were taken.

He couldn't recall when he started seeing her like that. Like the woman she was becoming instead of the petulant child, he had always known.

"I'm sorry," she said. Her voice cracked and was hoarse from the crying.

He shook his head and hugged her, managing what little comfort he could. If the roles were reversed, if he just put Killian in a hole, he wouldn't even be standing. He didn't know how she looked so strongly in the face of death and despair. He ran his hands up and down her back and squeezed his eyes shut.

"Pain is just a reminder you're alive," she said.

His eyes snapped open, and he held her at arm's length, studying her.

Her eyes widened in surprise at his reaction.

He heard those words a long time ago. Had said them to himself over the years, trying to dull the pain of his mom, of the city, of Angel. He never thought he would hear someone else say them.

"What?" he asked.

"Someone told me that a few moments ago. I think it kinda helped," she said.

Ryan scanned the trees and blinked, allowing his vision to change. He rarely searched for energy, but now was a good time to start.

Trying to use magik sent pain across the back of his leg, and the lines of energy vanished. He winced and pressed his weight onto his good side, rolling his ankle. Whatever Angel did to him, it wasn't healing.

"Are you alright?" Kara asked.

Ryan looked down at her and managed a curt nod. "Let's go back for now," he whispered. "It's not always safe."

She grabbed his hand before he could walk away. Her eyes met his, and the hardness he found surprised him. "I want to see my brother first."

"But Tory is-"

She slapped her hand over his mouth, cutting him off. "I don't want to hear his name. Not right now. Take me to my brother." She was commanding and authoritative.

Ryan found he didn't have any option but to agree.

His mom's warning whispered in his ear from long ago. *"When a Descendant first comes to power, their first emotions will set their path. You always have to be right. Do you understand me?"*

What would her path be if he let Kara continue as she was?

Ryan took her to a meadow on the other side of the woods.

She didn't say a word as they crossed over logs, passed intricate spider webs, and saw a few squirrels and chipmunks run by. Her eyes were set straight ahead.

They got to the small clearing, and Kara stared at the stone they had erected for Dawson. A shiny black rock that Ryan streaked blue paint along. He wanted the site to represent Dawson. There was a backpack next to the rock. The only thing the boy had on him in passing.

Kara walked over to it and clasped her hands to her chest, staring at the overturned earth. Her lip trembled, but she bit it to stop herself from crying.

Ryan didn't know whether he should turn away. What would he want if he were the one in mourning?

Kara knelt and pressed her palm to the earth, whispering to herself.

Ryan decided he didn't want to be a part of it. He didn't want to watch her break like this, not when he was the reason.

"He didn't blame you," Kara said, not turning to face him.

Ryan shot her a petrified stare. Fear and worry flooded his veins, and he wanted to run. That's what he always did, wasn't it? For once, it was time to face the consequences.

"He was never one to hold a grudge. He admired you in many ways," she whispered before her voice broke.

Ryan clenched his thighs and squeezed. They should blame him. Every single one of them. He opened his mouth to ask but shut it again. Ryan didn't want to know what she thought of him. He wasn't sure he could handle it.

"All that matters is that you were there. He was thrilled in the end. I could feel it." Kara wiped her hands on her pants and stood. "I'm ready to go back." She picked up her brother's bag and turned to face Ryan.

He flinched away from her dark stare and beckoned to the house. Dawson might not have blamed him for what happened, but Kara sure as Helwe did.

Chaos

KILLIAN LET TORY SHOW him around the cramped log house before they settled in the living room. A brick fireplace and coffee table were on a red rug in the center.

Killian sat on the couch behind the table, and Tory sat on the mantle with a huff. He needed to figure out what they were doing there. If Kara had been delivered to Nicholas, he should have gone with Ryan. They had to figure out the situation with their mom. It was possible they could still save her.

Justin was the first to walk through the door. Nicholas met him in the hall, and they talked about Kara. They didn't seem keen on hiding anything, so Killian supposed he should trust them a bit for that.

"I heard there was fighting. Did anyone get hurt?" Justin asked.

Tory shook his head. "We're fine. Worked it out." He hesitated like he was surprised he was being asked at all.

Killian had a lot to figure out with these people. Justin and Nicholas were related, and Tory was dating Nicholas. The three were odd, and Killian needed to figure out where he fit in.

The man stared in his direction, and Killian shifted uncomfortably. Even though Justin was blind, he had a creepy way of making it look like he could see. "You're going to be a problem," Justin said. He didn't bother to elaborate.

"How am I going to be a problem?" he asked.

"We'll work on it." Justin didn't bother explaining that, either.

Killian looked at Tory, and the brunette rolled his eyes. "You'll get used to him. He's a little hard to get along with."

"How hard?" Killian grew up with Ryan. He couldn't imagine someone was worse off.

"When we first met, he threatened to kill me," Tory said. "And I didn't do anything to deserve it that time, I swear."

Killian frowned. There was a fourth member of the odd family. "He has a kid?" he asked.

Tory nodded and pushed away from the wall as Nicholas and Justin walked away. "Yeah, hyperactive little boy. Descendant of Technology, but you'll not see him much. Justin's paranoid that something will happen to him."

"How old is he?" Killian asked.

"Cody's about thirteen. Maybe twelve. Honestly, I don't know. Never thought to ask. He strikes me as about Dawson's age..." Tory trailed off. Pain clouded his hazel eyes before he shook it off.

Killian looked out the window to his left by a spiral metal staircase. The forest beckoned just feet from the house. He wanted to be out there, hunting rabbits, building bases, and catching fish. He missed those days.

"Why're you waiting around here? It's been a decade," Tory said, nodding to the window.

Killian smiled bitterly. He wasn't sure. "I'm not ready," he said.

Tory stopped asking questions as if sensing Killian didn't want to talk about it. They watched the trees until Justin plopped beside him on the couch.

He nearly jumped but had the sense to reign in his terror. No one else was going to catch him off guard.

"Your brother has an interesting affliction. May I ask how long he's had it?" Justin asked, cocking his head.

A horizontal scar ran across both eyes, turning them a milky white. Bags and lines weathered his face, and he had black hair with silver strands peppering it. He didn't look old; he looked ancient.

Justin must've taken his silence as confusion because he shook his head and continued, "The cut on his calf."

Killian frowned in irritation. Perhaps he didn't want to share that kind of information. Plus, he didn't know the cut was still bothering Ryan. "He got that when we fought Angel before the school thing. It's already healed," he said.

Justin clicked his tongue and sat straight. "I dunno about that. Do you know what Angel is?" he asked.

Killian shrugged and scooted further down the cough, trying to put distance between them. "A Descendant."

Justin chuckled and waved his hand, egging him to continue. "What kind?"

"Shadow, I dunno," Killian said.

Justin grinned. Something feral and dark. "Ah, now that's where the fun lies. Have you ever heard of Descendants of Chaos?" he asked. His voice had bitter joy, as if he were enjoying himself.

Killian wracked his brain. "No."

Justin nodded again and sat back. He stared straight ahead, tapping his fingers against his legs as he pursed his lips in thought. "Some Descendants aren't attributed to elements," he said. It was like he was trying to figure out how much he wanted to say.

"Okay." Killian didn't know how much he could get from these strangers, but he would try to get the most from them.

Tory watched him for a long time before sighing. He obviously realized that Killian wouldn't try to pry for more information. "Chaos, Technology, and Energy," he said. "Those are the ones we know of that aren't associated with elements."

"What's the point of them?" Killian asked.

Justin chuckled. "Why does there have to be a point?"

There was a point to everything. Killian didn't know of anything that existed without purpose.

"It could mean magik is evolving, but no one really knows. It is what it is," Tory said. At least one of them was willing to answer his questions.

"How is chaos combated?" Killian asked. "It was like nothing I had ever seen before."

Tory chewed his lip and shrugged. They looked at Justin for more information, but he wasn't paying attention to them. His eyes were focused on something behind them, and he pursed his lips.

The front door opened again, and Ryan walked in with Kara. She clutched her brother's bag, and her eyes swept to Tory when he stood. She shook her head as she stared, her eyes darkening. "I don't want to talk to you."

"I just want to..."

"No," she shouted.

A light bulb overhead shattered and rained glass on him. Tory had the sense to shut his mouth.

Killian didn't imagine any of this was going to go well.

Justin was at Kara's side two seconds later. He could stand and move more quietly than any person Killian had met. "I have a room ready for all of you. Come with me."

"How do you know my parents?" she asked.

Justin smiled and reached out but stopped. As if sensing something no one else could, he dropped his hand. "I was their leader in the rebellion."

Ryan shook his head and stepped in front of her as if he could continue shielding her from the truth. "No."

The rest of the color drained from Kara's face. Her knuckles went white. "My parents fought in the rebellion?" she asked.

Justin stared at Ryan for a long time before he nodded. "Of course, they were Descendants. They had as much of a place in the war as anyone."

Ryan's shoulders sagged, and he closed his eyes.

Kara's energy whipped around the room but vanished when Justin waved his hand. "You knew about this," she said accusatoryly as she looked at Ryan. "How could you know and not tell me?"

"Kara-"

She hurried past them and ran up the stairwell without another word.

Ryan whirled on Justin, glaring. "Her world is already burning to the ground. Why are you making it worse?"

"I will not lie. Her magik will be more powerful than you know, and if she doesn't learn now, she could destroy every one of us," Justin said.

Ryan didn't move. He learned his lesson the first time they fought.

Killian looked up the stairs as Justin and his brother had a contest of wills. There was something more important than being the alpha.

He stood and climbed the stairs after her, ignoring the pathetic look Tory shot at him.

Kara was crumpled against the far wall on the second level, squeezing the Helwe out of the only thing she had left of her brother. Her shoulders shook as she sobbed quietly, and he huffed. This wasn't something he was used to doing. Even when Ryan was in a mood, Killian didn't do comfort.

Sometimes, people needed to be coddled, and while Killian wasn't the coddling type, he supposed he could try. He walked to her and slid down the wall.

"Leave me alone," she whispered, hiccupping.

Killian traced the patterns of the wood on the floor with his fingertips. They were smooth. "Nah, not gonna do that," he said.

Her eyes flashed angrily when she brought her head up. Her cheeks were puffy and red, but the tears didn't add to the intimidation factor. "Why?" she asked.

He stared back without flinching. Everyone was trying to tiptoe around her, and by doing so, they made that power worse. Killian wouldn't give her the satisfaction.

He pointed to her wrist where the bruises from a week ago were left. Had it even been that long? He could barely remember now. "When I was dying on your doorstep, you sat with me. Even after I left a bruise around your wrist."

Kara sniffled and looked away. "I'm angry," she said.

Killian nodded. If he thought he could tell her to pull her panties up and act like a woman, he would. Something inside his head said to him that would be a hazardous idea. "At whom?" he decided to ask more questions to help straighten out her head.

She waved her hand in a general direction. "Him, me, everyone," she said.

"Him as in my brother? Or him, as in the creepy guy's house we're in?" Killian wanted to make sure his record was straight, too.

"Both."

"I get that. Sometimes I hate the world too," he said.

Kara set her face on her knees. "Do you ever not hate the world?"

"Just because I hate the people in it doesn't mean I hate the world." Killian wasn't sure if he was offended or not. "Bad things happen. Without them, you can't see the good things."

"Can you stop talking?" she asked, straining not to yell. "I can't do this right now."

He rubbed the back of his neck and chewed on his lip. He wasn't doing great. Killian pushed himself to his feet. *You're going to regret this.* "Look, you wanna sit and whine and cry, fine. I get it, this sucks. You watched someone you love die, but wallowing isn't going to change anything."

Kara lifted her head and stared hard. Her eyes glowed like he just signed his death warrant. At least he didn't see any of the hollowness. That had to be a plus.

"My mom used to say that when a Descendant's powers woke, the emotions they had at that moment would set their path. You get to pick where you go," Killian said. He gestured around them. "Figure out where you're going to go, Kara, because if it's a path Ryan doesn't agree with, you'll lose us both."

Kara's chin rose, and her back straightened. "Is that so?" she asked.

Killian nodded.

"Then I'm going to watch the city burn," she hissed.

Well, at least he could still use her against Ryan. Killian wasn't sure how thrilled his brother would be to hear Kara gave zero craps about him right now. Then again, he shouldn't be as surprised as he was by that.

A Whole New World

KARA

KARA SAT ON THE bed in her new room and looked around. It was lifeless and cold. She missed her bed and the posters on her walls. Everything was so dull and unlived in. She pulled her knees to her chest and stared silently at the wall. *What am I supposed to do now? Everyone I've known is gone.*

Kara had never been in a situation like this alone. She didn't know what she was supposed to do. She fell back on the bed and closed her eyes. The anger from earlier left her body aching and stiff. Kara longed to hear Dawson's voice. He would know exactly what to say in this situation. There had to be something else she could focus on, like magik.

After a moment, Kara lifted her hands and stared at them. Her short, pudgy fingers didn't look any different, but at the same time, she didn't recognize them. There was a soft golden glow behind her hands. They were shrouded in a light she couldn't comprehend. Since her magik appeared, there was a faint glow behind everyone.

"What is happening to my life?" she asked.

There was a soft knock on her door, and it washed the room in blue. Kara rubbed her temple with a stifled groan. Tory. His calm energy poured over her until she breathed evenly again. She got off the bed and opened the door.

He hadn't tried to talk with her for hours. If anyone knew when she needed space, it was him, and now that she was dangerous, he seemed to take that to heart a little more. He stood with his hands tucked behind his pocket and rocked back and forth on the balls of his feet.

"I don't have the energy for this," she whispered.

He nodded and looked away. "You know they were my family, too. I didn't... how could I know something like this would happen?"

"You're alive," she said.

He winced and ran his fingers along the doorjamb.

She could slam it and break one or two of them. The thought hit her so fiercely that she almost flinched away from herself. That wasn't who she was. Kara didn't *want* to hurt people. Did she?

"My magik was getting out of control, and Angel was catching on," he said. "If I could change how I did things, I would."

Anger burst to life under her skin, and her light bulb flickered. She closed her eyes to calm herself before she could shatter another one. When it stopped, she opened them again and took another breath. "You let me think you were dead for four years. Forgive me if I'm not rushing to thank you," Kara said.

"How do I fix this?" he asked, his voice cracked with desperation.

Kara searched his eyes and curled her hands into fists at her sides. *Nothing. There's nothing you can do to fix that pain.* Her sneer must have said everything because he winced and hung his head.

"I'll wait until you're ready, then," he said, walking away.

Kara let her hands unfurl. She didn't want to be angry anymore, but that was all she could feel.

"He isn't a bad guy." Nicholas' voice startled her.

She looked down the hall and saw him at the top of the stairwell.

He looked at her with a curious glance. His brown and green energy danced around him, sporadic and restless. He still wasn't sure about her.

"I grew up with him. I know him better than anyone," she said.

Nicholas chuckled. "I dunno. Given my relationship with him, I might know a thing or two."

Kara cocked her head to the side. "A boyfriend? He found a boyfriend?"

Nicholas didn't try to hide his smile. He wasn't much older than her, maybe in his early twenties. His skin was bronzed and freckled from the sun. He had gentle, chocolate-colored eyes, and the right side of his head was shaved. The rest hung down his right shoulder.

"You sound pleased," he said.

Fear had taken hold of Tory when he first told her he liked boys. He thought it would ruin everything, but she was happy if he was. To think he could share a secret like that with her and vanish with another was heartbreaking.

"I know we don't know each other, but I want you to know he cares about you. Tory told me stories about your family for months after we met." Nicholas kept his voice quiet. He probably didn't want his boyfriend to hear their conversation.

Everyone was misinterpreting her anger. Wasn't she entitled to feeling things without being berated or questioned? Kara leaned on the door jam and frowned. "I don't doubt Tory's love for me, but he still left me. I'm allowed to be angry," she said.

Nicholas walked toward her, but she backed into the room. He stopped and sighed. "He wanted to protect you. He's a Descendant, and that's illegal. If they caught him, all of you would've been killed."

They were killed anyway. At least one of them was. She had no clue where or how to find her parents.

"I'm going to sleep," she said. "I'm tired."

He nodded, and she shut the door. Sleep. She needed to sleep. She wandered over to the bed with a slight shake of her head and fell onto her side, letting the mattress absorb her.

Someone shook her awake a few hours later. She woke up dazed until a flash of red clouded her vision. *Ryan.* She looked up at him with a slight frown.

He put a finger to his lips with a small smile. "I got something to show you. Come on," he whispered.

A million questions ran through her head, but she was too tired, so she settled for a groan and rolled over.

He chuckled under his breath and pulled the blanket off her. The cool night air whisked across her legs and arms, eliciting a slight whine.

She wanted to sleep.

He pulled her up by her hand. "I think you'll like this. Just follow me, Princess."

She scrunched her nose in her half-asleep state and followed him down the hall to his borrowed room. He pushed open a large window on the side. Her eyes traveled to Killian as he slept. It looked like they were sharing again.

Ryan beckoned her out, that grin still in place. The window was large enough to climb through, but she got skeptical.

She couldn't see anything past the sill. "It's pitch black," she whispered.

He snapped his fingers, and a flame popped up in his palm. He climbed through the window and landed on something just below. "I'm a walking lantern. Come on. Nothing is terrifying out here but you," he said.

She hesitated for a moment before rolling her eyes and following. Whatever he showed her had better be worth going out into the chilly night. She landed on a small platform beneath the window, and he led her over to a small area where he had set up some pillows and blankets. The light on his palm barely illuminated a few feet before them.

"What's this?" she asked.

He sat down and patted the spot next to him. "Since I tutored you all that time, it's time you gave me that date," he whispered.

She frowned. If this was his idea of a joke, she wasn't interested. "I don't feel like a shitty date."

Ryan patted the ground again. "I slightly changed it. Sit," he said.

She sat with a huff. "What are the new rules then?"

"I'm going to make this the best date you've ever had." He closed his hand, and the flame went out. He turned his head to the sky and nodded up.

Kara looked up and blinked in awe.

It was filled with stars. Stars as far as the eye could see. The sky was a mix of blue, purple, and pink amidst the black abyss. She assumed those were the galaxies she had read so much about.

Her eyes widened, and her mouth opened in a silent gasp as she stood and turned in circles. They never ended. Her chest swelled with emotion, and she reached up as if she could touch them.

"This is the best thing about my home," Ryan whispered. His voice barely cut through her thoughts, though.

Kara chuckled softly. "Okay, you're right. This was worth getting out of bed."

He nodded, leaned back on his hands, and closed his eyes. "Yeah, this is the first thing anyone should see. You can't put a price on freedom."

Freedom. That wasn't a word she had thought much about before. She looked back to admire the starry sky and thought of her little brother. They should have been able to enjoy it together.

He was the one who risked his life to get her books about The Wilds.

"Pictures don't do it justice," she said.

"Nothing quite like experiencing it for yourself." Ryan sounded sad.

She sat back down and leaned against him, not taking her eyes off the sky. Eventually, the sun would rise, and the sight would be gone.

"I'm sorry I couldn't bring Dawson here." He didn't dare look at her when he talked. "I wanted to."

Kara tensed and resisted the urge to cry again. She didn't want to feel that pain, not right now. "I know he's out there. He's seeing it too, and I bet he's dancing in the moonlight."

Ryan smirked.

She knew she had to believe in something, even if she didn't know what was true. Still, if she never found the light in things, her world would be like the night sky without the moon and stars. If she kept moving forward, she would see the light.

Kara studied Ryan's profile as he stared at the sky. "Can I ask one more favor?" she asked.

"What?"

Her voice trembled when she spoke despite her best efforts. "Don't let the darkness take me. I don't know what I'm doing, but I don't want to go down that path, alright?"

His eyes softened as he put an arm around her shoulder and squeezed. "If it wants you, it has to fight me," he said.

Kara smiled. She stood, and he gave her a questioning glance, but she held up her hand and crawled back inside.

Killian snorted and rolled over but didn't otherwise wake up.

Kara tiptoed down to Tory's room and hesitated. She didn't get the chance to make up with her mom. A lot between them went unsaid, and she didn't want to risk that again. Swallowing her pride, Kara knocked softly.

Tory opened the door with a mischievous smile and ran a bright red flower down his chest. "Hey baby, did you come for..." he stopped when he saw her. Tory's cheeks went red, and he threw the flower into the abyss of his room behind him. "Kara?"

She smiled and raised her eyebrows. "Let me guess, you were expecting someone with brown and green hair and long eyelashes. Which, by the way, I'm insulted. How does a man have such luxurious lashes?" she asked.

Tory held up a finger and scrambled back into his room. He reappeared with a shirt. "Are you alright?" he asked. His voice was no longer low and seductive.

She held out her hand. "I want to share something with you," she said.

He took it, and she led him to the twins' room and onto the balcony. She felt Ryan's anger before she saw him. It was like stepping into a sauna.

"Oh great, someone to brighten my evening," Ryan said.

Tory was about to climb back through the window, but Kara pulled him back to her side. "Tonight, I want to be happy and enjoy the stars with my two favorite people. Can we do that, please?" she asked.

When neither protested, she sat beside Ryan and took Tory with her. They both grumbled under their breaths but didn't otherwise say a thing. Kara grabbed Ryan's hand and fell onto her back. The boys followed suit in place of sitting and staring at one another.

Kara grinned despite the growing ache in her chest.

"Nick's gonna be pissed," Tory whispered.

Kara turned her head to look at him. "I'm more important than sex," she said.

He shrugged. "I can't for sure say that's true. When you've had good sex, tell me I'm more important."

Her cheeks heated at the thought. She pulled her hand out of Ryan's to smack Tory's arm and returned to watching the stars. It was quiet, but she swore Dawson laughed in her ear.

An Extended Hand

RYAN WAS IN THE hall when Justin walked upstairs. He caught the mess of bouncy red energy before it dimmed. Justin smirked and waved his hand. Obviously, the Descendant of Fire saw him. "Evening, you're up late," he said.

Ryan grunted in response. He wasn't much for a conversation.

Justin clicked his tongue and tapped his fingers on the banister. "I was wondering if we could talk."

"About what?" Ryan's voice was distrustful and soft.

"The cut on your calf."

Ryan scoffed. He obviously didn't think anyone knew about that. "I have no clue what you're talking about."

Justin didn't like teenagers. He prayed Cody was less stubborn the older he got. "You've been having nightmares, hearing voices you don't think are there. I'm curious. Have the hallucinations begun yet?" he asked.

Ryan hesitated before responding. His energy quaked, a pulse of violet streaking across the red and orange. Around his head was a swirling mass of black, like a starry sky without the beauty.

"The chaos infected you when she struck. It's a curse that her magik can use to control people," Justin said. If he gave information, he could get some in return.

A small thump indicated Ryan had kicked or leaned on the wall beside him. "She isn't going to be able to handle me," he said. There was a flash of arrogance in his tone.

"You're too arrogant," Justin said. "That doesn't bode well for your future."

Ryan chuckled without humor. "How long until this curse takes effect?"

"It already has, and if you don't learn to control yourself, it'll only speed up the process," Justin said.

Ryan had little to say to that. He didn't sound concerned or uncertain. His energy didn't waiver. He just stood there, waiting to be dismissed.

"I can see you won't care about what I have to say," Justin said.

"Why should I? I don't even know you. People have been warning me about myself for years," Ryan muttered. "You're no different."

There was a hint of something in his voice, maybe pain. Justin turned his head as he tried to pinpoint what thoughts ran through his head. It was harder to read people he knew nothing about.

"What does that mean?" Justin asked.

Ryan's voice rose a little. "It's not really any of your business, is it?" He tried hiding his anger, but Justin could see it growing. The sporadic waves of fire crackled and burned under his skin.

"I can't understand if you don't let me," Justin said.

"No one's asking you to understand. I'm just telling you to get off my back," Ryan replied.

Justin nodded. "If I could help you manage the chaos without questions. Would you let me?" he asked.

"No thanks, I don't need it," Ryan said.

"You can't do everything by yourself. Or is that not a lesson you've learned yet?" Justin asked, keeping his voice as innocent as possible.

The door to Ryan's bedroom opened, and he chuckled again. "Whatever. See you in the morning. It's late."

Justin heard the door close and watched the energy disperse. The tang of metal and chaos burned his tongue and tickled his nose. Even if he had a way to help, he couldn't do it without Ryan's consent.

Justin shook his head and walked back downstairs. Teenagers were stubborn and reckless. He hated dealing with Descendants of Fire during puberty. They were the most difficult.

"You're up late." Nick's voice met him as he walked into the living room.

Justin shrugged. "I thought I would extend a helping hand. It wasn't well received."

"The boys have been on their own for ages. I'm not sure they'll warm up," Nick said.

Justin wrinkled his nose. *Why couldn't they be adults?* "I'm aware."

"All we can do is keep an eye on him. After that, we'll figure it out. Maybe I can reach him," Nick said.

Justin smirked. Nick was always the more charming one, but even Ryan would be immune to those charms. After some bonding time with Kara, he could control Ryan through her. Or at least manage that attitude.

"You raised me. Just imagine it's the same thing," Nick said. "I turned out alright, didn't I?"

Justin chuckled. "I'm sorry. Do you remember the Helwe I went through with you? All the fighting, the drinking, the parties. You were a royal mess."

"Still, I'm self-sufficient and alive. I'm well-trained and have well-controlled emotions, *and* I'm still alive. Can you ask for more?" Nick asked.

Justin imagined he was blinking big brown eyes at him like he did as a kid. He waved a hand and walked out of the living room. It was late.

"All I'm saying is to trust your instincts. You're not new to this parenting thing." Nick's voice followed him all the way to his room.

Justin couldn't help but smirk. The people he was used to parenting
knew him as a parent. These kids had families out there, somewhere. They
wouldn't roll over to his will because he asked it of them. Then again, that
wasn't necessarily a bad thing.

"We have a long road ahead of us," he whispered.

The Mark of a Descendant

T HE BED SHOOK, AND Kara flopped onto her side, underestimating how close she was to the edge. She hit the floor with a 'bump' and groaned. The floor trembled beneath her, and she felt like she was in the ocean for a split second. Kara rubbed her eyes. Glass shattered somewhere downstairs, and Ryan cursed in the next room. She stood and swayed until the quake ceased.

She crossed to the window and looked outside. The sun was rising, so the sky was barely lit. She climbed the stairs with a muffled yawn and ignored how her world turned green. The colors were still disorienting, and she stumbled. Her foot caught on a step, and she fell forward, but Tory grabbed her arm.

"He's dramatic, isn't he?" Tory teased.

Kara frowned and entered the living room, only to find it empty. She mumbled a quick thanks and rubbed her eyes.

Tory went straight to the front door, but Ryan appeared before he could open it.

"It's too early for this shit," Ryan grumbled. "What's wrong with these people?"

As soon as he opened the front door, a rock the size of his fist was hurled at his head. He ducked, and it slammed into the back wall, showering pebbles over him. His gaze met Nicholas'.

"What the Helwe?" he spat.

"Let's have a talk! I've been dying to get some things off my chest, and I like routine," Nicholas said, showing his teeth in a charming smile. He held up a hand, and bits of vine and colored twine hung off his wrists.

Kara stepped out of the house and blinked in the blinding light of the morning sun. She got to sleep later than this in the city. "This couldn't wait until a little later?" she asked.

"It's not my fault you three were up all night watching the stars," Nicholas said, "I want to get a reading on everyone and their magik, so line up."

They all looked at each other, passing glances in mild irritation before lining up. She pursed her lips; he could use the word 'please.'

Ryan frowned and looked around. "What are we some sort of assembly line now?" he asked.

Nicholas walked over to them and ran a hand through his greasy hair. "You three have no clue what you're doing with magik," he said. "I don't care if you want to stay, but I can't send you into the world knowing you could hurt someone."

"Isn't that our decision?" Kara asked.

Nicholas shot her a look, and his smile faded. "Not anymore. Do you know what you did to the people in the city?" he asked.

Kara wrapped her arms around herself. On top of everything, she tried not to think about it.

He nodded when she went silent. "Exactly. Like I said, you don't have to stay, but you will get appropriate training before you leave."

Her mind worked too slowly this early. Kara thought through her words carefully. "What about the city?" she asked.

"The city isn't our problem. It's theirs."

Her parents could still be there, though. Plus, all the other countless people. They couldn't abandon everyone after that.

Nicholas held out his right leg and pointed at a tattoo around his ankle.

It was a green and brown yin-yang sign with rocks making up the yang side and leaves and vines making up the yin side. Vines protruded from the mark and wrapped all the way around his ankle.

Kara blinked and stared at the mark. She had never seen anything so beautiful.

"Since we have a new Descendant, I will explain how this works," Nicholas said. "Every Descendant has a mark of power. This is mine. Each mark tells others what power you have control of. As you can see, my mark has bits of nature and rock."

Kara looked at her arms and legs, expecting to find one on her body. She was disappointed. "I don't have one," she said.

Nicholas waved his hand and beckoned for Ryan. "Let me finish. Come here, hot head." When Ryan approached, Nicholas waved a hand up and down his body. "A real Descendant can find an opponent's mark of power through energy reading. Does someone want to demonstrate?"

Killian stepped forward, but Nicholas shook his head. "You already know where it is. Tory." Nicholas crooked his finger at his boyfriend.

Kara blinked and tried to keep up. *Energy reading. That must be the glow around everyone.*

Tory edged closer and looked Ryan up and down. He snuck a glance at Kara's confused face and smiled. "Channel your energy into your eyes. Let it show you another version of our world." He lifted Ryan's left arm sleeve and revealed a black mark.

A ball of fire with odd triangles and webbing underneath it nearly wrapped around his bicep.

"Our marks hold all our magik and disperse it throughout our body. The stronger your magik gets, the more this mark will change," Nicholas said.

Kara frowned. She pulled her shirt out to look down at her breasts and stomach. Still nothing. "I don't have one," she said again.

Nicholas rubbed the back of his neck. "Trust me, you–it's somewhere. Killian, why don't you find hers?"

Her cheeks heated, and she crossed her arms against her chest. "What if it's someplace indecent?"

Nicholas' cheeks went pink. He rubbed the back of his neck again and cleared his throat. "Then nobody will look."

Killian waved his hands over her and jolted when a line of purple electricity snapped at his hand. He yelped and jumped away from her. "Unnecessary," he said.

"I didn't do it." It felt like a violation of her privacy for someone to scope her out like that.

"Shadow and Energy are opposites. You two will have to learn to control your magik around each other. Just like Tory and Ryan," Nicholas said.

Killian tried again and pointed to her back, between her shoulder blades. "It's there."

Nicholas gestured to her shirt. "May I look?" he asked.

She turned around and pulled her hair over her shoulder for him. Nicholas peeked and let her shirt fall back into place.

She whirled around and beamed. "What does it look like?" she asked.

"A bunch of circles and triangles. We'll work on it," he said.

Justin walked out of the house, and Nicholas smiled. "Jay, will you take off your shirt?"

The man raised a brow. "What are you teaching them that needs me shirtless?"

"I want them to see the mark of a fully realized Descendant."

Ryan held up his hand. "Wait, wait, wait. You're telling me this man completely controls his magik and can't beat Angel?"

Justin seemed amused by the statement. He pulled his hair back into a short ponytail and stripped off his shirt. "All the power in the world doesn't mean you can do anything."

He turned his back to them, and Kara gasped. It was beautiful. In the middle of his back was a silver and sky-blue arrow, with the point of it being encased by three large circles. A half circle surrounded the arrow's tail, and three dots trailed behind it. Curves and loops cut through the mark and spread across his shoulders in beautiful blues and grays.

"I might have power, but I'm not invincible. Angel is powerful too, and while I have more of it, she has an advantage."

"And what's that?" Kara asked.

"She controls chaos."

Kara's head spun. There was so much she didn't know. "What's that? What's chaos?" she asked.

"It's a type of magik. There are eight types of magik in our world, and each is separated into two factions," Justin said as if that cleared everything up.

Kara wasn't following. The world of magik was more complicated than she realized. "What are the types?"

Nicholas smiled. "I'm going to give you a crash course. The factions are light and dark, and every bit of magik falls into those categories. For instance, I'm nature, so I'm in the faction of light. Creation often falls to light. Fire, energy, and wind are also considered elements of light and creation," Nicholas said. His body thrummed with energy when he talked.

Kara had never met anyone so excited to talk about magik before.

"The dark faction is shadow, chaos, technology, and water. Now, light and dark don't mean good and evil. We can use all magik for either. The factions were originally meant to balance the world. To make sure not one element was too strong. There was always an opposing force," he said.

Kara tried to keep up. "So, I'm energy?" she asked.

"Yes, which makes Killian your opposite. Mine is wind, which is Justin's magik. Angel is chaos, so her opposite is technology," he said.

Technology. Kara couldn't even imagine what magik that would encompass. Tech didn't follow the elemental pattern. "Okay," she said, not understanding anything.

Justin and his brother began whispering. After their brief conversation, Justin smiled at her. "I'll be training you separately."

She scrunched her nose. How was she supposed to learn alone? Her eyes fell on Ryan, but he whispered something to Killian. She didn't want to be isolated.

Kara looked at Justin. "No," she said.

Everyone looked at her.

"I want to train with everyone else. I'm behind, but I can learn from them. Ryan's been my tutor before. He can help me," she said.

Justin waved a hand and shook his head. His energy didn't change from its calm, steady stream. "That would be fine if he knew what he was doing himself."

"Then we'll all learn together." She wasn't going to bend on it. Kara wanted to learn with the others. If she was going to do anything, learn how to be anything, she needed those she trusted.

Justin pursed his lips and looked at Nicholas. "What do you think?" he asked.

"You don't even know spells, Kara. How do you plan on training with us when you can't produce the basics?" Nicholas asked.

"I'll figure it out. I might be behind for a while, but I'm not sitting in the background," she said.

Angel could do terrible things. Her magik was terrifying and ruining lives. If Kara could learn how to help them, she would. All she wanted was to stop this from happening to others.

Screams of the dying resonated through her head. She had a lot to make up for. Kara hardened her gaze and straightened her back. "I want to help people, but I'm not going to be able to by being coddled." Her eyes flicked to Killian. She didn't want to be a burden and wouldn't let people fight her battles anymore. "I've chosen my path."

Justin hummed before nodding. "Alright, we'll try it. If you want to train with the others, you can."

She beamed. *Don't worry, Dawson. Your big sis is going to make things right.*

Justin clapped his hands and smiled. "Well then, consider you all my guests. I will be sure to provide your basic needs, and you'll be sure not to kill anyone on my property." His eyes went to Killian when he spoke.

Ryan's eyes were on Kara. "You sure you want to do this?" he asked.

"I have to. I'm not leaving the city as it is. Someone needs to do something about Angel, and if no one else will, I am going to." Her voice wasn't as strong as she hoped.

Nicholas shot a look toward his brother, but Justin didn't notice. "You want to fight Angel alone?" he asked.

Kara kept her gaze firm. "No, but I will." For Dawson and her parents. For everyone who lost someone because of that witch and her magik.

"She won't be alone," Ryan said. "Because I'm going to help."

Killian tensed but didn't say anything. He would go where his brother went, they all knew that. He just didn't look happy about it.

"Well then, it sounds like we have a lot of work to do," Justin said.

Thus was the beginning of Kara's new life.

About the Author

SLMcGinnis writes Young Adult Fantasy and Coming of Age Stories featuring female leads who grow into the role of strong heroine with an emphasis on mental health in both boys and girls. She promises to make her readers laugh and cry as they connect with their inner child with relatable characters.

This American writer holds an MFA in English and Creative Writing with a minor in Fantasy and Fiction from Southern New Hampshire University. Her love of all things literature encouraged her to leave the safety of the medical field and pursue a career as a college educator with success. As a happy educator in Northeast Texas, SLMcGinnis brings her love of writing to a new level.

She loves writing in her bed in her free time with a cup of coffee and her favorite pillow. She started her writing career as a self-published author and found some success.

She is now represented by Castle Drum Publishing, so she has more time to caffeinate, write, teach, and love on her three dogs and two cats as she suffers the Texas heat.

You can follow her through her linktr.ee/slmcginnis and find more by her.